BLOOD THIRSTY

BLOOD THIRSTY

CHELSEA BURTON DUNN

DEAD MAN'S HAND
BOOK 1

4 Horsemen
Publications, Inc.

4 Horsemen
Publications, Inc.

1497 Main St. Suite 169
Dunedin, FL 34698
4horsemenpublications.com
info@4horsemenpublications.com

Cover by J. Kotick
Typesetting by Niki Tantillo
Edited by Blair Parke

Library of Congress Control Number: 2023936540

Paperback ISBN-13: 978-1-64450-986-9
Hardcover ISBN-13: 978-1-64450-862-6
Audiobook ISBN-13: 978-1-64450-985-2
Ebook ISBN-13: 978-1-64450-987-6

DEDICATION

To my teenage self: I fixed it, and it's really getting published now. Your dreams are coming true. I'm glad we never stopped.

And to my Mandy: I love you and our craziness. Hope you love this new version of BT as much as I do. This victory is as much yours as it is mine. You are my Six of Diamonds, my dear.

TABLE OF CONTENTS

CHAPTER 1

The night was dark. Clouds loomed over the city, casting away the silver light of the moon for the harsh glow of streetlights below. The air was heavy, damp with mist, and collected on Ace's hair and jacket, dripping to the street floors below. She was perched on the tin roof of a manufacturing warehouse, shadowed by a tall exhaust pipe; her partner Makiut was at her side, eyes scouring the people coming and going from the club below. The Gast was a nightclub that had popped up a few years previous. Some enterprising person had situated this club in the heart of Harringay Warehouse District. Word had traveled in fringe groups that the club catered to more intriguing guests, with rooms tucked in the back for illegal gambling, drug deals, and even more taboo entertainment.

What the humans below failed to realize was that this was essentially a lure. A draw to bring warm bodies to a place where they could become a convenient snack to others. It wasn't just Vampires who partook here. This place had become an unofficial neutral zone where Immortals kept to themselves. The war between them essentially paused, once within the four walls of this club.

1

Ace and Makiut, though Vampires themselves, weren't there to prey on the innocent, if not naive mortals, tonight, as it was most nights they were hunting for Werewolves. Recently, they had observed some odd behavior from the local Werewolf den, as the Werewolves had been seen following a certain mortal, not attacking him but more trying to convince him to come along. The previous Necare had been unable to get close enough to distinguish who this mortal was and why they were deemed so important that the Werewolves simply wouldn't just attack him. That's where Ace and Makiut came in.

Though Necare, the soldiers and assassins of the Vampires, had a keener ability to be able to get closer to their targets without detection, there would be no fighting within the assumed sacred ground of The Gast. But Ace could at least find out what these Werewolves were up to.

"There they are," Makiut murmured, gesturing toward the entrance to the alley where they spotted two Werewolves. To a human, they wouldn't have seemed any different from the other club goers, but Immortals could always sense the presence of an Other. Both Werewolves looked rough, clothes worn and not good protection against the mist, which was slowly becoming more like spitting. They lurked down the alley, eyes targeted on the spray-painted metal door of the club entrance.

"Give them a moment to go in," Ace said, letting her silver eyes follow their trajectory.

The Werewolves pushed through the crowd of humans eagerly waiting in line to enter the club. A few looked like they voiced their displeasure at being pushed aside, but quickly seemed to shrink back when it became obvious these were not the men to be starting a fight with. Ace could hear the low growl vibrate from one of them, even at her distance. Perhaps that was a little overkill, but there was no denying the mortal shrank back, their instincts telling them what their mind hadn't. This creature would kill them.

The Werewolves entered the club not a moment later, and that was Ace's cue. She deftly jumped from the tin roof, boots landing against the pavement soundlessly and unnoticed by the line. Makiut joined her a moment later, flicking his long dark hair out of his face.

"We could have ambushed them before they went in," Makiut grumbled beside her.

"And then we wouldn't find out why they came here in the first place," Ace replied coldly, moving ahead toward the door.

Ace didn't need to shove her way through like the Werewolves had; the line parted without even noticing her, as if they were repelled by her. Repelled by the innate sense that she was a predator. The doorman's eyes glowed slightly as he took her in. These days he went by Don, but he had many names over the years. He was a Vampire, but not one within her coven. Domainless, apart from the war. It was Immortals like him that had made The Gast in the first place. It made hunting their prey easier, if they weren't potentially finding themselves in the middle of warring factions.

"Ace," he said as a greeting. "Not going to cause trouble in there tonight, are you?"

"I don't cause the trouble. Just taking a look, maybe a listen. We'll see what happens," she told him, black eyebrow rising on her forehead as a smirk graced her lips. He chuckled and gestured with his head for her to enter.

Ace and Makiut pressed through the poorly painted door, immediately overwhelmed with the intense bass from the music blasting through the speakers and the stench of warm human sweat, cigarettes, and spilled alcohol entering their noses and tongues. Makiut's face wrinkled at the smell, but Ace, ever the cool head, simply slinked to the outskirts of the room, Makiut in toe, to lean against a dark, unused corner to scope out the scene.

There wasn't much to see other than the usual. Werewolf, Vampire, and even Witches were here, hunting both the unsuspecting and well-versed mortals. For example, Ace not only could see the faint scars left behind on the bartender's neck and arms, marks meaning he had been a Vampire's dinner at some point, but he bore more signs he was acquainted with more than Vampires. Ace saw the faint outline of a bandage at his side, indicating either a Werewolf got a chunk out of him or a Witch had gotten him to sacrifice some flesh for a dark ritual. Whichever it was, he was well-versed in the Masquerade that the Immortals played at. Most, however, were none the wiser, eagerly flirting with dangerous creatures. Instinctually, they could probably feel the threat they were under, but it merely boosted their adrenaline and gave them a thrill instead of having them running in the opposite direction, as they should have been.

The Werewolves they were tailing were talking at the bar. Ace couldn't make out what they were saying, but they gestured to the door directly beside it. There were a number of doors that littered the walls surrounding. Makeshift walls had been created within the old warehouse, making the main space much smaller than the exterior would suggest. Ace had never utilized these rooms, but she knew what they were for. Some of the more frequenting Immortals would use these rooms to do what they wanted with their prey. Though Ace never desired to take any of these mortals, she would certainly never drink from someone in such a place.

Ace pushed off the wall just as she saw one of the Werewolves move around the bar edge and head straight for the door they had just been gesturing to. Odd, since he had no mortal companion, nor had either of them even attempted to get anyone's attention since they arrived.

Briefly, Ace took her eyes off the pair at the bar, feeling someone watching her. Across the room, near the dance floor, Ace locked eyes with a man in the shadows. His eyes were slightly glowing out from under the dark hood he wore. Those eyes seemed familiar to Ace, hauntingly so. In fact, as she scoured her memories of her recent times out, this figure was certainly in the background. He was like a shadow. A ghost. Never close enough for Ace to identify, but always seeming to be there, waiting and watching her. If she had time to waste, she would have thought about the person's presence more, perhaps even approached him to find out why he had been following her, but that wasn't her current objective.

"I'll distract the other one," Makiut said, bringing Ace's focus back to the duo at the bar. There was something in that room that they were after, and if nothing else, Ace intended to find out what was happening.

The partners split, Ace heading to the bar while Makiut made his way toward the opposite side of the room, their path making a semicircle, giving them distance, while still being capable of watching each other's backs. It didn't take much to antagonize the waiting brute. Makiut merely stared at him menacingly, eyes aglow and body tensed with the promise of a good fight, a fight that they couldn't do within the walls of the club.

"I'll lick your blood from my fingers before you've even hit me, dog," Makiut said, his voice carrying through the thumping music to only the Immortals ears. Every one of them stopped and perked up, eyes drawn to the two Immortals facing one another through the crowded room, everyone but Ace that was. She resisted rolling her eyes at the blatant display of ego. Makiut could be a touch dramatic, and she didn't particularly like having a scene drawn, but it served its purpose, allowing her to slip through the crowd and around the bar.

"If you weren't so filthy, bloodsucker, I'd gladly crunch on your bones."

"Outside," Don's voice came from the front of the club.

"It was the Vampire, Don," the Werewolf said, his voice little more than a growl.

"I don't care. Outside. Both of you," Don said. With his words, the other Immortals who worked there seemed to come to attention. If they had to physically remove Makiut and this Werewolf, they would. Makiut smirked, beckoning the Werewolf to follow, before he turned abruptly and left the club.

A distraction was all Ace had needed, not for the Werewolf to be taken from the club altogether. And she wasn't too pleased to be separated from her partner. Not that she couldn't handle herself; it was him she was more concerned about, but they came here to see what the Werewolves were up to, and she wasn't leaving without something of information.

Ace moved to the door, pressing her ear against it to hear what was happening within. It wasn't very common, but sometimes if she focused hard enough, she could actually see what was happening somewhere she was listening to. She wasn't sure if it was a function of her superior hearing and concentration, or something she was gifted with separate from other Vampires, but she tried to use it now.

"You have to come with us," growled the voice of the Werewolf.

"I left. I'm not going back there, Jack," came the voice of someone unfamiliar. Ace's brows furrowed as she tried to concentrate on his face. He was young, in his twenties, built and strong but not overly so.

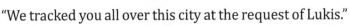

"We tracked you all over this city at the request of Lukis."

Ace's brows shot up in mild surprise. Lukis was the leader of the Werewolves. Not just the Werewolves of London, but of them all.

"And you'll be searching again."

"You know you're important."

"That's what you all keep saying." The sneer that spread over this man's face made Ace smirk in response. "I'm not going. You'd have to drag me out kicking and screaming, and I don't think Don will appreciate that much." Jack, the Werewolf, growled angrily, fists clenching as he glared at the man.

Ace focused on the unknown man's face. It was familiar, but not perfectly so. His hair hung at his shoulders, rough and shaggy, while his clothes were ill-fitting, as if he'd either dropped weight at some point or they weren't his clothes. If nothing else, Ace knew she had to remember his face. Jack said he was important to Lukis; well, that meant he was now important to her. What did Lukis need from this man, who, for all she could see and hear, was nothing more than a mortal?

"We've found you once, and we'll do it again. Next time you won't be hidden behind Don's apron strings for protection, Lu—"

But the hair-raising sound of a wolf howl and the subsequent muted sound of suppressed gunfire cut through the thumping music of the club. Without a second thought, Ace raced through the crowd, pulling the door open to see Don about to usher the humans waiting in line inside. They'd still be in danger of the creatures within, but at least they wouldn't be witnesses to whatever chaos Makiut and the other brute were reeking.

"You should control your kin better," Don hissed as Ace passed him. Her eyes blazed as she glared at him for a moment, but she didn't have the time to correct him, as another horrifying sound seemed to rip through the air; this time, it was the unmistakable sound of Makiut.

She kept her pace a mortal sprint but broke out into a full-fledged run as she turned the corner out of view of any humans whose eyes may stray her way. There, in a fairly narrow alley between warehouses, was Makiut, his gun drawn with his less dominant hand and pointing at the Werewolf. He didn't even look up at her as he proceeded to empty the remaining clip into the beast, eyes white and fangs extended.

"What did you think you were doing?" Ace hissed, as the Werewolf's body started to crumble against the wetted street stones.

"Distraction, or that's what it was supposed to be. Took a bit more off me than I was expecting," Makiut admitted, turning so she could see the full gore. Where his right arm should have been was quite a distinct hole. Dark blood oozed, saturating the side of his shirt.

"Idiot," Ace grumbled as she bent over, ripping the sleeve from his severed arm before it started to disintegrate and moving toward him so she could wrap the gaping hole. Something about the magic that made these creatures Immortal, seemed to dissolve their bodies when that magic was cast out. The only Immortal that didn't turn to dust upon death was the Chenja, but there were few things about the Chenjas that fell into the same categories that the other Immortals did. "This will have to do until we get back to Kurome."

"He had a blade," Makiut said mildly defensively, gesturing to the machete that was lying on the ground, clearly having been tossed aside.

"You may have gotten us banned from The Gast."

"Killing the dog was worth it," Makiut hissed, spitting where the Werewolf's body had once been, before cringing as Ace tightened the makeshift bandage roughly.

"Worth the time it will take for this to heal?" Ace snapped, stepping back and glaring at her partner.

"We'll see what Minshin has to say," he murmured, following her out of the alley.

"That will need to wait a bit longer," Ace whispered, pausing at the corner that led back to The Gast. Ace waited in the shadows, eyes on the entrance that was no longer crowded with the line of mortals. Jack, the Werewolf Ace had been listening in on, stepped out, eyes scanning the surrounding area while he sniffed the air. He disappeared around another corner instead of heading where Ace and Makiut stood.

Ace waited, watching. For some reason, she just knew that the man he had been talking to would be coming out. And she wasn't disappointed. Moments later, he emerged. Seeing him in the flesh was wholly different than visualizing him as she had through the door. From his face, his coloring, and the odd way his eyes looked like that of a changed Werewolf, all told Ace exactly who he was. This was Lucef, the leader of the Werewolves's son.

After Lucef left, Ace and Makiut walked through London, heading back toward Kurome Mansion. They had run most of the journey, but now that they were getting nearer, Makiut had slowed to a very human-paced walk from the obvious blood loss. Ace walked beside him on his left, letting him prop himself against her.

"How long do you think it will take to heal this?" Makiut asked quietly, as they began approaching the overgrown gate.

"A while," Ace grumbled, pushing him against the wall so he wouldn't fall over as she pressed her hand against the hidden pad and watched the gate open. Normally, they would have just jumped over the high stone walls, but Makiut was in no condition.

Once the gate opened, Ace pulled him off the wall again, putting most of his weight against her. He glanced down at her, face slightly dazed but amused.

"So many memories for such small brains to hold," he said aloud randomly, making her glance up at his face.

"Yes, much more than I'd like to remember," she murmured, making her way up the path. The grounds were slightly overgrown, obscuring the buildings hidden behind them. Ace knew this perfectly, though. She had lived here for centuries, even before she had become a Vampire.

"Do you remember when you woke up in the mansion all those years ago? You were so frightened of us. A tiny, little human against a coven of Vampires," he said softly.

"I remember."

"I never would have thought then you'd become stronger than me," Makiut murmured, eyes drifting from her face to the massive building that was finally coming into view.

Kurome Mansion sat imposing against the dark night sky. While they were still technically in London, this was tucked away, one of the few estates that sat amongst various golf courses. The magic that kept mortal eyes from paying attention to Vampires and the Others also kept them from noticing or straying into Kurome's territory. Kurome's grey stone façade was well-maintained, though it still looked old. It had stood for hundreds of years, years before Ace had become what she was now.

It was the largest and strongest coven in the world, housing the Elders, the Vampires who commanded the rest of their kind, and Ace, though a Necare, was the Judge of this coven. Being Coven Judge was not exactly what she had wanted when she set out to join the ranks of the Necare.

Transitioning from a House Vampire to one of the warriors for the Vampires had been her ultimate goal, but it was when her sire, Nero, had been chosen to become an Elder that she was given his role as Coven Judge. The Elders made most of the big decisions, so she had just become the easier go-between for the lower ranks.

Though Ace didn't particularly love her additional responsibilities as a judge, she did love her coven. This mansion, and most of the inhabitants, had been a safe place for her before she had even become a Vampire, as Makiut had astutely reminded her. Initially she had been afraid, but it hadn't taken her long to feel at home here, secure from the outside forces that had ripped her human life from her behind these stone walls.

"Makiut," she snapped, noticing his eyes had started glazing over a bit when they had finally reached the large front doors. "Hold it together just a bit longer, would you?" She hastened her steps, holding her partner tighter as she hollered at the doors, impatiently waiting for them to open.

CHAPTER 2

The massive wooden doors of Kurome Mansion's main entrance opened, revealing William, one of the younger House Vampires. She had instructed him to keep watch of the door while most of the Necare had gone out. It wasn't frequent, but injuries did tend to happen from time to time, and she was rather happy she had made this a standard practice. She wasn't certain what would happen to Makiut if she released him before he was in Minshin's capable hands.

"What's happened to him?" William asked, eyes widening as he took in the bloody and poorly bandaged place where Makiut's arm once was.

"Werewolf," Ace snarled, pushing past him and walking through the parlor, now dragging Makiut along with her, the toes of his boots scraping heavily against the floor.

Dava, another House Vampire, stood up quickly from the chair she had been lounging on to follow behind them.

"Wasn't this just a reconnaissance outing?" she asked Ace, her voice sweet but clearly laced with smugness.

"It was supposed to be, but Makiut here couldn't seem to help himself," Ace said, turning down a wide hallway.

"You two always seem to get into the most trouble."

"Perhaps Makiut and I take the most difficult missions, Dava. Had you thought of that?" Ace hissed, stopping just outside the doors where the Medicus worked. Dava visibly cowed, backing away from Ace and the door and bowing her head.

"I didn't mean to insult," Dava said, but Ace turned away from her sharply, barging through the doors. The room was large with very high ceilings. Stainless steel tables and shelving littered with various equipment were only broken up with large refrigerators and incubators. The Medicus served many functions for them. They were their doctors, predominantly, helping the healing process of ill or injured Vampires, but they were also their smiths and techs. For years, they had only perfected the art of metalsmithing but as technology grew with humans, the Vampires took full advantage.

Guns, blades, specialized gadgets, and even internally integrated weapons had been created and employed by the Medicus. Ace had even had special weapons integrated into her hands and fingers, blades that she could protract and retract at will. It had come in handy quite a few times when her weapons of choice had been lost in a fight.

"Minshin," Ace said, spotting her in the furthest corner of the room, her short black hair swayed slightly as she turned her head. Minshin, though a fairly young Vampire by their standards, had been schooled in medicine as a human. Giftedly blessed, but curse in a male- dominated world, she took on the role of head of Medicus with fervent passion upon becoming a Vampire. Her dark hair was still kept in a short bob, like it had been since the day she had been turned, and her long, slender frame held far more strength than it would have outwardly appeared.

"What did you do to him?" Minshin asked, smirking lightly as she helped Ace get Makiut situated on top of a cleared-off table.

"He got himself into a fight he wasn't prepared for," Ace said, watching as Minshin pulled the soaked shirt sleeve from his wound to take a closer look.

"He'd going to need blood, a lot of it," Minshin murmured, gesturing to one of the refrigerators that sat against the nearest wall.

Ace went to it in a flash, pulling out numerous bags and bringing them back to the table.

A few decades earlier, Nero, Ace's sire, had decided that in this day and age, it was harder to kill humans without attracting attention to mortal public. Unsolved murders and mysterious sightings were becoming too numerous to be safe. There were also far too many humans with cameras at any given time that they simply couldn't risk the Masquerade being broken.

There were several families with genetic abnormalities that allowed them to produce more blood than their bodies could handle. They had worked for the Vampires for years, offering their blood off and on to preserve their lives and the eternal lives of the Vampires. But there weren't enough of them to sustain the entire Vampire population of the world. That was when the Elders had convinced a blood bank to donate blood to them. It was done legitimately enough that no agency could find fault with the bank.

Soon, though, there were some mortals that knew the truth and actually volunteered to donate blood for the express purpose of donating to Vampires. Ace had always wondered about that. Instead of being scared or trying to go to the public with their knowledge, these people wanted to give their blood to them. It had become quite the enterprise once the Medicus developed a drug shortly after that enabled these donors to produce extreme amounts of blood. Families in dire financial situations could decide to go to a facility they had created in Sweden, take the drug, and have a month-long holiday with a spa-like experience, as long as they donated their blood each day they were there.

The humans would come away with plenty of money, while the Vampires around the world would have blood to sustain them between times they could truly hunt without being exposed. It worked fabulously, for the most part, to demolish vampiric hunger, but the urge to hunt was in their nature. Ace chose to take out her urges on Werewolves, only very occasionally finding a human to prey on, but many Vampires, like Nero, hadn't hunted for years.

Makiut grumbled, eyes still foggy, as Ace pressed a bag to his lips.

"Drink it," Ace commanded, pressing it until it broke through his lips, and he began drinking the cold, thick liquid slowly.

"It's going to take some time," Minshin said, still inspecting the arm joint. "He's going to need a lot more blood and constant monitoring until it's mostly healed.

"How long?' Ace asked, glancing down at Makiut's strained face.

"A week. Perhaps more."

A week. That would have seemed far less troubling if Ace didn't feel like she needed to immediately go back out. She could feel it with every fiber of her being. Lukis was planning something, and it was going to be big. But Ace knew she wouldn't be allowed to patrol without her partner. House Judge and Leader of the Necare or not, Ace was still held to the same expectations that all her Necare were. They all went out in pairs.

"Makiut," Ace said, leaning her face over his, her silver eyes shining with irritation. "You will focus all your energy into heal this, do you hear me?"

"Ace, I..."

"No. You will, Makiut. There's too much to do," she said, her voice rough with frustration, before she stood up and looked at Minshin.

"A week," Minshin reaffirmed, eyebrows up, as if tempting Ace to challenge her.

"Fine," Ace snapped, turning abruptly on her heel and storming from the room.

Once out in the hall, she realized Dava still stood there, though she was now leaning against the opposite wall, her entire being exuding boredom. Ace didn't know what Dava wanted and, quite frankly, didn't care. Though previously an integral part of the machine that was a coven, verses a nest, House Vampires were now made practically worthless with the blood bank system they had developed. Prior to that, it was the job of the House Vampires to procure humans for the busier ranks to take; now they just sat about, being useless, as far as Ace was concerned.

"Ace, wait!" Dava said, scrambling to keep up with her as she briskly moved back toward the parlor.

"What do you want, Dava?"

"Nero wants to speak with you," she said, causing Ace to stop abruptly. It had been weeks since she had seen him, months since they had spoken of anything other than updates on their current situation in the war.

Ace didn't have much to tell him about her mostly failed mission she and Makiut had just been on, so she wasn't sure what he could possibly want to discuss. Discussions about anything but their duties often placed her in quite a frustrated state. She had long ago decided to focus on being a Necare and a Coven Judge over anything emotional, while

he tended to push that carefully laid boundary simply by being himself.

"Did he mention why?" Ace asked, hands curling into fists.

"He didn't say," Dava said, her voice taking on an oddly taunting tone. Dava, bored as she had to be in her role, was a well-known gossip, and her favorite topic seemed to be Ace and Nero's relationship. She had been made a Vampire shortly after Ace had taken on the role of Judge, and Nero, Elder, giving her no direct insight into how they had been previously but hearing it all had intrigued her. Now, it seemed to be her greatest entertainment to make Ace squirm about it.

Without another word, Ace turned, changing her destination from her rooms to the Elder Council Room, which was located on the lower level. As she descended the winding stone stairs below, she could feel the change in energy. There had always seemed to be a magnetic draw between Ace and her sire. It was so very hard for them to stay away from one another, which is why Ace tried so hard not to tempt herself. With each additional step closer to where her body instinctually knew he was, it became harder to ignore.

With a hesitant step off the final stair step, she glanced down the dimly lit corridor, eyes resting on the symbols that were engraved on the stones there. These were the wards for this place, powerful stones gifted to this coven by the first Vampire to keep them safe. She had been here many times before, felt the pull of her sire and the surge of power from these wards, but it never ceased to give her pause.

With a deep breath, she moved through the corridor with purpose, passing several other doors. Some were Elder chambers, though most of them chose to live on the upper floors. Some doors held antiquities, items of power or powerful knowledge that they had acquired over the years. And some were merely for interrogation, though it had been a century since they had brought a Werewolf or Witch into Kurome. It wasn't worth the possible breech to bring their enemies there.

She paused at the double doors in the center of the corridor, glancing down at herself for a moment and realizing she was still covered in Makiut's blood. Not particularly presentable, but certainly not the worst state Nero or any of the other Elders had ever seen her in before. They were all Vampires after all.

She raised one of those bloody hands to knock on the door but was stopped when she heard familiar, deep velvet tones say, "Enter."

She did, pushing the door open and closing it silently behind her before she slowly moved further into the large space. The room was expansive, meant to be intimidating. It was mostly empty, making every sound echo noticeably against the marble floors and pillars. At the center of the room was a stone platform that held the seats of the Council of Elders. Each one was adorned with specific symbols associated with their bloodline. Only two held a circlet of thorns: the seats of Srinta and Nero, signifying their specific line. If Ace were ever to become an Elder, her seat would also share the same symbol.

Ace kept herself steady, despite the instinct to let her breath hitch when she realized Nero was alone. This was not a summons of the whole council, but a summons from her sire. He sat, elbows on knees, clear blue eyes trained on her face as she moved closer. His long black hair cascaded over his shoulders, partially falling in front of his face. His face was long, but his jaw was squared, with his prominent Roman nose sitting perfectly on his face. Ace kept her face neutral; seeing him after several weeks was always somewhat of a shock to her system. It was as if she was missing a piece of herself that only his presence made her aware she had lost.

Dropping her eyes from his gaze before she gave herself away, Ace bent her knee and bowed while keeping her eyes fixed on the floor instead of on him. A rumble came from him at her gesture, and he swiftly stood, closing the distance between them.

"Ace," he murmured, as he stood before her.

"Nero," she said, still not moving. He was so close. Her fingers tingled with the urge to touch him, but she knew that would only lead her away from what she wanted.

He knelt down and brought his hand to cup her chin, lifting her face back to his. Their eyes locked, and the combination of skin on skin, however small it might have been, and eyes meeting reduced the remainder of Ace's careful control. Her steely mask fell away, and her brows drew up vulnerably, unnecessary breaths coming out as shallow pants.

"Why are you bowing to me?" he asked, letting his fingers trail to her cheek lightly.

"You are an Elder," she whispered in response, unable to make her voice any louder in her current state.

"I am not just an Elder to you," Nero said, eyes narrowing slightly. He withdrew his hand, standing and stepping away from her. "I'd prefer if you stood."

She did, meeting his eyes again to see the displeasure there and fought the wince that that the expression gave her. There would always be a part of her that desired to please him, but the logical and independent part made her question if that was *her* or the power he could wield over her by being her sire. She made an effort to make her face expressionless again.

"Why did you call for me?" she asked, watching as his brows pinched together a bit more. He seemed startled by her direct question, but he crossed his arms and looked resigned after a brief sigh.

"I happened to *see* earlier. Not very much, but it intrigued me. None of us on the council have gotten an update on current hunts or outings in some time," he told her.

There were two things wrong with this admission. One was the very obvious question of why was he alone calling for her and not the council? Two, that he had used the sire-progeny connection they had to look into her mind. It was not a common connection between sire and progeny. In fact, Ace only knew of one other pair that had that connection, and it was Nero and his sire, Srinta.

Ace and Nero had promised to push that ability away during their ... time apart. They had once been together, centuries together. Nero had brought her there as a human, changed her at her request, and they had reveled in their connection for years. But the war began to ramp up, Nero had been elevated to Elder, and mutually, they had agreed it would be better to focus their efforts and attention on the war instead of themselves.

Using their connection that way was a direct violation of the separation they had agreed upon for the good of their kind. It was selfish of him to have looked into her mind, making Ace's eyes glow with anger.

"I'll write up a report for you. Unless you want to just take a peek and find out for yourself," Ace said stiffly, one eyebrow rising on her forehead provokingly.

"It wasn't my intention; it caught me off guard," Nero snapped, eyes lightening to a slightly brighter shade of blue with his own anger.

"I suppose I don't want to waste any more of my time making a report," Ace said coldly, taking a deliberate step back so he was no longer close enough to touch her without pursuing her. "I saw Lukis's son tonight. His men approached him at Don's club."

"Why were you there?"

"We got a tip that they had been clearly out searching mixed Immortal haunts. For what, we didn't know until this evening."

"I heard he had a son, but I don't have anything concrete to say about him. He's only been alive for thirty years, maybe less," Nero said, bringing his hand up to his chin to rub as he thought.

"I don't think he's fully Werewolf," Ace said, glad that the tension seemed to have melted away for now.

Her impulse to give into whatever he wanted was what truly scared her. Though they had been together for centuries, she hadn't known if it was of her own free will or his. Ever since he made her, she felt like she could hide nothing from him, the man who had given her this life after she had no one and nothing left. She was already damned, her human life destroyed, when he gave her a new life and purpose. But that came with the price of wondering if her feelings were real or fabricated by the power of her sire.

"That doesn't surprise me. Rumors about Lukis's human wife have been going about the Immortal world for years," Nero told her, giving her a small, amused smile briefly.

"Human? How?"

"He keeps her alive somehow but hasn't changed her. I imagine she's gone mad over the years. The change helps us adapt, changes our brains so we're capable of handling living for such a long time. He either loves her dearly and can't let her go, or he enjoys watching her in torment," Nero said quietly.

"Perhaps that's why his son left?" But Nero didn't seem to hear her, his eyes distant as if he were lost in his own thoughts.

"Curious… Why would Lukis be tracking him down in such a way? And for what reason?" Nero pondered aloud.

"I haven't the slightest idea. But he looked frustrated and didn't want to leave with the men his father sent. Had Makiut managed to keep himself from getting in an actual fight with the other one, I may have learned a bit more information," Ace said, a grumble in her voice. She knew the fault didn't lie strictly with her partner, but it felt like she was about to overhear something that was interrupted quite thoroughly with the outbreak of their fight.

"You two separated?" Nero asked, eyes once again focusing on her, making her still heart ache slightly in her chest.

"He was distracting the one that was going to post by the door so I could listen," Ace said, watching as his eyes lightened with anger once again.

"You aren't to be alone."

"I'm quite capable, Nero, and so is Makiut. He killed the *single* Werewolf he was fighting. Nothing either of us couldn't handle," Ace said, crossing her arms and glaring at him.

"He killed the wolf without a scratch?" Nero questioned, looking down at her blood- saturated clothes and hands. Ace rolled her eyes.

"He lost an arm. But *I* have not a scratch! I am fine on my own," Ace insisted.

"No," Nero said, turning away from her and heading toward a door on the side of the council room.

"You can't keep me from my duty, Nero. I'm the judge of this coven!" Ace yelled, causing him to pause.

"It's because you are judge, and you are important to this coven, that I can't allow you without a partner. You'll wait until Makiut is well before you leave again," he said without looking at her, resuming his stride and leaving Ace alone in the council room.

CHAPTER 3

Ace glared daggers at the closed door Nero exited in, her hands in tight fists at her sides. She took the role of Coven Judge only because of him. For him. Now he was using it against her. Never before had she been prohibited to hunt on her own. Not when she was a new Necare, nor when she became a judge. There was some other reason for him barring her from leaving the mansion, and she needed to know what. But now was not the time. She was far too angry, and her reactions to him weren't to be trusted; another confrontation would only make things worse. Instead, she would scour the intel they had gathered recently and try to ascertain more about Lukis's son.

She turned on her heel, walking back through the large main doors of the council room and briskly back up the stairs to the main corridor. The House Vampires were lounging in the parlor when she passed through, heading toward the main stairs. Dava's eyes, full of devious light, watched as she passed. Dava, the snake, regularly tried inserting herself where she wasn't needed and incited rumors throughout the coven. That look she gave her made Ace suspicious at how or why Dava, of all Vampires, was chosen to deliver Nero's message.

Ace paused only a moment to let her eyes glow in warning toward Dava, before she continued up the stairs, moving past the other chambers before finally reaching her own. She immediately set her trajectory to her computer. She could get lost in her work and would put it all there, because *this* was what she was good at.

The dark room she called her own was nothing but black tapestries, a huge black desk with various weapons, papers, and her laptop placed on it, and a few black velvet chairs. She was a minimalist at heart. Her role was a judge and a Necare, and she didn't need other frivolous things getting in her way of that. Other Vampires she knew had other hobbies, their rooms filled with their other ministrations, but she didn't afford herself any additional luxuries. It was simply not who she was.

The date flashed across the screen before she entered her password. She hadn't thought much about the time of year, but it caused her to pause. The Harvest would be happening soon and with it, the Judges would converge. She sat back against her chair, eyes staring beyond the screen. The Harvest meant several things. She had to entertain the other judges and their companions, hosting them in her home as the leader here. It also meant that Six would once again be at Kurome. Though it happened once a year, each time Six returned, it made the blood curdle in her veins.

It wasn't because Six and Ace were so different. In actuality, they were quite similar: both powerful, respected, and high-ranking female Vampires. But where Ace was reserved, Six was very much the opposite, with a reputation for being rather mad. Six had originated at Kurome but was sent to the Americas to have a coven of her own because of her relentless thirst for power. Taking direction from others was not something she did well, often opting to kill anyone who got in her way before following their orders.

Too young, as far as Vampires were concerned, to be an Elder, and having committed atrocities against her own kind in pursuit of her own will, Six had been spared because of the bloodline she came from. The same bloodline as Ace. Six's disposition was something that always seemed to strike Ace with guilt, because had Ace been a bit more focused on her blood-kin and less on her own sense of purpose, perhaps Six would have turned out differently.

Perhaps that was what Lukis was trying to do with his son? Mend a bridge that he had damaged by being so focused and driven to win the war?

Ace pushed herself from her leaning position, pulling up the photos that had recently been taken of other Werewolves who had been suspiciously moving through the city over the last few weeks. There, in the background of several of the photos, Ace could see Lukis's son. Often, he was just out of view of the wolves, fleeing before they had a chance to corner him. The look on his face told Ace everything she needed to know. This man wanted nothing to do with the Werewolves, but they were working *very* hard to get ahold of him.

She pulled up a map of the city, looking at each of the locations where the man appeared in the photos. He wasn't going very far. He seemed to maintain a circle, remaining near ... what? He clearly had a central location he either lived at or he liked to frequent. It would have been a lot easier on her if she knew his name to track him down more easily.

It was only when the sun's rays were glowing from the bottom of the thick velvet curtains that Ace realized how much time she had spent feverishly working at tracing his movements. If she could gather all this information from the Werewolves being tracked, how much did they know about his whereabouts? She clenched her fists, glaring at the window as if it were the sun that was keeping her locked away in the mansion, not Nero. Makiut's dried blood crack and flaked from her knuckles onto the keyboard, and she suddenly realized that not only was she still disgustingly caked in her partner's blood but she was desperately hungry.

With a quick wash and change of clothes, she set off back down to the Medicus to secure some blood. The coven was quiet, as most of the others had gone to sleep with the sun. She moved silently through the building, coming to the doors of the Medicus, expecting to be the only one still alive for the day. But as she opened the door, there stood Nero at the little cot where Makiut slept. He turned his gaze from Makiut's face to her, watching as she moved briskly to the refrigerators, grabbing the closest bag she could find, and then left the room once again.

She was already at her door before she felt his hand on her arm, halting her before she could enter.

"Ace, I wanted to—"

"Scold me? Imprison me?" Ace interrupted, whirling to face him.

"Imprison you?" he snapped back.

"That's what you've done by banning me from leaving the mansion. I cannot make any difference from here," she said, gesturing to her room. Though she loved her Necare, she couldn't trust anyone else to go out searching for Lukis's son. There was something big here, something monumental in whatever Lukis was planning with his son. She didn't know how she knew it, but she could just feel it.

"You cannot make a difference if you're dead!" Nero hissed, tightening his grip. A rustling indicated someone in one of the nearby rooms was stirring. The mansion was quite silent at this time of day normally, so despite their hushed voices, the conversation was bound to alert someone if they continued in the hall. Nero narrowed his eyes at her, opening her door and shoving her forcefully inside before stepping in himself.

"Why are you so concerned about me going out alone all of the sudden?" Ace asked as she strolled over to her desk, letting the blood bag flop on top of a stack of papers she had left there.

"It's not all of the sudden," he growled. Ace turned back to him. He was practically vibrating, frustration and possessive energy rolling off him. "I have always worried, and I will always worry," he said a bit more softly, moving a few paces closer to her. The look in his eyes, that same look she had seen a thousand times, was there. The same eyes that she saw first through her weak mortal view were staring at her once again. She didn't know how she managed to stay away from him so well for so many years, but her strength in that regard was falling away each moment they continued making eye contact.

"Don't," she whispered, turning away from him again. She placed her hands on the edge of her desk, leaning over and willing herself to stare at the bubbles in the cold blood bag instead.

"I can't keep doing this."

"You'll have to."

"Look at me," he growled, taking her around the waist to turn her back to him. Her eyes shown vulnerability to his face. He was so close, the feel of his arms around her, his face mere inches from her own made her stomach clench. "I want you," he whispered, his voice a low rumble against her chest.

"We decided—"

"We decided we would pause while we transitioned to our new roles, Ace," he chided, pulling her even more firmly against him.

"I..." She forced her gaze from his, turning her head to look anywhere but his face, searching for some distraction from how good it felt to be in his arms again. What she so desperately wanted to tell him was that she wasn't sure anymore what was real and what was his manipulation. Hundreds of years of manipulation, potentially. But she couldn't bring herself to admit that to him. If she said those words, asked that question, and he answered with a yes, it would shatter the illusion of what she thought they had before.

But he was right, of course. They couldn't go on this way.

"How do I know this isn't your influence on me?" Ace asked, her voice more timid and shakier than she would have liked. Nero's face changed with the question, frustration and desire giving way to horror.

"You think I'd do that?" he asked, pulling away just a bit more to see her face fully.

"I don't know."

Nero searched her eyes for a long moment, seeing the sincerity in her confusion. He had clearly failed, failed her in so many ways that had become utterly clear with her last declaration. With much regret, he pulled himself away, putting a bit of space between them.

"Ace, I ... I have never used any influence on you. Never. Not even when you were human," he said solemnly, giving her a mournful look before he turned and left the room without another word.

Ace let out a breath, the sounds coming out as a strangle sob from her lips.

Ace threw herself into her work for the next several days. She had gathered her two best Necare, Nyprat and Lotte, sending them out with the map she had created to monitor. There was still a lot of territory to cover, even with having it somewhat narrowed down, but she hoped they would be able to catch a glimpse of Lukis's son. It would at least help her determine where she could potentially pick up the trail once Makiut was healed, or her duties as Coven Judge were concluded with the end of the Harvest.

Dava appeared in her doorway without knocking on the third night. The sun had just set not long before, and Ace knew she would be wanted at the weekly summons, the "dinner" they had once a week. Often the Elders didn't join this occasion; it was simply an opportunity for the coven members to commune. Before the blood bank and the subsequent farming facility, the House Vampires would acquire mortals for them to feast on together, which had been quite the bonding experience. Ace smiled lightly at the memories of sharing her meals with Nero that way, eyes locked in hunger and ecstasy.

"What are you doing?" Dava asked, her voice ripping Ace from her thoughts abruptly.

"Working," Ace said, gesturing to the computer in front of her.

"You have to make an appearance this week. It's not like you are out on a hunt with Makiut. You don't have an excuse not to come," Dava said, smirking as Ace's eyes narrowed.

"I suppose I don't have that excuse," Ace grumbled, standing from her chair.

"Should I help pick a dress out for you?"

"A dress? Whatever for?" Ace asked, annoyed and bewildered. Dava had, on a few occasions, been put in charge of purchasing attire for Ace, who found the whole business of shopping rather abhorrent. A dress for a weekly summons was, however, completely unnecessary and out of character for Ace. She had exactly two dresses, and one she was saving for the Harvest, when it was expected that she dress formally.

"I hear the Elders are joining us tonight," Dava told her, giving her a rather suggestive stare. Ace shook her head, her lip curling with irritation.

"My normal attire will do just fine," she said firmly, waving her hands to shoo Dava away, as she made her way to her bathroom. Within the room was a large wardrobe. Large enough for Ace to walk into. She didn't have much variety, but since she detested shopping, she usually got a number of the same pieces so when one was inevitably torn or stained with blood beyond cleaning or repair, she would have a replacement at the ready.

Pulling on a black jacket over the black camisole she had been wearing, she found that good enough and headed down to the dining hall, which sat just on the other side of the Medicus. Most of the coven was already in attendance. Even Makiut sat in his normal position near Ace's spot, though Minshin was clearly hovering and keeping an eye on him.

"Makiut. You're moving about, I see. How's the progress?" Ace asked, as she sat beside him. She could see the thin form of an arm tucked and bandaged to his side. A few days of very direct care from Minshin had proven to do him well, but she could tell there was still a long way yet in his healing.

"Painful," Makiut said roughly. He seemed to wince with each movement, eyes never leaving the glass of blood before him.

"I can imagine," Ace murmured, deciding to turn her attention to the warming pitcher of blood at the center of the table and pour herself some instead of pestering him with questions. She was eager to get back out once the

Harvest was over, but his progress didn't look promising for that to occur as she had been expecting.

"I heard a few of the other Judges are coming in a day early," said a high-pitched voice that broke over the murmurs of others chatting. Ace whipped her head around to find the source. She hadn't heard any news like that, and if that was the case, she'd need to make sure there were rooms to accommodate the early ones. Her eyes homed in on Melody and Melony, twin sisters who had been changed together. They were annoying and perhaps a bit stupid, but otherwise Ace had nothing against them. Their more aggravating attributes seemed to stem from the fact that their twin link enhanced once they became Vampires, the two of them often talking as one or in tandem.

"Who did you hear that from?" William asked, clearly distraught. Ace had put Dava and William in charge of preparing for their guests. She supposed the rooms had not yet been fully readied, or he would not have been so uncomfortable with the idea.

"Damin told us," Melody said, as she and Melony both flicked their strawberry blonde hair over their shoulders at the same time.

"Why on earth would Damin tell you before—?" but William was cut off as the doors to the dining hall banged open. The room went still and silent as the Elders filed in. Srinta entered first, her small form not taking away from the absolute power she commanded with her presence. Her long black hair flowed around her in thick curls, golden eyes peering out at the silenced coven with indifference. She made her way to Ace's table, sitting directly across from her, which prompted the other Elders to follow behind.

Nero made his appearance in the doorway a moment later, eyes scanning the room before ultimately coming to rest on Ace's mildly surprised expression.

"Ace," Srinta said as a greeting, reaching for the pitcher between them as Nero took the last seat at the table, which happened to be beside Ace. "Are the preparations underway for the Harvest?"

"I instructed my House Vampires to the task. Everything should be prepared before the Judges arrive. That is, unless there are some that are coming earlier than we previously thought," Ace said, pointedly glancing at Damin, who was seated beside Srinta. His pinched face seemed to contract even more, as his gaze looked everywhere but at Ace.

"Mmm, yes. I believe some information was supposed to pass to you. Apparently, it wasn't," Srinta said, her voice sharp as she looked up at Nero.

It didn't surprise Ace that the whole council knew. Most Coven Judges dealt only directly with the Elders, instead of using her as a go-between; she preferred it that way. It also didn't surprise her that Nero had failed to mention this to her. They hadn't seen or spoken to each other since their daytime encounter, but it shouldn't have stopped him from performing his duty to his own kind, and that was a large part of the reason Ace felt it necessary for them to continue to remain apart.

"It seems Racid and Six will be joining us early. They both wanted private audiences with us before the others arrived," Srinta continued, bringing the glass goblet, now filled delicately with blood, to her lips. Makiut groaned quietly beside Ace, but it didn't draw anyone's gaze his way. It was well known that Makiut and Six did not mix well.

"I'll make sure William and Dava get those rooms prepared before the others," Ace said, knowing full well that both heard her. The room was still devoid of the previous conversations, everyone listening quite intently to what the Elders had to say.

"They're arriving tonight," Nero murmured, letting his fingers nervously fiddle with the stem of his still empty glass.

Ace stiffened a bit.

Tonight.

There was no possible way for the number of rooms to be fully prepared in a few hours for the companions Six and Racid would bring along with them, even if every House Vampire pitched in. Ace took a deep breath, trying to keep herself from the rage-filled outburst she wanted to have. Downing her cup in one gulp, she stood from the table, and bowed her head respectfully to each of the Elders, save Nero.

"House Vampires, come to the guest wing to assist me as soon as you're finished with your meal," Ace instructed, her voice carrying louder than required through the room before she left the dining hall without another glance.

CHAPTER 4

Ace retreated back to her room once the preparations had gotten to a point where she no longer needed to keep hovering over the House Vampires. Racid traditionally brought with him three of his Necare, while Six would bring two. Each Vampire would be given their own room, but Six, in her demanding-as-usual nature, had very specific requirements. Her room was not to be in the guest wing but in Ace's, with the other Necare and the odd House Vampire or two. The room she usually occupied on these visits had been hers when she lived at Kurome before. On her first return to Kurome, after she had been given her own coven, she had thrown a tantrum that could have alerted all of London, seeing that her former space had been altered.

Never again had they made that mistake, instead keeping the red decorations and furniture exactly where she had left it. But since it would sit empty for a year, it required additional steps for cleaning and preparations. Six also would insist that one of the Vampires she brought along be in the room beside hers, a room that was now being occupied by William. He hadn't made a fuss about having to relinquish his space to an outside Vampire, but

Ace knew the instinctual urge to protect one's territory, and Six's coven was infringing on that.

Six would be arriving any minute, and as the Coven Judge, Ace would need to be present to greet her. She quickly changed her clothes once again, having acquired some dust on them from the cleaning, before swiftly moving toward the parlor to await the arrival of her ... guests.

She heard the sound of the car tires crunching up the side gravel drive from the other hidden entrance to the south of the property long before the headlights pierced the darkness through the large windows. She held herself back from the nervous fidgeting she wanted to do, now that the parlor had become flooded with the rest of the coven. Makiut and Minshin were scarce, back in the Medicus, Ace assumed. At least he had a good reason to be absent from events this year. Normally, he would make the briefest of appearances at the Harvest and only to see his sire, Aknot.

William opened the doors at the barely audible sound of footsteps approaching, and there stood Six just inside the threshold. Her appearance was exactly as it normally was, flaming red hair done up with massive amounts of teasing and gel, reaching high over her head like a crown of crimson thorns. Her equally red attire and eyes would seem shocking to most, especially against her paper-white skin, but Ace had watched this girl change from human to Immortal right before her eyes. Her appearance was engrained in her, much like Nero's was.

"Ace!" Six said excitedly, eyes alight as she walked forward. "You look the same as usual," Six continued, peeking around Ace's face as if she expected some small change to be missed.

"The same to you," Ace replied dryly, glancing at the two companions that entered behind her.

Lin was expected. The last several years, he had been tagging along with Six under the guise of being her Head Necare; however, everyone who met them knew he had become her regular plaything, and he was absolutely infatuated with her. The other, however, was completely unknown to Ace. He looked young, as if he had been turned right at the end of his teenage years. He stood, looking somehow both arrogant and anxious, a step behind Lin with his shoulder-length blond hair drooping slightly in his face.

"I expect my room is prepared for me?" Six asked, turning to head up the stairs before she got her answer.

"Of course. Which of your flock will be staying in the guest wing?" Ace asked, eyes flowing Six's course. Ace already knew who Six would keep close, but the formality was for the House Vampires who weren't privy to that information.

"Jacob. Lin will stay beside me." And without another word or any of the customary formalities, Six disappeared into the depths of the mansion as if this were still her home.

Nero paced angrily in the lower library. These books were old, ancient in some cases. The scent of them usually put him at ease, but this time it was not the case. Six's presence complicated things. He hadn't planned on trying to reunite with Ace before the Harvest for this very reason; Six was always a complication. Her ties to both Ace and Nero were strange, and she had always had a destructive desire to *have* Nero.

Six's overt attempts had only increased when Ace and Nero had decided to pause their relationship to focus on their duties, as Six saw this as an opportunity to snatch Nero. But thankfully, her thirst for power had won out, and she was subsequently sent to the States before her attempts at seduction had become too overt. So soon after their separation, Nero imagined Ace would have taken Six's attempts far worse than she did in later years, the wound having been so much fresher at that time.

But he was more frustrated with what Ace had said before. He had been tormenting himself with it for days.

She thought he was using his power as her sire to influence her.

It was one thing that he had never utilized; in fact, he wasn't sure that he even could. There were certain things about Ace that were so unlike other Vampires, a power in and of herself that seemed to shatter norms. She had taken to her life as a Vampire so much more quickly than anyone he had ever known, been able to control herself and her instincts with ease. And most surprisingly, she had the ability to move things with her mind.

She used it rarely, as it wasn't a skill Ace liked to advertise. But having been with her when it first manifested, Nero remembered the surge of power he felt through his own body, through the innate connection they had, when she would use it. He pressed his hands on the inlaid leather of the desk before him, leaning onto it as he closed his eyes and pictured her as she was before. Newly changed, Ace's eyes opened to show a brilliant silver, instead of the grey they had been in her mortal life. She had been worried, he recalled, that he wouldn't love her anymore once she was a Vampire like him, but she had been concerned for nothing.

She was still his Ace, only now they fit together far better than they had before. She would not age and wither away, but would remain with him through the ages. She could match his strength now, and his need for her only grew.

With a hiss, he held himself back from throwing the short stack of books that were beside his now closed fist across the room. It had been her suggestion that they break from each other, her need to feel herself in independence, but he should have fought harder to keep her. Now she was blinded with worries and thoughts he hadn't even entertained as a possibility, and Six ... Six was just the catalyst to push Ace's misgivings over the edge.

"Six has arrived," came Srinta's voice from the door. Nero had felt her drawing closer but had chosen to ignore it. Srinta was his sire, but they were equals now and had been for some time. He had no obligation to acknowledge her.

"I thought as much," Nero grumbled, standing to look at where she leaned in the doorframe. She pushed herself off, wandering over to a pedestal at the center of the room where a book sat. It was closed but propped, as if ready to be cracked open. The book was one of the most important relics that they held within the mansion, old and full of terrible and powerful knowledge.

"You didn't tell Ace that Six was coming early," she said as a statement, opening the book cover leisurely. Nero watched the casual way with which she touched it and cringed. She was older than him by nearly a thousand years, which apparently made her care far less about being careful with something so aged.

"I didn't have an opportunity," he said, turning his back on her to pace the room.

"I think you were avoiding it. Just as you have been avoiding fixing things with her for years," Srinta said, snapping the book shut so it made an awful slapping sound. Nero's head snapped to glare at her for the noise, which only made Srinta smirk. "You have certainly put yourself in a strange position, haven't you?"

"I'm going to fix it," he hissed.

"Men. So proud of themselves for their stoicism. Feigned strength with anger and harsh reactions. It's that pride that makes you stumble," Srinta said, inclining her head with clear judgement. "Is it pride in herself, as it is with you, or fear of you that causes her to hold back?"

Nero went rigid.

"Don't be stupid and let this go on forever. You're both absolutely miserable, and I'm tired of it," Srinta said with a growl, before leaving the room with a flutter of her flowing skirt.

With Six disappearing to her room, Ace could finally see what results Nyprat and Lotte had gathered since she set them on the task of tracking down Lukis's son. She moved through to the training room on the south side of the mansion, away from the other main rooms mostly because it ultimately became the Necares' area. Ace hadn't spent nearly as much time training since she had become the Coven Judge, but she felt a small rush of comfort as she passed through the doors. The familiar clang of metal on metal as a few newer Necares sparred could be heard, as well as the low murmur of voices.

Ace found Nyprat at one of the desks, clearly scrutinizing something on the screen. Nyprat was not one who hid her emotions well.

"New developments?" Ace asked as she approached. Nyprat looked up, startled by Ace's presence.

"Yes," Nyprat said, her voice a little shaky as she gestured for Ace to come look at her screen. Ace came around the desk, peering at the footage that Nyprat had apparently been watching repeatedly.

The video was returned to the start and played, where it showed a narrow street below, indicating Lotte and Nyprat had been perched above, simply watching. This street was so narrow, the buildings were close enough that even a well-trained mortal would have been able to jump from one rooftop to the other. Not suitable for vehicle traffic. The foot traffic was fairly sparse, as it seemed to be quite late in the evening. The camera, which Nyprat had clearly been handling, was focusing on the window of a little café.

"He's coming out," came Lotte's voice over the inferior laptop speakers. Moments later, their target emerged from the glass door, wrapping his oversized coat closer to his body. His eyes darted up and down the street nervously before he turned right. *"We should follow,"* Lotte said, coming into the camera's view as she appeared to be preparing to jump to the street below.

"It's just recon, Lotte. Ace wouldn't want us to get involved. He's still too close," Nyprat said, her hand coming into frame to grasp at Nyprat's sleeve.

"We'll lose him!" But Lotte's voice carried too much. Just past Lotte's shoulder, Ace could see two Werewolves coming down the narrow lane, opposite from where Lukis's son had come from. One sent up glowing blue eyes that seemed like they connected directly with the camera. Almost as if they were looking through the lens, through time, right at Ace.

"Pause it right there," Ace whispered, leaning in to try to make him out.

There was no face to be seen, just simply eyes piercing through. His silhouette was exactly like the Werewolf from The Gast. This wasn't Lukis; she'd know his build anywhere. This shadowy ghost of a Werewolf was someone else. Someone Ace hadn't come across, at least not face to face, but she knew, with the utmost certainty based on the feeling she got from looking at him, that she *would* be coming across him at some point.

"It gets worse," Nyprat murmured, pulling Ace from her trance-like state.

"What happened?" Ace asked.

Nyprat resumed the video, turning her head from the screen as Lotte jumped from the roof, pulling her gun and pointing it directly at the two approaching Werewolves.

Ace watched in horror as Lotte, one of her most trusted and prized Necare, went against everything she had been taught. There was no stealth as her body dropped before the café. No subtlety when she drew her weapon at the two Werewolves, causing a mortal woman who had been crossing in front of them to scream and run. Ace's eyes glowed in fury as Lotte stood, preparing to face these two enemies with nothing weighing in her favor.

"Stop it," Ace hissed. Nyprat did, putting her head in her hands. "Is she dead?" Ace asked through gritted teeth.

"In the Medicus," Nyprat murmured, still not looking up.

"Send me the video. Your investigation is done," Ace said with a finality that rang through the whole of the training room. Everyone had stopped to listen, so the room was eerily still as Ace stormed out, leaving Nyprat utterly distraught.

CHAPTER 5

Six heard the commotion in the training room as she came out to find something or someone to eat. She knew Kurome had long since stopped keeping mortals in the house for feeding, but a girl could hope. She peered down the banister into the parlor, where she watched Ace storm through, her eyes glowing with rage and her hands clenched into fists. Whoever caused Ace to be so livid was in for it, which made Six's face lit up with delight.

"We should follow," Six said to Lin, who was at her side.

"That seems like a coven matter, Six. We should—" Lin started.

"Then *I* will follow. Feel free to stay here and be boring," Six said with a scowl, before rapidly descending the stairs.

She, though not visual subtle, was quite skilled at being deathly silent. She crept swiftly behind Ace, following her to the Medicus.

Ace burst through the doors, eyes rapidly searching for Lotte, who was on a cot just beside Makiut.

"*What* were you thinking, Lotte?" Ace thundered, moving through the space so rapidly that even Makiut seemed startled when Ace suddenly appeared beside them.

"I—"

"So many things wrong with what you did! You endangered yourself. You bloody tossed the Masquerade aside as if it meant *nothing*. You abandoned your partner. You lost sight of the objective. Need I go on?" Ace asked, standing stiffly with her hands on her hips.

"She had additional orders, Ace," came Nero's voice from the other end of the room, where he had been watching the footage Ace had watched earlier diswith Minshin. Ace whirled around, looking at him with a face contorted with disbelief.

"I'm sorry..." Ace paused, holding her hand up in the air as she processed what he said for a mere moment. "I thought I heard you say *my* Necare, Lotte, had additional orders that didn't come from me."

"I gave her an additional objective once I had heard what you sent them out to do," Nero confirmed, gaining a frightening brightening of Ace's eyes as they went from glowing silver to white rage.

"And what, may I ask, were those orders?" Ace said, her voice too calm, too controlled for comfort.

"I was to keep Lukis's men from being able to follow his son if we were to come across them," Lotte offered, though her voice was quite rough. Ace looked back to see part of her throat had been torn at and clearly damaged.

"And that was the best way you thought of doing that?" Ace hissed. "You could have deterred them much more safely from your perch. There was no need for you to leave Nyprat behind and try to take two Werewolves on by yourself."

"They would have caught his scent. I..." Lotte let out a strange hiss of air, wincing as she did so. "I jumped down to mask it with my own."

Now Ace felt a bit dull for not having realized that was a possibility for her actions, but it was still utterly reckless. Was Lukis's son's life more important than one of her Necare? Presently, that answer was no. He may be important to Lukis's plans, but Lotte's life was far more precious to Ace than some half-blood.

"You are more important to this coven than Lukis's son. I trust you to remember that the next time I decide to let you out," Ace said quietly, glaring at Lotte until she nodded her head slowly in understanding.

"It could have been done a bit differently, Lotte. On that, Ace and I agree," Nero said, coming to stand beside Ace before Lotte's bed. Ace shook a bit with how hard it was to control the impulse to yell at Nero in front of everyone.

Six listened from the hall, not wanting to give away that she was eavesdropping. At first, she had been amused by this situation, even a little proud of Ace. Ace, who throughout Six's time at Kurome had always had a rage seething under the surface but so rarely let it out for anyone to see, was actively raging on one of her Necare, and Six was simply relishing in it. It had become somewhat of a game to her in the past, how could she best misbehave and cause Ace to lose her mind, but she had never fully succeeded.

But what was odd was the visceral reaction Six had to Nero saying the words, "Ace and I." She had made no attempts to hide her intentions, as Six had always imagined Nero would someday choose to favor her, or if nothing else take her to his bed, even if it was only once. It was often that way with sires and their progeny. Upon opening her new eyes at her rebirth as a Vampire, Nero and Ace had been everything to her, and yet he had only had eyes for *her*. It had become a sick goal for Six that she would have him and discard him, just as she felt he discarded her.

And yet, here he was, continuing with this odd pining after Ace. Years they had not been together now, and each time Six returned to Kurome for the Harvest, he never gave in to her advances. Never gave in to anyone's advances, as far as Six had heard. Dava was quite the gossip and confidant to Six when she came to the mansion, and even she, with her aesthetically perfect body, had not been able to convince Nero to stray. Not even once.

Nero's words "Ace and I" continued to ping in Six's head. It was always her. Always her. What was so special about Ace? She vibrated with a rage that was barely contained, as she turned back down the hall just as she heard Nero say, "I need to speak with you privately," to Ace.

Ace, too, was infuriated, as she blindly allowed Nero to steer her out of the Medicus and through the mansion. Her eyes were barely seeing where they were going as she was consumed with irritation, Ace suddenly found her gently pushed through a door. She paused for a moment, taking a sharp intake of air when she realized where she was: Nero's room.

She had been in this room many times before; it had been her room too for many years. But two particular occasions would always stand out specifically in her memory of being there: when Nero was making her a Vampire and when he was ill. His room looked somewhat different now than it did when she was mortal, but then all things eventually change when one lives an extraordinarily long life, and she had spent quite a long time avoiding this room in recent years.

Ace stood by the door hesitantly and watched Nero as he moved to his desk, pulling the cufflinks from his sleeves and tossing them, before sitting on the edge of the desk and turning his eyes toward her. His long black hair fell over his shoulders gently as his gaze moved over her body.

"You undermined me," Ace said, her body still tense with frustration as she glared back at him. It was not so much that he, an Elder, had given her Necare additional orders, but more that she hadn't known about them.

"I did no such thing. Lotte acted foolishly. It was against what either of us would have wanted," Nero said.

"You gave *my* Necare orders without telling me. You barely had interest in what I did or how I ran things since you became Elder, and now you suddenly feel as though you need to interfere?" Ace hissed. Nero suddenly stood up, coming before her, and grasping her chin so she met his eyes.

"I've always had interest, Ace. I have always checked in, consulted the members of the coven as to your plans. I always know what's going on," Nero whispered. "I did not interfere. I did not take away your power, but I *always* knew." Ace pulled her face from his grasp, stepping back a pace.

"You..."

"We agreed on many things when we decided to take time apart," Nero started, turning away from her once again, but this time to approach the back of the Victorian sofa that was placed before his unused fireplace. His gaze lifted to the painting over the mantle. It was a piece he had done of her many years ago, a painting Ace hadn't been sure he kept but her eyes also lifted to it, taking in the vision of her fresh from a hunt, blood spattered and eyes glowing. "We agreed to take time apart to focus. To let *you* focus. I never had such a compulsion or need. I never wanted this."

"Your duties as an Elder—"

"My duties as an Elder pale in comparison to my desire for you!" Nero snapped as he whirled back around to look at her.

"You speak of desire as if I'm some object to possess," Ace said coldly. He tensed with frustration, walking back over to her and grasping either side of her face forcefully.

"Not an object to possess, the person who haunts my every thought. The woman who, from the first moment I looked upon you, I knew I couldn't go on without. These years, being so near to you in this bloody mansion, covered by the same roof, but not *with* you. I could not come to you to ask about your missions. I could not call you to my chamber to simply talk to you and know what's going on within your mind. It has been utter torture for me to stay away from you. You are no mere object to me. You are the only air I wish to breathe."

"Nero..." she whispered, eyes wide as he leaned forward, pressing his lips to her forehead gently, his hands going softer against her face. With his lips upon her flesh, memories rushed back to her, sending a shockwave throughout her whole body. His lips found their way to the tip of her nose, to her chin, and back to her forehead. Featherlight kisses everywhere on her face, except her lips.

Her mind was spinning. She had been the one to push away. She had been the one that needed to halt their relationship. She had needed to know who she was and if everything she had thought herself to be was because of him. And she had found that. She was powerful in her own right. A leader. A warrior.

His breath cascaded over her face, the scent sending her mind and body on alert. She wanted him. She missed him. She loved him in a way that was overwhelming. Ace realized she had loved him from the moment she saw him through her window, her dull human eyes not fully grasping his beauty at the time.

She tilted her head up just slightly, catching his lips with hers. The sensation was overwhelming. A kiss that was years overdue. He let a small moan release from his throat as he deepened the kiss, their arms snaking around the other as Nero pressed her against his chest so nothing but a hair could come between them.

But as the kiss became more frenzied, hands clutching, fangs scraping against one another, Ace realized this was not the time. No, the war would not end overnight, but with the other Judges arriving and the fact that she knew she was at the precipice of getting to the bottom of Lukis's current plan, she couldn't afford this distraction. She couldn't afford to lose herself in Nero, as she so wanted to.

It was a great effort, but she pulled herself from him, releasing her lips from his and stepping away, hand extended to halt him from pursuing her.

"No. Not now. I can't," she murmured, glancing up at him with eyes begging him to understand. She had no way of knowing otherwise, but some small piece of her felt that if she gave into what she wanted, it would distract far too much. Her duties and responsibilities were imperative to success. Right now, she had to remain alone and unattached. If the Vampires were to win against the Werewolves, she could not let her attention get diverted.

"Just give in to what you want, Ace," he whispered, stepping closer to her again, but she stepped back another pace.

"I want us to win," she told him, letting her eyes get lost in his for a moment. Had her heart still beat within her chest, she was certain it would have been pounding as she hesitantly stepped forward, placing a final kiss on his cheek, before she walked out of the room, closing the door softly behind her and leaving Nero behind, a very confused and exasperated expression on his face.

She moved down the hall a bit, stopping when out of view of his chamber door to lean back on the wall and stare at the ceiling for a few minutes. She wasn't certain all her concerns were gone about manipulation, but one thing was certain: she didn't really *care* anymore. That kiss, the first they had shared in over fifty years, left her ... wanting.

But she had made her choice, at least for the time being. She chose the war, and because of that, she would not delay. She pushed herself from the wall, walking through the mansion back to her room. Nyprat would have sent her that footage by now, along with any other pertinent information the two of them had gathered while out. Ace would need to scrutinize each frame to see if she could glean any additional information on Lukis's son. She walked up to the second floor and back to her room to find Six there, sitting in one of her black velvet chairs. The red spikes gave her away, even though the backs of the chairs were tall.

"You don't seem disheveled. Turn down poor Nero?" Six asked in her southern drawl as Ace walked around to face her. Six smirked, though her eyes hinted at a fiery anger that smoldered just under the surface.

"We simply talked," Ace said, sitting in her chair and waking her computer from its sleep. Yes, Nyprat had sent everything and had some additional notes.

"The way you smell, I doubt that," Six said, though her voice was cutting.

"Is there a reason you've come to my room?" Ace asked.

"Is there some reason you keep turning him down? He hasn't taken any other lovers, the House Vampires would undoubtedly know of it, and they tell me that he takes none to his bed. He just sits there and pines for you, of all people," Six said disgustedly, crossing her arms over her chest.

"Is there some reason you are so fascinated in my or Nero's lovers?" Ace asked, returning Six's look with a vehement glare.

Ace knew, of course, why Six was so interested. Six had made it abundantly clear for many years that she wanted Nero, even before Ace and Nero had separated. It was an irritation, but one that never held much weight for Ace, because at the time that Six lived at Kurome and could have been considered a threat, they were together; and Ace would have been damned if Six had touched him.

What Ace hadn't known, and what she had tried very hard to keep herself from thinking about all these years, was that he wasn't taking others to his bed. She had assumed he would have at some point. Decades of loneliness would have been difficult for anyone; it had been for her, but especially for a Vampire of the likes of him. He had quite the appetite. Just because she had kept herself isolated didn't mean her instincts were any less intact. She hungered for touch just as much as she hungered for blood.

Six let out a laugh.

"You didn't know?" Six asked, her face changing from angry to surprise and delight. "You had no idea he's been keeping himself for you. How funny." But her face turned sour again. "At least you're the *special* one. The one he chose. The one he actually wants. I was made by pure chance, but you know that," Six said, scowling and averting her gaze to the window.

Ace and Nero had never told Six that Ace was the one who had truly changed her. It would probably be the death of them both if she ever found out. Who one's sire is and the mental state of the person who's being changed were large, contributing factors on how they reacted upon awakening as a Vampire. That may have been why Six was a bit more ruthless than the average Vampire. Ace, herself, was not a merciful Vampire. When they hunted mortals in the past, she loved the kill and the blood. She loved what she had become. Those traits were often passed down from sire to progeny.

And from what little Ace knew of Six's mortal past, Six had not been altogether sane. The combination in the flesh before her was a quite volatile Vampire.

"It wasn't chance, Six. You were chosen too," Ace said, finishing off a glass of blood that she had left on her desk earlier that evening. It was thick and beginning to congeal from the open air, but she hated to waste it.

Ace had chosen her for Nero to feed on. He hadn't been able to leave the mansion, as ill as he was. Vampire illnesses were rare, but often brought on due to human disease. The unfortunate House Vampire that had brought the diseased human into the mansion had been disposed of, but the damage had been done.

An illness in a Vampire as old and powerful as Nero was especially troubling. Ace found the innocent girl walking by herself on the streets of London, near the library she had passed earlier in the night. So innocent, so pure; Nero had to have her. Ace had smelled how clean her blood had been, simply by walking past her. *She* could barely resist the impulse to drink her dry, but she knew that was exactly what Nero needed. She had hungrily watched as Nero drank greedily from her, so sick he was unable to be neat about it, and the girl's blood had cascaded over her chest, saturating them both.

It was after he had finished, as his body was visibly taking in her clean blood and healing itself, that Ace had looked at the girl, connecting to her in a way she had never connected to another mortal. She looked upon the dying girl, eyes growing foggy and already distant. The look on her face told Ace this was not the worst pain she had ever faced. No, this mortal had lived in misery, and now she was dying before she had a chance to live any other way. It was at that moment Ace knew she couldn't let her die.

In a way, Ace and Nero were both Six's parents in blood. Nero took her life, and Ace gave it back to her. Ace looked upon her progeny with a mixture of pride and sadness until Six's head turned back.

"I wasn't chosen by him," Six said, before she stood and departed from the room, leaving Ace with an ominous chill.

CHAPTER 6

Six bitterly made her way down the hall toward her room. It was just a few doors away from Ace's. When Six had lived at Kurome before, Ace had always stayed with Nero, but oddly, having Ace in such close proximity when she visited every year put her at ease. They were sisters, she supposed, and Ace had been her most present teacher when Six was learning about her new life as a Vampire. However, it was an odd sense of calm that she didn't feel around anyone else, not even Nero.

Despite the ease she felt near Ace, she still hated that Nero favored her. Six entered her room, letting the comforting color of red overtake her. She wasn't sure why red had always been her particular color. Even the few memories she had of her time as a mortal, she recalled she loved the color, which had been considered an improper color at the time, at least for a lady. Ace had always encouraged her to be herself, though now, Six thought with a smirk, Ace perhaps thought her a bit too outlandish with the way she chose to dress.

It was hard enough for her to come back to this place that both held so many good and bad memories. Six had never quite fit in with the more subdued and reserved

Vampires of this coven, and she made it quite clear that *her* coven would not have to behave so formally. But most of her feelings of being an outcast here had more to do with her abilities. Abilities she shared with Ace.

As far as Six knew, she and Ace were the only two Vampires that could move things with their minds. They also seemed to be impervious to fire, Six even having created sparks from her own fingers a time or two. Ace seemed to rarely use these talents, but Six had made them an integral part of her life, and perhaps that was why these Kurome Vampires feared her so. She knew she was scary. She knew her anger and desires got the best of her, but it was hard for her to care. If she *wanted* something, she would *have* it. Why would she let anything or anyone get in the way of that?

"Ah, you're back," Lin said, as he opened the door to her room. She turned to glance at him and smiled. *He* didn't fear her. If there was one thing she knew with certainty, it was that he was hers to do what she wanted. He would dress how she wanted him to, grow his hair if she desired it, touch her in just the way that she wanted, anything. He was convenient, attractive, and never argued. These were good traits, if not boring. The only thing that annoyed her was how increasingly attached Lin seemed to be getting, and that was a large part of the reason she had plans to discard him. Too much longer, and he'd expect commitment and affection. Things she had no interest in giving anyone, except perhaps Nero if he had wanted her.

"Sun will be coming up soon," Six murmured, moving through to her trunks of attire as she began loosening her corset. Thinking of Nero again irked her.

"I wasn't sure when your meeting with the Elders was—"

"At nightfall," Six said, interrupting him with a bit of exasperation.

"Are you going to ask—?"

"Are you going to question my every decision?" she hissed.

"No ... I just..."

"I will do what needs to be done. I will get the necessary support, because *I* am the Coven Judge," Six told him, daring him with her eyes to say yet one more thing. It was with a nod that he turned around, eyes downcast to the ground, before he quietly slipped from the room, leaving Six to continue disrobing in peace.

The sun had risen, and the mansion went still. Ace had spent the remainder of the night looking over every detail of the intel they had already gotten. Werewolf moments were strange; not only was Lukis spending an absorbent amount of time and effort to get his hands on his own son, but Werewolves were also leaving London almost daily and not returning. She had no idea where they were being sent to, but wherever it was, her spies and other covens' spies on coastal cities didn't seem to have the slightest clue.

She pulled her boots on and had gone to grab her hooded jacket and gloves from her closet when she heard her door open. The sun was not the immediate killer of Vampires as many myths eluded. Over time, direct sunlight would burn them, but they didn't turn to dust in moments. It felt like knives were piercing into them everywhere it made contact. It was painful, and long exposure would be an excruciatingly slow torture that would ultimately end in a pile of ash after many hours, but they could remain mostly protected with hooded jackets or cloaks. Ace was usually not one to do daytime hunts, but this was a true exception. Two Necare down and the mysteries with the Werewolves mounting, she couldn't remain locked away in her room with only her laptop to work from.

"Just a moment and we'll go," she said, assuming it was Nyprat coming to collect her.

"Where do you think you're going?" came Nero's voice instead from behind her. Ace sighed, turning to face him as she pulled the gloves over her hands.

"Out?"

"I told you—"

"You said I couldn't go alone. I'm taking Nyprat with me," she said, pushing past him to exit her closet.

"What are you going to do during the day? The other Judges arrive tonight. You have to present for the Harvest." Ace turned back to him, watching the way his eyes burned. This wasn't because she could potentially miss the Harvest; it was clear in the possessive way he was looking at her.

"I can't do anymore from this room, Nero. We need to get more information, and the only way to do that is in the field. I'll be back long before the sun goes down," Ace assured him, trying to restrain herself from the urge to brush his hair over his shoulder. He looked at her, eyes still hardened with frustration, but he couldn't very well tell her no. She wouldn't be alone and because it was daylight, he knew she wouldn't be reckless.

"You must be careful. Take one of the cars," he said stiffly. She nodded, turning sharply and heading to the parlor where she and Nyprat had agreed to meet.

Ace wasn't sure why, but she just *knew* she needed to go to the café where Nyprat had taken the video footage. They made their way as far as they could with the car, parking it and walking the rest of the way.

"The itch," Nyprat hissed quietly about the sun exposure, pulling the sleeves of her jacket over her gloved hands.

"You need to get heavier gloves," Ace said, as they rounded the corner to the narrow lane.

"Do you think he'd be here? It's so early," Nyprat whined.

"I don't know," Ace snapped, shooting a glare at Nyprat, who flinched.

"I'm sorry. With Lotte and now daylight hunting ... I'm a bit..."

"Anxious, yes. I noticed. Just be quiet. I only took you with me so Nero wouldn't have an aneurysm," Ace said, slowing a bit as they approached the café entrance. Ace glanced through the large windows. *He* wasn't there, but two other Werewolves were.

They were two she had seen before: one was a female, long blonde hair that went to her waist and lean muscles. The other was a brutish looking male Werewolf. Ace glanced at the lane, spotting a small gap between buildings that would be good cover, while still allowing them to watch the window. She wasn't sure what her plan was, only that she needed *something* else. Something more to go off.

Her break seemed to come when she watched the male partner get up and come out of the restaurant for a smoke. Yes, she had definitely seen this one before. Perhaps even fought him. If she recalled correctly, he was Kyle, one of the wolves that Lukis kept close. As close as Lukis let anyone to him, anyway. Ace reached behind her, taking out the gun she had stashed in the waistband of her pants.

"What are you—?" Nyprat started, but Ace had fired before the question could be fully formed. Kyle flinched, hand going directly to his neck as if he were stung by a bee.

"Tranc-chip," Ace whispered to Nyprat, moving closer. Kyle looked with unseeing eyes past Ace as she approached.

He was just out of view of his partner through the café window, and the opportunity was right at hand.

"We're taking him?" Nyprat asked as Ace grabbed his arm, pulling it over her shoulders and bracing his weight.

"I have questions," Ace said, as she began pulling him back toward the car.

The room was dark, the scents were reminiscent of death, blood, and earth. Kyle's eyes focused more, taking in the stone walls. His heartbeat loudly in his chest. What was the last thing he remembered?

The café.

Kira had been with him. They were on watch, and he stepped out for a smoke before...

The door to the room opened, revealing a tiny woman. Her hair was cut short, so he could see her thin neck. Her body seemed slight, but from her smell, he could tell she was a Vampire, and strength was not always what it seemed with them. She approached, hands clasped in front of her. He tried to move, realizing now that when he did so, the silver on the chains burned into his flesh.

"Silver. You may want to stay still," she said, crouching to be more at his eye level a meter or so away. He looked up into her glowing silver eyes and knew immediately who she was. There was no Werewolf in all of London who didn't know of Ace.

"Are you going to torture me?" he asked, hardening himself to the possibility. He had heard rumors before. Werewolves who had been caught being tortured for information.

"Only if I must. You're Kyle, yes?"

"Why would you like to know?"

"You're as close as they come to Lukis, aren't you?" she asked, tilting her head in question.

"As close as he will allow." She nodded, threading her fingers together before her.

"What will he do when he hears you've been taken?"

Kyle stiffened at the question. In normal situations, Kyle would have been left for dead, but there were already plans in place. Many plans were already set in motion, and his capturing could be a helpful coincidence.

"I don't know. It varies from wolf to wolf, who he deems worthy to be saved," Kyle decided to say after a moment's pause. It wasn't a lie so much as a very vague truth. Ace nodded, standing and looking down at him.

"Dietris," Ace said, turning her head slightly toward the open door. A man's figure then filled the doorway, coming in and standing beside Ace. He towered over her, and his eyes showed green in the dim light. "Dietris will ask you questions. How you choose to answer will determine how much he will hurt you," she said, crouching once again, this time a bit closer, casting her face in the small sliver of light coming from the corridor outside the cell. "And let me remind you, Kyle, we can hear your heart beating within your chest, so your lies will be clear." And with that, she stood and walked out of the room, leaving Kyle to his fate.

Nero had stayed in Ace's room while she was gone. He didn't often force the connection to see what she was up to, having rarely used it in their decades apart until recently, but the idea of her out during the day ... he loathed it. He had paced and glared at her sparse room, hating every-thing he saw. She had far more personality than this bland, abysmal space. She didn't even have a bed, simply a few pieces of furniture and a tapestry to hide her coffin.

When she returned with her prisoner, he shut the connection back down, feeling almost guilty for having peeked there in the first place. He was breaking too many boundaries between them lately, and if he wanted her back, he would need to stop before she found out.

She walked into her room, stopping as soon as she saw him sitting at her desk.

"Did you stay here the entire time?" she asked warily, closing the door and putting her jacket and gloves on one of the empty chairs.

"I worried," he admitted, watching her.

"Nothing to worry about," she admonished, coming around to grab her laptop.

"Did you gain something from this unnecessarily dangerous outing?" he asked, eyes a bit narrowed.

"I gained a Werewolf who may come to tell us a few things we didn't know before. It's on Dietris to ask the right questions now," she said, sending him a quick but aggressive glance before returning to her laptop.

"He's not going to give you any information."

"He might let something useful slip."

"Doubtful."

"Don't you have somewhere to be?" Ace hissed, snapping her laptop closed a bit too forcefully. Nero stood from her chair, buttoning his jacket and challenging her anger with a powerful stare that he only used on lesser Vampires. Ace didn't like it at all, staring back and trying very hard not to lash out more than she already had. He *never* used that look on her.

"The sun will be setting soon, Ace. The other Judges will be arriving. Do make time to greet them," Nero said after several tense moments between them, leaving the room in the blink of an eye.

CHAPTER 7

Six stood before the council, her red form standing out in the sea of black marble that surrounded her. There was a still silence in the cold room, not a rustle of clothing nor the shift of position. Finally, after several seconds, Nero spoke, "You have asked to come before the council in advance of the Harvest for what reason, Six?"

"I need more Necare. We only have three in New Orleans, and it is growing steadily difficult to gain control over the local Werewolf den. They seem to be growing in number," Six replied.

"Your coven is relativity small for a reason, Six. That den has had a notoriously insignificant number for decades. We do not need to burden the other covens by taking away their strongest Necare—" Nero started to state. Though his words were firm, his voice carried a softness, trying to keep Six calm. Her short-tempered nature was part of the reason she was sent away in the first place.

"Let alone without an Elder. Need we remind that you are a *minor* Coven Judge. You are not permitted to have more than three Necare and three Medicus without an Elder with you," Damin interrupted, his tone rather condescending. Nero's eyes snapped over to Damin, disgust and mild horror on his face. Silence permeated the room for a beat, all of the other Elders waiting. Six's reactions were unpredictable. There had been times she would laugh off such disrespect, but most often, it was the opposite.

Six's eyes began glowing bright red with rage, the air around her seeming to vibrate with it.

"*Minor?* MINOR! I AM NOT A MINOR JUDGE, ELDER DAMIN!" she screamed at him, her voice echoing through the large, circular council room. Her voice seemed to overtake the cavernous space.

All the Elders, save for Nero, were taken aback. Nero merely closed his eyes. This was precisely what he had hoped to avoid.

Six's fingers began to spark, an inferno building within her. The moment she had stepped back into Kurome Mansion, her rage had been growing. They all saw her as weak. They all chose others over her. Nero chose Ace. The council chose other Judges. Being spoken to in such a way by an Elder was simply the final straw. It was enough to make her want to murder. She felt the heat start to build and her feet slowly lifted from the floor. She was quite a sight to behold, glowing red eyes like churning magma, sparks spitting from her fingertips, and levitating as she stared at the row of Elders atop their thrones.

"I am more powerful than any of you," she whispered coldly. "Call me *minor* again and I'll kill you where you sit," Six snapped, eyes burning as she glared directly at Damin's head.

"Six..." Nero started, but she was too far gone, her hands barely noticeable behind the blazing flames that burst there. Nero let a small gasp escape his lips. He had only seen one other Vampire exhibit such power, and he had spoken of it to no one.

"Minor Judge Six—" Damin started again, though horrified, as he was continuing to try and instruct her.

But the word had left his lips, and Six didn't hesitate. She began releasing small orbs of fire that for a moment seemed to encircle her, like small candle flames or fireflies. The Elders watched in wonder and dread, unsure of what to make of this display. Most of them had never seen something like this from a Vampire. Srinta gasped quietly in horror as several orbs seemed to join together, creating one large orb that seemed to pause before Six for a moment, which lasted for an eternity, before it shot toward Damin. He was unable to react, merely staring in absolute terror as the ball of fire slammed into his neck, burning through his ancient skin and completely obliterating his throat. In doing this, she combined his blood with fire, causing it to evaporate from his body. His eyes were melting in their sockets, and the fire and blood that was pouring out of his mouth was muffling the sound of his screams. The other Elders just sat and watched, shocked and terrified as they sat back on their black thrones, still as statues.

When, at last, Damin had become nothing more than a pile of dust, slightly smoldering, the remaining Elders turned back to Six. She stood, still slightly hovering over the ground, looking at the rest of them like an impatient child, one eyebrow quirked expectantly.

"Well?" Six hissed.

Nero leaned forward and put his elbows on his knees, looking at her with narrowed eyes. He was deciding what to do with her, because surely if he said no to her, she would end up killing every single one of the Elders in the room, save for him. If he sent Necare without an Elder, it could lead to descension amongst the covens. They needed to remain unified, especially now that Lukis was planning something. But any Elder they would send would be dead almost immediately. He could smell the acrid stench of Damin's ashes beside him. This wasn't the first Elder Six had killed, and it wouldn't be the last, unless he kept it from happening.

The only thing that kept him from making this seemingly easy decision was Ace. He was trying desperately to rekindle what they once had. The idea of leaving her behind now, jeopardizing his chance...

Nero's eyes burned into Six's as she waited for an answer. He would regret this decision, but there was no other to be made.

"Six. I know you. I know that I am the only Elder that you will not kill," he started, leaning back into his throne and sighing. Six's lips quirked up into a smirk, looking over the other Elders, who averted their eyes from her. "Because of that, several of the covens will give a Necare to your coven, and I will join you in New Orleans," he said very definitively. He needed no other Elders to start speaking up again. Six could not be given any more reasons to harm the Elders. At least not on this day.

Six started to slowly drift back down to the floor, letting her lips curl into a grin. It looked evil and deranged, her eyes wide, as she felt glee for getting what she wanted and mild pleasure for having killed Damin. Nero kept his lip from twisting with disgust. She wasn't just happy; she was hungry, and he was the meal that was being delivered.

"Thank you, Nero," she said, giving each Elder one final smug glance before she turned sharply on her stiletto heels and walked out of the council room. She would have Nero to herself in New Orleans to do what she wanted with him. No Ace to ruin things for her this time.

They all seemed to sag once the great wooden doors of the room closed behind Six.

"This is a disaster," Fredric, an Elder, murmured, eyeing the pile of dust that was once Damin. Damin was no great loss to the council, though, as his thoughts were always far more contradictory to what the rest of them wanted, and he remained far more isolated than the others, preferring not to join with the other ranks or even step foot outside of the mansion. But for Six to have killed one of them and not only remain unpunished, but get rewarded?

"What will Ace think about this, Nero? You're going to Redeamond? She will be furious," Srinta's voice rang throughout the room, echoing loudly off the walls. Nero sighed, raking his hands through his hair in frustration.

"Ace will understand," Nero said, even though he was worried about what Ace would do as well. Would she completely shut him out? Would she ever trust him again after this?

"Srinta is right, Ace will be greatly taken aback by your decision—" Fredric started, but Nero cut him off.

"Would you all be quiet? I chose what is best for the Vampires! I will speak with Ace. Our business is not yours, as you both seem to be greatly forgetting," he growled, standing and storming out of the room.

As Nero approached Ace's room, he thought of what to say to her. How would he tell her he was going to Redeamond where he would, undoubtedly, be asked many a time to join Six in bed? He knew he could turn her down—as he had every time she had asked him in the past—but there was something about this time that made him uneasy. He opened the door a bit to find Ace hunched behind her laptop, looking at an enhanced picture of Lukis's son.

"Has Dietris gotten any information from the wolf?" Nero asked, coming to sit at the chair across from her. She glanced up at him briefly before looking again at the picture on her screen.

"His name is Lucef. Lukis's son. He apparently is needed for some ritual, but that seems to be the only information Dietris could get from him," Ace told him.

She had found herself completely absorbed in her work, trying to decipher what was so special about Lucef that Lukis would be seeking him out so aggressively. What could they be planning to do with him? What ritual?

Nero sat quietly for a moment, just absorbing her. He loved the way her silver eyes grew so intensely focused under her furrowed brow while she worked. Her sheer determination throughout the years continued to amaze him. She felt his eyes on her, pulling her from the screen to look up at him.

"Just going to stare?" she asked, curious as to why he didn't approach. He let his face show a bit of his concern as he pressed his fingers into his temple. "I thought Six was wanting to speak with the council?" she asked him, taking her fingers from the keyboard slowly and placing them on the arms of her chair. Something about his expression made a pit form in her stomach. Something was wrong.

"She did," Nero replied.

"And what did she want?" Ace asked cautiously, her instincts now on high alert, as if there was an imminent attack.

"Ace..." he sighed and looked down at the floor for a moment, placing an expression on his face, as if he was damning himself for even saying the words to her. She just looked at him, waiting. Whatever he was going to say was going to be bad. "I need to go back to New Orleans with Six, to Redeamond. She needs more Necare and can't have more than three without an Elder there." As he had been speaking, her eyes turned bright with anger and her fingers clenched against the armrests of her chair. The wood whined against the strength of her grip, threatening to break.

"You're joking. You're going to Redeamond? With Six?" Ace hissed.

"I am, but—"

"You're leaving this coven. You're leaving—" She snapped her lips closed before she allowed herself to say more than she wanted to. She had been battling with herself and Nero about these wants and desires she had. He had been persistent, almost irritatingly so, and she had nearly given in to him. Wants and desires she knew Nero also had, but it wouldn't matter now. He would be an ocean away with Six, someone who seemed to always get what she wanted.

"We don't have any other choice. I must go. If another Elder went, they wouldn't last a day. She thinks I made her; that's the only reason that she won't try to kill me," Nero said, standing up and moving quickly around the desk to kneel before her.

"I'd like to see her try," Ace grumbled, trying to avert her eyes from his stare.

"It would be quite the task," he murmured, smiling lightly. He reached over and cupped her cheek, turning her face back to him and forcing her gaze to meet his. "I wouldn't be doing this if there was another way." His words were heavy with promise, eyes pleading for her to understand.

"You're right, of course," she grumbled, hating herself for feeling so angry about him leaving, and for not being able to pull herself away from his touch.

"I will come back to you, Ace," he whispered, his fingers snaking around to the back of her head. Against her better judgement, she allowed him to pull her closer, their noses touching for a moment before his lips pressed against hers. She hated him for this. Every moment of this was blissful and yet accompanied by horrible pain. The Judges would leave following the Harvest, meaning by tomorrow he would be gone.

She pulled away, stifling the whimper that threatened to escape her throat.

"I need you," he whispered, trying to chase her lips as she leaned back in her chair.

"You'll be gone tomorrow," she said bitterly, turning her eyes to the screen where the picture of Lucef was still displayed. Nero dropped his hand, standing lithely and looking down at her face, his chest feeling tight with the emotion he saw there.

"I need to speak to the other Elders anyway. We have to make some decisions regarding what we're going to do about Damin," he said, realizing she was dismissing him, at least for now. The Damin comment caught her attention, though, and she turned back to him, curious.

"What's wrong with Damin?" she asked, not exactly worried about him, since he was her least favorite of the Elders, but more intrigued there may be something amiss.

"Oh. Six killed him. You know she's not good at controlling her emotions." He breathed in deeply, thinking of the mountain of work he would have to do, recording Damin's death, appealing to the other Judges for Necare. "Quite a mess she's made for us," he said, snarling momentarily.

"You realize that is why we sent her to New Orleans, with her *own* coven," Ace reminded, crossing her arms with smug satisfaction.

"The only reason she still lives after she killed Cara and Tahmores is because I'm supposed to be her sire," Nero said, as a retort. Ace raised her eyebrows and shrugged with mild guilt. Six's invulnerability to punishment was based on the lie that she and Nero had kept going for quite some time. The only other person who knew that Six wasn't Nero's progeny was Srinta, and she was simply happy they had yet another in their line.

Nero's eyes lit up, recalling Six's show of powers in the council room. He hadn't seen her use them before, certainly not during her time spent at Kurome when she was a young Vampire.

"Six seems to have inherited some gifts from you, Ace," Nero told her.

"Hm?"

"In the meeting, she killed Damin with fire she produced from her hands, and she levitated." Ace's eyes widened a fraction. Her powers were always kept a secret; only Nero knew the full extent of them. She rarely ever used them when she was on a mission, and if she did so, it was when Makiut and the other Necare were out of sight. She hadn't ever brought up Six having abilities like hers to him before.

"I see," Ace said, averting her eyes. She was mildly disappointed Six had revealed that particular skill, but there was little she could do about it now.

"It was quite the surprise," Nero admitted, watching Ace's eyes and realizing she had known. He frowned a fraction, pausing just a moment, as if to give her the opportunity to say something else to him, but when it was obvious she wasn't going to, he turned to leave.

She didn't watch him as he left the room, her thoughts muddled now. Nero was leaving, Six, and of course the new developments with Lukis and his Werewolves. How had she let herself get so distracted? For so long she knew what her goal was. She was a weapon and instrument to win this war. No good would come of her splitting her focus. With a sigh, she turned her eyes back to the picture of the strange man in the photo on her computer screen. His shoulder-length hair and eyes black and blue were like that of a changed Werewolf staring back at her. She decided she would keep herself busy with this Lucef character while Nero was gone.

In fact, it was a good thing he was leaving. Now she'd have no distractions.

CHAPTER 8

There was a large full moon in the sky and the keen ears of the Vampires could hear many Werewolves out on the loose, letting themselves get lost as the moon called their beasts to the surface. The properties around the mansion were mostly golf courses and small pockets of woodland, so the city Werewolves often spent their full moon changes in the surrounding area. Normally, this would be prime killing time for Ace's Necare, but since the Harvest was upon them and so many prominent Vampires were in attendance, they couldn't chance leaving the mansion unguarded. Having them all at the mansion wasn't a comfort to Ace, who was trying not to feel resentful she had to stay indoors on such a night.

Nero sent Dava by Ace's room earlier in the evening to let Ace know he planned to escort her down to the event. It was customary that she would be expected to be seen with the Head Elder, as she was the Coven Judge and, therefore, both were seen as hosting this event. She didn't care for the appearance it showed the other Vampires, though. It was well known that Ace and Nero were no longer a couple, but that wouldn't stop the rumors from spreading, as they usually did following the Harvest. Each year, she had to contend with a new bout of questioning, asking if they had rekindled their relationship, and each year she would have to dissuade them from those assumptions.

Ace moved to her closet, glancing at the dress that was hanging there, waiting for this very event. It was black silk, and not at all anything Ace would normally have chosen for herself. It was a dress Dava had ordered for her and had surprised her when she decided she liked it. Often, she hated the clothing Dava picked out for her, but Ace also wasn't one for shopping for herself either. She quickly pulled off her pants and black shirt she had been wearing and slipped the dress up as she heard her door opening.

"We should be making our entrance," came Nero's voice.

"One moment," she murmured, putting her boots back on. They may not have gone with the dress, but she would be damned if she was forgoing pockets *and* her footwear. She had cleaned them off after her and Nyprat's daytime expedition, so they were at least free of dirt and debris.

She peeked out from her closet, watching the moment as Nero moved gracefully through the space, pausing at her desk. He was dressed in a green silk shirt, black dress pants, and a duster length evening jacket with intricate embroidery. He looked handsome, regal, hungry, and somewhat uneasy at the same time.

Ace stepped out, watching Nero's expression deepen from mild desire to consuming. His eyes looked over her hungrily. The dress was long, black silk, flowing to the floor. It clasped behind her neck with an ornate broach, but the rest of her back was unfettered, showing off her pale perfect skin. There was nothing to be done about her hair; it was mostly short and heavily layered. She didn't have the slightest idea of how to make it dressy nor did she want to make any effort to try. She approached him, letting the silk flow over her legs like warm butter.

"You look…"

"Not like myself at all?" Ace supplied.

"Delicious," he said finally to her, reaching out his hand. "I had no idea we would match." She tried to hold back the smile that threatened to form, realizing the silk of his shirt and her dress, along with his accompanied pants and jacket, did make them match.

"Nor did I," she said.

"I wish we could just stay here," Nero murmured, grabbing her waist and pulling her closer to him. Ace took in his scent, the feel of his body on hers, the look in his eyes, and almost considered it.

"I wish we could sneak away and hunt," Ace countered, with a playful raise of her eyebrow as she pulled away, putting some distance between them. Nero chuckled lightly. Of course, Ace would rather go hunting.

"We'll hunt together again one day," he said as a promise, though Ace doubted it would ever happen again. Elders' lives were so valued, they almost never went hunting or battling, leaving that to the lower ranks.

They left her room, her arm trapped in his, and slowly walked to the stairs. There was a pregnant silence. Words that they wanted to say to one another, but there wasn't time. Nero would be leaving after this event and Ace … Ace was struggling with how she felt about it. Keeping him at a distance was far easier than giving in and revealing how his leaving really made her feel. The low murmur of conversation down in the parlor quieted somewhat as they approached the banister. Ace stopped to look out at the crowd of Vampires. So many of them piled into one room, and all their eyes were on them.

As they descended, their footsteps were muffled by the deep red carpet that covered the stone stairs. Nero looked around at the silent crowd of seemingly glowing beings.

They were all watching the two of them. He stopped Ace in the middle of the stairs and turned toward the crowd. She wanted to meld into it, not continue to be the center of attention, but with Nero beside her, she could hardly do that. And as Judge of Kurome, she was technically their host.

"We shall discuss important things at a later time. Right now, we enjoy each other's company. Please, as you were," he said loudly, his voice echoing around the hall. They had been expecting some great speech, Ace realized, some grand entrance announcement. Conversations started up again, and there was once again a low mumble of voices, but the eyes stayed on them.

What's going on? Ace wondered to herself. The eyes continued to stare as the two of them walked through the room, side by side. Soon, the curiosity became too unbearable. She turned to Nero quite suddenly and stopped him in the middle of a step.

"Nero, what—?" Ace began, but he cut her off by holding up a hand.

"I believe Dava started a nasty rumor on the wrong day," he told her quietly. Ace's eyes widened, and her eyebrow rose to a violent height on her forehead. "She began murmuring to the guests that we have become a couple again. I suppose I may have enflamed that by drawing you to my chamber the other day." Her eyes narrowed and she shook her head with rage. The *last* thing she needed that evening was more questions about their relationship. "No anger!" he whispered into her ear, subsequently pulling her closer to do so. "Nothing good will come of your rage here and now. We'll dispel the rumors in due time," he said stiffly, clearly wishing he didn't have to dispel them. He led her into a dance, gesturing to the others to join in as they had been before.

The music started and the two didn't speak for a bit until Ace broke the silence with her mumbles. "They'll be on me all night, the vultures," she hissed under her breath, eyes glaring out at the eyes upon them. The only eyes that didn't seem to be watching them dance were the humans that had volunteered to join them for the evening.

"I'll try to keep them from you. It would be much easier to just tell them we are, then we'd field less questions," he whispered. When he pulled away to look into her silver eyes, she was clearly staggered. His eyes glowed warmly, his face full of amusement.

"We'd be mad to do that, Nero," she murmured, glancing around at the eyes still firmly placed on the two of them.

"I seem to have a very specific madness when it comes to you."

"And what madness is that?" Ace asked him, letting the corner of her mouth turn up in a subtle smile.

"I love you," Nero said, eyes shimmering between dark and light blue. Ace opened her mouth a bit, but a shock of red amongst the sea of darker colors caught her eye from over Nero's shoulder.

"Six is coming," Ace hissed, pulling away from him slightly. Within seconds, Six was right beside them. Her heart-shaped face looked more dramatic than usual, with harsh and dramatic red makeup. She was adorned in a corset, as usual, but it was ornamented with elaborate diamond embroidery in silk. The skirt that accompanied the corset was similarly decorated, but was voluptuous and flowing, as opposed to her usual skintight preference. She was shocking to look at, both for how out of place and alien she looked in comparison to the other Vampires in the room, but for how strange she looked to those who knew her standard dress.

"May I steal your partner, Ace?" Six asked, not waiting for a greeting or even the awkward pause that would accompany her interrupting their conversation. Ace nodded, unwrapping her arm from Nero's and stepping aside.

"It will only be for a moment," Nero said to Six, narrowing his eyes.

"Only a moment tonight, but don't forget who you're going home with tomorrow, Nero," Six said with a wide grin.

Ace kept her face neutral, moving quickly away from them. She was stopped a few times by other Coven Judges who thanked her or made strange innuendo illuding to the rumor previously mentioned. She finally made it to the outer rim of the crowd successfully and had started for a chair when the scent of Werewolf stopped her in her tracks. The sound of voices and music faded away as she searched for where the wolf was in the mansion from where she stood. The scent seemed to fade but came back strongly every few seconds. There were too many Vampires in the room to make out exactly where it was coming from.

The likelihood that Kyle had escaped his confinement was minimal. Even with the harvest moon outside, those cells were specifically designed to hold Werewolves. He could not have changed and broken out within its confines. It had to be another Werewolf. She had to get out of the parlor.

This time, her push through the crowd was not hindered by those that wanted to speak with her. She merely broke through them, ignoring whatever drivel they wanted to say to her as she pursued the intruder. There was no other reason she would be smelling a Werewolf like this, so there had to be one in the mansion. As she closed the door behind her in the main hall, the wolf stepped out to the middle of the room and started to walk toward her slowly, carefully stepping on the carpet as if he expected a trap to pop out at him.

"Not a smart thing, is it?" said the Werewolf, as he smiled smugly at her. "Having a great gathering like this." His blond hair was wet from the rain and stuck to his scruffy face. There was a mud trail behind him from his boots, and his jeans were soaked to mid-thigh. The brown leather jacket that was tattered and worn fell past his hands so only the tips of his fingers could be seen. Ace was walking toward him as well, but slowly, not because she was afraid of a trap but as if begging him to come closer. "But you're the smart one, the one who found me before we both made our escape, and I went to tell my master. Too bad you're just a woman," he said to her snickering.

Her suspicions were correct, at least. He had come to release Kyle from his confinement, but she was uncertain if this man had already finished his task, or if he was expecting to defeat her and follow through with his original mission. Regardless, he was obviously an ignorant and arrogant Werewolf; the worst kind, the kind that pissed Ace off the most. Her nails had begun to grow into very long, pointed, silver spikes on the ends of her fingers. Some years ago, she had Dietris and Minshin take out her natural nails and replace them with a mainly silver compound so she could lengthen them and use them in close combat.

It had been a little while since she had the opportunity to use them, and she stretched her neck and flexed her fingers, letting an eerie smile emerge on her lips. She held her nails up for him to see, showing off her knives, as she liked to call them.

"This is new," he said, looking at her nails, confusion forming on his face. She was now not but two feet away from him, having used the distraction of her reveal to close the distance between them.

"Not new for me," Ace said, smirking as his eyes widened.

He opened his mouth as if to say something, lifting his foot to take a step back, but she was too fast for him. She pounced, and he couldn't dodge the attack. His detached head hit the carpeted floor of the hall, a thick spray of blood arching over the walls, before he had a chance to even think about screaming. His body went a moment later, crumbling to the ground. She retracked her nails before shaking her hands quickly to rid them of most of his blood.

"Just a woman, hm?" Ace murmured to the dead Werewolf.

She quietly walked to the stairwell that descended to the lower level, racing to the cell where Kyle had been held. As she rounded the corner in the corridor, she saw the destruction. The door had been torn apart, ripped from its hinges, and her prisoner was nowhere to be found. Without missing a beat, she raced to the training room. One of the smaller, adjacent rooms was where they kept their surveillance equipment. The room was empty, and suddenly Ace panicked, not sure who was supposed to be on duty there.

"Gate guards. I just killed a Werewolf in the main hall, and our prisoner has escaped. Who is supposed to be in the control room right now?" Ace demanded through the comms.

"Makiut was on comms, but he left to greet Aknot about twenty minutes ago," came Dartri's voice. "I'm on the South Gate. We haven't seen anything other than the stray wolf changed by the moon. No one has attempted to come over our walls on this end."

"East Gate is clear," came Trunist's voice. And on it went until all gates and watches were accounted for. No one was dead or had seen anything out of the ordinary. Somehow the Werewolf had slipped past them in this perfect window when Makiut was not watching the cameras. She slammed her fist into the stone wall, raining dust over the room.

"Keep your eyes on your jobs. When day guard changes over, make sure they have extra protection," Ace growled into the microphone, getting an affirmative from all her Necare out keeping them safe.

She took her time walking back to the parlor, so slow her gait was that of a human's pace as she tried to control her anger. Not only had their enemy breached their walls, but their prisoner had also escaped without notice. She slipped back into the room, happily unnoticed by the crowd; it was far easier for her to go undetected without Nero at her side. She made her way over to one of the seats along the wall, after snatching a glass of blood from one of the tables. She took a sip, speculating on what she should do next. She couldn't just announce that she had killed a Werewolf in the mansion; that could lead to chaos.

There were plenty of Vampires in attendance who hadn't fought a day in their lives, or if they had, it had been so long ago they were reluctant to have to do so again. It was a source of contention for her. When she was made Vampire, *every* Vampire learned how to defend themselves from other Immortals, if not kill them outright, not just how to attack their prey. Now House Vampires were little better than mortals with eternal youth and additional strength.

She scanned the crowd, searching for Nero, who was undoubtedly still with Six. Once she found him, she would be able to tell him what happened and hopefully excuse herself for the remainder of the evening. William came over to her slowly, nervously, standing before her and blocking her view. She looked up at him annoyed.

"What can I do for you, William?" Ace asked, gesturing for him to step aside so she could resume scanning the crowd.

"Would you care to dance?" he asked hesitantly. At first, Ace was confused by the suggestion. There hadn't been people dancing when she left minutes ago, but then she heard the small orchestra from the Venetian coven playing and saw through the mass of bodies that there were couples dancing in the center of the room. She looked back up at William's very sincere face, still stuck in an innocent questioning position.

"William, I'm so sorry, but I have to find Nero," she told him, giving him the briefest of sympathetic glances and cringing internally, knowing this would only enhance the rumors.

"It's because I'm so young, isn't it?" he asked, dejected a bit, turning away from her. That was definitely part of it, that and he was barely into his twentieth year of his new life, but there were also factors such as her need to remain vigilant presently, and that she had no desire to have him ruminate on any potential feelings she may or may not have by allowing that gesture.

"I simply need to speak to Nero right now," she told him, standing to get a better view over the heads of the crowd.

William opened his mouth to say something more, but Ace felt an arm snaking around her waist, finding its resting place at her hip.

"Ah, William. Enjoying the crowd this evening?" Nero asked, giving a look at the younger Vampire with a hint of warning. William's head drooped, and he nodded shortly before melting quickly into the crowd and out of sight.

"How was Six treating you?" Ace asked, sipping lazily at her glass.

"As Six does. I only got rid of her when Racid asked her to dance," Nero said, finally pulling his gaze away from the bulk of the room and letting his eyes fall on Ace, more specifically her hand that was still slightly coated in blood. He reached and took her glass from her hand, setting it on a table beside them, before bringing her sullied digits closer to his face. "Why is there Werewolf blood on you?"

"There was a Werewolf in the hall. I killed him before he could send word to his den, and the prisoner has escaped," she said, pulling her hand away from his as his expression distorted into disgust at the scent.

"What?" he asked, as if he was making sure he had heard her correctly.

"He was in the hall," she said, as the tinkling of nails on glass started, and the room began to quiet. It was time for Nero's speech. He hissed quietly, his blue eyes glowing slightly as he glanced at the large doors that led out into the hall.

"How did a fully transformed Werewolf get into the mansion unnoticed?" The room was growing too quiet for them to have much of a private conversation now.

"Speech. I'll go," Ace whispered, pulling away from him. He quickly took everyone's notice in his direction, as he moved toward the center of the room, giving Ace an opportunity to slip back out, mostly undetected. Six's eyes watched her the whole way through the crowd, suspicion bubbling within her.

Ace stopped in the hall once she reached the remains. It hadn't dawned on her at the time, but he should have been in his wolf form. It was the full moon, after all. The change was irresistible to them. How was he able to maintain his human shape to sneak into the mansion?

She crouched down at the pile of dust he had eventually dissolved into and collected some of it carefully, examining it for a moment. It was oddly clumpy. Not the usual consistency of the Werewolves she killed. Younger Werewolves usually changed back into their human shape at death, while very old ones would disintegrate into dust, much like Vampires. The dust was usually a fine power, but this was...

No, she must not be looking at it correctly. She stood again and took it to the Medicus station just a few doors away, examining it closer under a microscope. But when she looked at its structure under the magnified lens, she realized she had been correct. This dust was sticky, not at all a normal sample from their foes. There was a very distinct and odd difference in this chemical makeup. She would need further testing done.

Ace secured the sample, leaving a detailed note to Dietris. She needed whatever information that sample yielded now, but he was with the rest of their coven in the parlor, and she couldn't risk the upset that could occur if she revealed what had transpired that evening. Her mind was racing, trying to understand what happened. What was Lukis up to with his son? And now this revelation that their change may not be forced or dependent on the moon.

She had no desire to go back and pretend for the rest of the evening. Ace clearly had work to do. She was missing some vital component of this puzzle and wanted to find it. No time for frivolous parties. Slinking up a secondary set of stairs, she went back to her room where she could look over everything once again. She got dressed in more practical clothes, pants and a red tank top, and was sitting at her desk once again.

She had years of research, centuries of knowing her enemy, but clearly she was forgetting something or failing to see something hidden there. She knew how they hunted, who they preyed on, how their power structure worked. She thought she knew it all, but maybe...

She pulled the drive that had the recently digitized version of their shared history. Werewolves, she was certain, had their own version of this history, but this was the knowledge base she had. She scrolled through until she had the den in London's information pulled up. That's when she stopped short, reading it again, several times over to make sure she wasn't interpreting it incorrectly. But no... Her eyes widened suddenly with astonishment. The Werewolves were headquartered in New Orleans, not London.

New Orleans is the base? she thought to herself. *No wonder Six has been having trouble.*

If there was one bit of knowledge she was certain of, it was that Lukis called London home, so why would the base be across the Atlantic in New Orleans? She leaned back in her chair, speculating what this could mean and occasionally hunching forward toward the computer to reread things she had looked over a thousand times.

Ace was briefly pulled from her thoughts as she heard light footsteps outside her door. Her eyes looked over it, watching the shadow at the bottom. He was standing out there, not knocking, not speaking, just standing.

She wanted to go to the door. To pull him in and tell him he couldn't go, at least not without her. But she gripped the armrests of her chair instead, holding herself against her impulses.

Nero pressed his hand to her closed door. He had no doubt in his mind of what she truly wanted. He had known her for so long it was almost laughable that she was being so stubborn. But what good would it do to press the issue when he would be leaving this coven, not knowing when he would return?

He let his hand curl into a fist, the frustration eating at him. He could step inside that room, whisper his good-byes to her, and then leave her here, or he could simply walk away.

Which option was better?

He knew she heard him. He knew she was, right now, watching his shadow at the base of her door, waiting to see what he would do. She would not come. She would not open this door and beg him to stay, because she was still fighting against them.

He took a deep breath, angry with himself for leaving and her for letting him. His fist hit the wall beside the door before he had even contemplated doing so, and with a sharp turn on his heel, he left, heading to the cars that would take them on the plane to the Americas, the Harvest still in full swing below.

Ace startled just a little at the sound of his angry breath and his fist breaking a piece of wall outside her room. She hadn't seen him that volatile in many years. He was usually so calm and collected, but not, apparently, when it came to her. She waited, watching, even though she knew he was gone. Would she have wanted him to barge in? For him to forgo his patience at her never-ending push back and simply take her?

She let herself take in a shaky breath several minutes after he had already clearly gone, turning back to her work.

The sun began peeking through the curtains onto her papers, pulling Ace from the histories she was starting to see in a new light. Slowly, as if it pained her to leave her desk, she went to the tapestry that her coffin sat behind. She realized Nero should nearly be arriving in the Americas by now, and her stomach dropped. She clutched the coffin lid for a moment as she realized at some point, she was going to have to go to New Orleans.

From everything she had read the night before, she knew there was no possible way she would be able to miss out on all the action that was bound to take place there. If it was truly the headquarters for the Werewolves, and what Six had told the Elders was true, Ace needed to be in the midst of whatever Lukis was planning.

But as she began to climb in, Ace heard screams and gunshots from the parlor. If the sun was up, there should have been no one but the day guard moving about, let alone gunshots and screams. She ran out of her room and to the main upstairs hallway where she saw bullets flying from automatic guns. There were pieces of stone and other debris raining through the air.

She ducked, peeking over the balcony's edge to see what exactly was taking place. There, in the middle of the parlor, seemed to be quite a large group of Werewolves, more terrorizing the lingering House Vampires that had remained in the parlor after the party than actually hurting them. There did seem to be a few bodies that had begun crumbling on the floor, but otherwise the intention seemed to be to scare rather than incur damage.

"Your leader! An Elder! Bring them to me!" came the booming voice of the man in the front. His was large, just as bulky as his voice would suggest. His hair was cut short, dusty brown against sun-tanned skin. Everything about his appearance screamed brute, from the squared jaw to the breadth of his shoulders.

"Lukis," Ace said under her breath. She certainly wasn't an Elder, but she was a Necare and the Judge of this coven. She wasn't about to let these filthy beasts roam within her walls without her having a say.

She stood, using the balcony railing to jump and project herself to the center of the atrium, landing before Lukis himself. He looked down at her with a smug look on his face, eyes glittering with delight, before he held up his hand, halting the gunfire.

"Are you an Elder?" he asked, crossing his arms in an almost defiant way. Her lips curled into a snarl as she stared up at him with utmost disgust.

"No," she replied, mirroring his stance. "What do you want with our Elders, dog?" she hissed.

"Negotiations, sweet thing," he cooed, bending lower as he would a child with a sneer spread across his face. "If you aren't an Elder, then get out of my way."

His gaze fell behind her once again, seeing the large doors that lead out to the hall. They had been broken either by a Werewolf or a fleeing House Vampire, Ace didn't know. With his new goal set, he began trying to push her aside with his large hand, but it didn't work in the least. She still stood there, holding her ground and not letting him pass her. Their mansion was breeched, but there was no way Ace was going to let any of them get further than where they stood now.

"I am the Judge of this coven. You will address me. Your scum doesn't even deserve to stand on Vampire ground, Lukis," she said, spitting at him. He let out a bellowing laugh, prompting the others with him to chuckle as well.

"Little fiery isn't she, boys?" he said, turning his head toward his men, but keeping his eyes firmly on Ace's. "You have something we need in this mansion, Judge. Give it to me, and I promise we'll only kill a few more of you, instead of burning this whole place to the ground."

As he spoke, he stepped closer, his boots crunching splintered wood and glass that had scattered the floor from the previous gunfire. In her periphery, Ace could see the other Necare hovering in the shadows, having finally made their way to the room. Several of them had begun shielding and pulling the remaining House Vampires from the room to the relative safety of the main hall.

"What is it that you want?" Ace hissed, her silver eyes glowing, body preparing for a battle she knew was closing in. Each step closer to her and away from his own, she felt the anticipation of the coming fight.

"There's one among you. I need them," Lukis said. Cryptic.

"Why would I give you anything? Let alone when you speak in such a way without meaning?"

His hand shot out, large thick fingers wrapping tightly around her throat. She saw the flicker of momentary movement from Trunist to her left, but she quickly signaled her to stand down. No, Ace had a plan. Not a great one, but given the circumstances, she had more to lose by not attempting it than she did letting her Necare try to assist her.

"You'll give me what I want because look what we've done." He gestured his free hand, glancing around the atrium briefly before setting his eyes back on hers. "We've breached your domain midday. You are weak, exposed. Don't let your pride get the best of you. You can't win this one." The last few words he spoke in barely a whisper, having pulled her close so she could feel his breath on her face. She held back a shiver of revulsion, instead letting her lips curl up in clear disgust, displaying her fangs blatantly for him to see.

"Weak?" she asked, eyebrow rising on her forehead. "You may have breached our domain, in daylight no less, but we are far from weak, Lukis," she said, finally taking the opportunity that had presented itself before her. As he had been talking, Ace had made her nails lengthen as her hands hung at her sides. He was so close, having felt so in control of the situation, that she had a perfect shot at his soft belly. In the blink of an eye, she plunged her right hand's blades within the forgiving flesh there. She smirked as she watched his eyes widen in surprise and pain, the silver burning at his wound.

She began twisting her hand, listening to the snapping and squishing of his organs and ligaments within. This wouldn't be a mortal wound for a Werewolf, but it would hurt him, nonetheless. The brief moment of shocked silence that had filled the room was broken as a small gasp rasped from his lips, prompting his Werewolves into action. None got close to her and Lukis, as her Necare swarmed from the shadows, filling the once-still room with growls and roars.

Lukis's fingers fell away from her neck, so he could use both hands to rip hers from where it was buried in his stomach. He cursed loudly once her blades were free from within him, but he kept her hand crushed in one of his fists as he panted.

"Full of surprises," he growled out, panting as he towered over her.

"I'd like to think so," she said, smirking up at him slightly. She was momentarily trapped there, his grip like a vice, as his other hand flashed within his jacket before he pulled out a gun he had hidden there.

"My men made the bullets in this gun just a few days ago. They don't allow Immortals to heal. I wonder..." He scratched his cheek with feigned curiosity. "Will sunlight kill you if it comes into contact with your blood?" Of course, it would. And Lukis grinned as he pointed the weapon directly at her face.

Ace quickly placed her feet on his thighs and pushed off, ripping her fingers from his grasp and landing so she faced him once again. He began to shoot at her with the bullets that seemed to be made of a green-tinted metal. She had been dodging the bullets, but it was becoming somewhat difficult, considering he was catching onto her movement patterns. Instinctively, she reached her hands out to two very large silver blades from the wall to her right. She didn't often use her telekinesis, but this had become somewhat of a dire situation. The blades flew to her hands, and she immediately began swinging them in front of her, blocking the bullets and forcing them off in other directions, mainly toward his Werewolves. The Werewolf Dartri was struggling with dropped like a stone when a bullet rico-cheted right into his head. She was moving too fast for a mortal's eye, and, at some point, even Lukis seemed con-fused, watching the blades spin before her.

"Coven Judge here, you say?" Lukis asked, pausing his firing for a moment to look over her. His expression was oddly impressed. "May I know your name?" he asked, his eyes oddly alight. Ace glanced at his weapons. He hadn't stopped firing to ask her, just run out of bullets. And the odd expression on his face told her he knew exactly who she was. If he had scouts nearly half as skilled as hers, they would certainly know who she was.

"I'm sure I don't have to tell you," she said, stepping closer to him, her blades at the ready.

"Ace," he murmured with a sneer. He was excited to be fighting her. Proud, even. "Your reputation doesn't do you justice."

With a smirk of her own, she stepped further forward, bracing to attack. But he dropped the gun quite suddenly and pulled a long blade of his own from behind his back. She had expected an old werewolf like him to have the older methods, such as wrist gear that allowed him to call blades out at a clenched fist, but these were a bit longer than a dagger would be, yet not long enough to be swords. She came after him quite suddenly, with a calm yet determined look upon her face. He backed up and buckled slightly under the amount of strength she had with those blades.

"Having fun?" she asked him, her eyes flashing with blood lust. He may have been physically larger than her, but that mattered little when dealing with Immortals.

"Oh of course. Though it would be much easier if you just got me an Elder, like I asked," he grunted in reply, his face was showing signs of strain.

Ace managed to twist his blade from his grasp, letting it skitter across the floor loudly, even amongst the other fighting. It was then that the action seemed to pause, as if everyone in the room knew how monumental it was that Ace had gotten the upper hand. She pointed the end of her blade at his throat, her eyes nearly white with the expected blood that was about to be spilled.

She could end it here and now.

Lukis would be dead by her hand.

The Werewolves would be so crippled from it, the Vampires could overtake it all.

Her mission would be complete.

Lukis's breath came in sharp pants as he looked boldly at the blade.

"Are you going to do it, Ace?" he asked quietly. She grinned wildly, opening her mouth for her fangs to end fully, as she reeled back, preparing for her final strike, the strike that would finish this war. Once he was dead, the Werewolves would be easy to take down. It would be nothing but simply pulling a thread and letting it all fall apart.

But she froze, a split second before she would have cut his head from his neck, the shrill scream of a human woman sounded. Lukis used the opportunity to push away from her in the shelter of his men.

"Stop! Lucef wouldn't approve, Lukis!" the woman shrieked to the nearly silent room. Everyone had been watching the finality of what had been about to happen, and this woman... Well, Ace had never been so distracted in a kill. The woman ran, seemingly unafraid, or perhaps simply oblivious to the dangers surrounding her, through the crowded parlor and to Lukis. Her hair was long and black, tumbling around her pink-clad shoulders. She was so small and frail in comparison to Lukis that when she finally stood before him, before the blade Ace still had poised toward his face, he seemed nearly double her size in both height and girth.

"Dammit, woman! Lucef doesn't care anymore," he growled, still eyeing Ace as he pulled the woman away from harm, or at least as much as he could.

"You brought your human wife to this?" Ace hissed, eyes narrowed with disgust. For all the rumors about how protective he was of her, this was far from keeping her safe, bringing her to a coven, even in the middle of the day. He glared back at Ace, having effectively put enough distance between them as he moved his wife away so Ace's strike was no longer possible at the distance.

"Who is that?" the woman said, her eyes finally falling on Ace.

"Come now, Deca. We should leave," he said, not acknowledging Ace or Deca's previous words.

"This isn't over," Ace growled, stepping closer again and lunging to stab him, somewhere, anywhere, but she missed as he scooped Deca off her feet and ran through the crowd and out the front door, his remaining living Werewolves following behind him.

The sunlight flooded the atrium like water through a broken dam. Many vampires that were either trapped in the room or had been fighting ran to get away from the piercing, suffocating light. Ace dropped her blades immediately and met with Nyprat halfway to the doors. Quickly they closed them, locking them thoroughly and leaning against the hard wooden surface.

"Unexpected," Nyprat said, slightly out of breath.

Ace glanced at her, then around the room at the destruction that was had just been wrought by their invasion.

"He's either gotten far bolder or he's gone mad," Ace said, before she set about to triple the day guard.

CHAPTER 9

A ce seemed to be tallying up quite a mass of information with little to connect the dots, and it was becoming rather infuriating. The remaining daylight hours after Lukis's attack, Ace had forgone sleep to scrutinize the cameras from the night before and this morning before returning to her research. So many unanswered questions behind the Werewolves' motives.

For example, who or what had Lukis been searching for when he stormed the house during the day? He kept demanding an Elder, saying there was *something* in the mansion that he wanted. What could he possibly want that was within their walls?

Why was he hunting his own son? There was little to go on, and Ace couldn't contain her frustration at needing her partner before she could go out and investigate for herself. Some of the other Necare were reliable at gathering information, of course, but after what happened with Lotte recently and her desire to leave the mansion herself, she was crawling out of her skin to do it herself.

Ace had even gone to Makiut's room to check on him, partially for her own selfish need to be out of the mansion, hunting and, if not killing, at least trying to answer some of the many questions she had about what the Werewolves were up to.

"Ace, my fingers finished growing back yesterday. I'm still not in any shape to go out just yet," Makiut grumbled from where he lounged on his settee. He held up his arm, which other than some odd blue colorations around the joints, looked perfectly normal to Ace.

"I cannot just sit around here. Lucef, the attack on us ... now Nero and Six are gone, and apparently the Werewolf headquarters are in New Orleans, *not* here in London as we were led to believe," Ace hissed, pacing in front of him.

"What?" he asked, sitting up suddenly.

"You heard me," Ace snapped, her fists clenching with a sort of pent-up energy. Makiut sighed, running his hands through his tussled hair.

"Go, then," he said quietly, watching intently as she halted mid-step at his words.

"It's against the rules."

"The only Elder who cared to enforce that rule is now an ocean away from us. And we know he only made that rule for your protection." Ace stared at him for a beat or two.

"You'll not speak of this to anyone," Ace murmured, saying nothing more before she stormed from his room unceremoniously, much like how she entered a few minutes before.

"Good luck!" he called to her back.

She moved through the halls like a ghost, slipping briefly into her own chambers to make sure she had all the supplies she would need, before gliding quietly from the window and down to the unguarded side of the gates. Trunist was on comms in the control room and would most likely have spotted Ace on the cameras, but she knew no one would actually stop her.

Once she reached the cobblestone path, she took in the night air, letting herself smile for just a moment to relish the feeling of being out like this alone. She liked it better without a partner. She had partnered with Nero as he trained her both upon her transformation, and when she started her journey to becoming a Necare, but there were years where she hunted in solitude. The only things that she would run into would be her unwitting prey.

It was only after Makiut's partner died that she agreed to take him on. He was quite a bit older than her, yet he still refused to hunt alone. They had a rough relationship at first. Several times Ace was certain he would try to find another partner to take her place, since they rarely seemed to agree on anything, but he never did. Ace had grown used to him, but she still had secretly hoped she would be able to hunt like this, with no one influencing or affecting her decisions simply by being there.

The rain came down a bit heavier as she moved further into the city. She decided to peek at The Gast, perhaps to pick up the trail of a Werewolf while she was there. But instead, she caught an odd scent from a hooded passerby, just as she was nearing the alley where the club entrance stood. He was tall and broad but was clearly hunching and trying to look unintimidating, keeping himself hidden from prying eyes. His scent wasn't overtly odd, but more of a hint of something other. She knew she probably could have attributed that to having brushed up against an Immortal, especially with how close he had been to the club when she first came across him, but she was certain that wasn't it.

He appeared normal, but he acted different; his energy flowed differently than that of a human. She had felt energy that way before. There was an alleyway that he turned into, and she followed silently. The sound of water dripping from metal stairs and balconies echoed around her as she made her way into the shadowy recesses behind him. He was just walking along this dark, wet alley when he suddenly stopped and turned around to face her.

"Why are you following me?" he asked her, his voice gruff as it raised with anger. She looked at him, his pale fingers clenched into fists, turning his knuckles chalk white, with a mild growl in his voice to accompany the snarling lip she could see from beneath the hood.

"You sensed me," she murmured, amused. "You're not human." His face was covered in the shadows; she still couldn't see who he was in this darkness, not to mention the water that was still pouring between them.

"Then neither are you," he said, stepping forward revealing his face. He took her by surprise. Her eyes widened as she looked upon his face.

Lucef.

"Lucef Lynae," Ace murmured, smirking to herself. Her first time out to gather information, and here she happens to stumble on one of the biggest pieces to the ever-growing puzzle.

"And you're the Vampire wench they're all talking about," Lucef replied, crossing his arms and smirking back at her.

"Wench?" She made a sour face at him. She supposed there were worse things to be called than a wench by her enemies, but she felt like they should have been more creative than that.

"My father fought you. I heard through the grapevine. They say you were harder than the last Head Elder he fought," he said, seeming to assess her with interest rather than disdain or fear.

"I suppose I should be flattered?" Ace questioned.

"I don't know what he was getting at, trying to go into the Kurome and raid it. Didn't work, did it?" Lucef sneered, shaking his head at his father's actions. Ace took him in for a moment. He looked like the spitting image of his father, but she could see the undercurrent of anger smoldering there. Lukis angered him, both for his foolish actions, and for what?

"Well, obviously not. If it wasn't for your *mother*, you wouldn't have a father now," Ace said, crossing her own arms. He smiled and snapped his fingers over dramatically.

"Drat. I've wanted to get rid of him for quite some time, now. Damn that woman," Lucef told her. Ace raised her eyebrow.

"So, it's true then? You hate your parents?" she asked, stepping forward a bit, perhaps a bit too eagerly. She was strangely exhilarated that she was talking to him, and he wasn't running away or outright attacking her.

"I'd say 'hate' is a strong word. More that they disgust me."

"Disgust?"

"They are hypocrites. All Immortals are. Doesn't make much sense for you all to be fighting one another, does it?" he told her. "But more than that … my mother is kept alive by drinking the blood of Werewolves … just like you're kept alive by drinking mortals' blood." Ace shrugged a bit, nodding to indicate she understood his reservations, however naïve they may have been. All Immortals dealt in death and blood; that was the way of them. In fact, Ace thought they were all more alike than they were different. Perhaps if they could come to common ground…

She nearly shook her head physically at the thought that had been forming. She didn't need to be distracting herself when Lucef was here before her, talking rather than running in the opposite direction.

"Why are you in London, right under your father's nose? You could be so many other places where he wouldn't find you. And why is he sending people to fetch you?" Ace asked, now realizing she couldn't let this opportunity pass her by. Mindless chatting with him would lead her nowhere. He sighed, leaning against the alley wall and glancing up toward the sky.

"Can we go somewhere else? This is an odd place to be talking about all of this," he murmured, eyes slowly shifting back to her. She looked around and back at him. Ace had questioned many Werewolves and Witches in locations very similar to this, but she also, strangely, had no intention of killing him. They didn't have to be cloistered in the drenched alley for her to gather the intel she needed.

"Sure," she said slowly, gesturing for him to lead the way. She may not have intended to kill him, but she still didn't trust him or know all his motivations. Why would the leader of the Werewolves own son be so generously answering every question she asked? Even if he was disgusted by them, why would he choose their enemy?

Ace's suspiciousness of him only seemed to become more muddled as he happily moved through the wet streets, murmuring little tidbits of information about the neighborhood. Ace had no interest in the vacant building that once held one of the oldest bakeries in town. Nor did she particularly find it necessary to know that the Werewolves usually ate a group breakfast at one of pubs just down the corner from them. Breakfast meant daylight, and there was little possibility she'd be using that information in the future.

Lucef led her to a café not far away from the aforementioned pub, the same one Nyprat and Lotte had tracked him to, and they sat down. The café was small and bright, the colors were vibrant, with blue beanbags and mismatched table and chair sets about the room. He smiled at her as she grimaced at the place.

"I never thought I would be sitting down and having a civilized conversation with a Vampire," he told her, as he pulled his rain-covered jacket off and set it on one of the seats between them.

"I can't say I thought this conversation would be happening either," she murmured slowly, casting her eyes around at the few mortals sitting around before leaning her elbows on the table to stare at him. He ordered a coffee when the server came over. The girl looked at Ace, almost becoming mesmerized by the porcelain skin that seemed to give off a glow. When asked if she wanted anything, Ace merely shook her head and turned to look at Lucef, watching his movements.

"Vampires only drink blood?" Lucef asked, curious. Ace raised her eyebrow. For someone raised by Werewolves, it was quite odd he seemed to know nothing about their enemy.

"No, we can drink other things. Even eat human food on occasion if we must, but not much and not often. Not only does it provide nothing for us, some beverages, like coffee, could dry us out. Not a pretty sight, let me tell you," she replied. He chuckled, his eyes sparking happily. The server came back a moment later, steaming mug of coffee in hand, and he thanked her before taking a quick sip.

"Now, where were we in our conversation?" he asked, setting his coffee down on a flowery doily and looking back up at her.

"Why is Lukis sending his men after you?" Ace asked, leaning closer. Lucef sighed and leaned back in his seat, running his hands through his red-tipped hair.

"My father thinks I'm some sort of key to something."

"A key?" Ace asked, furrowing her brow in concentration.

"I don't know the full of it. Whatever his plans for me are, they aren't in my best interest," Lucef told her, letting a slight shiver run over him at the thought of it.

"Why you? What's so special about you that he would use his own son? Kill you potentially?"

"I don't exactly know. My mother's mother was a Witch when she was alive, but my mother has no powers of her own, nor is she an Immortal. That's why she has been fed Werewolf and sometimes Witch blood to keep her alive. I don't know how long they've been doing this, but her blood, and my father's, made me different enough, it's convinced him I am meant for something."

"Really, now?" Ace asked him in surprise, eyebrow raised. Well, if he wasn't important before, Lukis had certainly made him important by seeking him out so unabashedly. Lucef held a surprising lack of knowledge of the Immortals, but she couldn't quite be sure if that was his fault or the fault of his father. It seemed Lukis had been planning to use his son as nothing more than a vessel for his own aspirations. "How old are you, Lucef?" she asked suddenly.

"Older than I look. I don't appear to be getting any older than this," he said, spreading his arms. He seemed somewhat sad about this fact. She didn't know why; she liked to stay the same, that she could always expect to remain as she was, though she hadn't always been that way. It had taken her several hundred years to grow to appreciate that she was always going to look exactly as she did. The only thing that plagued her still was the knowledge that unless she was killed, she would be around forever.

"It seems your father has kept you in the dark on many very important aspects of the world you live in," she said, sitting up in her chair.

"I don't think it was necessary for me to know. Not for what he intends," Lucef grumbled in agreement.

"I should go," she said abruptly, standing and turning to leave, careful not to make her movements too quickly, what with the humans around. He stood up too and grabbed her hand, which surprised her.

"Why?" he asked, his face strained, as if it pained him to see her leave.

"You want me to stay?" she asked, recoiling from him, but his grip only tightened.

"I…" He seemed to hesitate at her question, eyes shifting nervously. She got the impression he was stronger than he seemed but broken in a much more internal way.

"I'll contact you if I need more information," she said with a smirk, twisting her wrist to free her hand from his hold, before moving swiftly out the door and then suddenly was nowhere to be seen.

A moment later, Lucef realized that a slim phone had been placed in his hand as she had been wringing her hand free from his grasp.

Contact *him,* she certainly would.

CHAPTER 10

Weeks passed with Nero at Six's manor and her group of odd Vampires. She had collected quite an odd array of individuals to make up her ranks. Each was loud and obnoxious, like Six, and each wore bright colors, which he never really understood, considering it was far more prudent for Vampires to stay in the shadows and not attract unnecessary attention to themselves. But Six had told him it was to their advantage in a place like this. The tourists and the youth of this city especially were more inclined to follow along with whatever they wished if they were more like them. In that way, those of her coven seemed to blend in just as well, if not more so than the Necare that had joined them from other covens.

It made Nero feel oddly out of touch, realizing that Six, perhaps, was right about that. Ace did not conform to tradition either, finding ways to either blend in with the way modern mortals viewed the world, or be embraced by them, given she did not exactly have a traditional look to her either. But Ace was more subtle and certainly could hide within the shadows and go undetected, when necessary, while Six was ... not.

His transition to Elder had held him back, and he found himself out of step with how this world was now. He wondered if that was part of the reason Ace seemed so much more distant from him now too.

Nero's items he asked to be shipped from Kurome had just arrived the previous evening, and, along with it, was work. He and Six were in the extravagant study at the Redeamond manor, a large room filled with all sorts of miscellaneous things, not simply books. There were intricate vases probably almost as old as he was, jars filled with various anomalous body parts, and, of course, various items of voodoo charms and dolls. The room was covered with very elaborate designs in gold on the red wallpaper. It was overt and gawdy. Very much Six's style. There was nothing subtle about Six. She flaunted herself and what she was with little care for the intricate rules that the rest of the Vampires had to live by.

Nero was finishing the paperwork for Damin's death at a large wooden desk that he suspected rarely saw use until he took up residence. Recording an Elder's death was tedious. Another Elder was required to properly document every detail of how the death occurred and why, then seal it in blood. It was rather odd that he had to describe in detail, for their permanent records, that Six had not continued her rampage with the others because he had given into her demands. A part of history that he thought would be a low point for the Elders when looked back on in the future.

Six was standing right over his shoulder, reading everything he wrote. She had said, when he questioned her positioning so near to him before, that the reason was because she didn't want him saying something bad about her, but her real intention was something completely different. She slyly slipped her hands over his shoulders and down his chest, causing him to stop. He looked over his shoulder and up at her with a sigh.

"You know—" he started, pausing to fully turn, which caused her to move in front of him instead of behind him, though she didn't remove her hands from his chest. He took a moment to fully absorb her overall appearance. She was donned in her usual red leather corset and mini skirt. It left almost nothing to the imagination. "That's terribly annoying."

Nodding with a sultry smile, she slowly slipped her hands off him and walked around the desk to the chair directly across, sitting and letting her eyes lock on his hands as he wrote. He stopped with another sigh, as he felt her eyes gazing at the words he was scratched out on the page.

"That really isn't any better," he said, looking back up at her, hair hanging in his face from bending over the paper. She scowled at him and got up, walking around the room and examining the things he brought along with him: swords that killed major Werewolf leaders, heads of important Vampires that had been stonecast before they could turn to ashes, and armor worn by the first Vampire. Her fingers ran along each item she passed, and soon she was lost within the very full room.

When he finally finished the report, he stood up and looking around to see if she was occupied with something else. He had hoped she was so he could leave without detection, and it was his lucky day. He smirked when he saw her engrossed with the armor, so he left the room quietly. Six was entranced with the black metal that adorned the armor; it was reminiscent of the demon metal she had acquired some years ago.

<It is demon metal,> came a voice. The voice was inhuman, as if many voices were speaking at once. It didn't

scare her or deter her, but the suddenness always made her jump a bit.

"I didn't know Ramses used it," Six said quietly, still thinking Nero was in the room, letting her fingers run over it with reverence.

<It was a demon that made your Ramses what he was. A demon and a god,> came the voice.

"Is that what you are? A demon and a god?" Six asked. A spine-tingling laugh resounded.

<Only a demon, Six.>

Six lifted her hand, summoning six diamond-shaped blades from within her sparse clothing. They came together before her, melding into one large diamond piece and revealing the distorted face of the one who had been speaking. Multiple vertical slits made up the void-like eyes that glared through the metal at her, while its mouth was row after row of jagged, sharp teeth. Blackened skin stretched over misshapen bones and horns shifted with a sinister smile.

"Vehekan, you can't talk to me here. He'll hear us," Six hissed at the face before her.

<He's been gone for several minutes, and you didn't even notice. How could we have chosen you for this. You've barely scratched the surface of what we've asked of you,> Vehekan said, though the lips and teeth moved oddly and out of sync from the words that she heard.

"He's gone?" she asked, whipping her head around and moving back to the open space in the room, seeing that Nero was, in fact, no longer in the room. She hissed, waving her hand to try to summon the blades back to their homes within her bodice, but they remained whole, hovering in the air as Vehekan's face glared out at her.

<Your task, Six. You cannot forget it,> Vehekan growled.

"I'm working on it," she snapped back, once again flicking her fingers so they would return to their resting places. With clenched fists, she took a deep breath, trying to calm herself before leaving the room to pursue Nero. Her goal was to win him over, not to scare him away. And once she did, though it pained her, she would complete the task Vehekan had asked of her. She would kill Nero, as she had promised.

Nero had gone to the room that was declared his, a large room with a bed of red silk sheets and walls of the same wallpaper that had been in the study. He shut the door and locked it, wanting to be alone, something Six obviously didn't want to allow.

He knew exactly the thing to take his mind off Six's intrusive attentions. His eyes caught a painting. If he could have only brought one thing with him, it would have been this. It was the same painting that usually sat over his fire-place at Kurome, of Ace a few centuries after he made her. He remembered vividly how he had tried to persuade her to let him do the portrait, though with his recall, he hadn't really needed her to sit for him.

"No, Nero," Ace had said, her hands on her hip, a silver blade still clutched within her fist.

"But this image of you just now is perfect. I want to have a reminder forever," he had told her, running his fingers down her pale cheek. Her long, black dress had some dirt on it around the hem, and her fingers were still running with blood from a hunt. Nero went to her and sat her down in a chair, with black cushions on the armrests, seat, and back. A fire was lit in the hearth of the library in Kurome, not for comfort but the flames still had their appeal, and of course cast beautiful shadows. Perfect for painting. "Sit and stay," he ordered her with a shake of a finger and a smile. Ace rolled

her eyes and looked at him with a furious glare as he picked up his brush and began to paint.

The sound of the door rattling pulled him from his memory, but he remained where he stood. Six undid the lock with ease, keys in hand as she came into the room. He continued to look at the painting with longing, ignoring Six's presence. Infuriating as it was, he was trapped in this situation indefinitely. He didn't wish to speak with her; she only made him feel worse about leaving Ace in London.

"Did you paint that?" Six asked him, after sauntering up beside him and following his gaze to the painting. A brief scowl graced her face as she saw Ace's glare through the canvas, as if Ace were glaring directly at her.

"Yes," he said coldly, turning away and sitting in a chair, with its back to Six and the painting, to his dismay.

"Looks just like her. Was that when...?" Six began, but Nero interrupted her, a subject he obviously didn't want to touch on with her.

"Must I speak of these things with you?" he asked, his voice cold and his face folding into a deep scowl. It was none of her business what happened between him and Ace, as much as she liked to delude herself that it was. Six shrugged and sat across from him once more, hands folded and legs crossed, letting as much of her legs show in her short, tight skirt as possible.

"I find it difficult to get past, Nero. It strikes me curious why you would favor one progeny over another." Struck her curious was quite the understatement. It was frequently in her thoughts. A tormentor. There was no reason that she could see why they were different, her and Ace. They were both his, both bound to him the same way.

He was glaring at her, wishing he could simply force her to leave him be. Some sires did have control over their progenies that way. But he had never wielded that power over Ace, and he wasn't in a position to do that with Six. His glare turned deeper momentarily, resenting this entire situation. He shouldn't have had to be in New Orleans in the first place. He hated this place, the temperature, the people, this coven: he felt out of place. But he knew he had to be there, so there wasn't another dead Elder.

But Six's gaze held, and he sighed, his glare turning weary.

"I needn't tell you such things, Six. It is not for me to say, not on my own at least," he told her. It was for him *and* Ace to tell, and unfortunately it was going to be very difficult to do so with how he and Ace seemed to be at odds often as of late. Six frowned and her eyes twitched momentarily before she took in a deep and rather unnecessary breath. Her hands clenched several times in a row as she tried to gain control over her anger, but it didn't work.

"FINE!" she yelled, after several moments of obvious frustration and lack of control over her emotions. She got out of the chair, which wasn't hard because she had begun levitating slightly, in her angry state, and started to glide out of the room, slamming the door behind her.

Nero watched her leave, oddly pleased that she seemed to have been trying to remain calm. It was like a toddler, learning how to regulate their tantrums, though she was much more deadly than a soft human babe. He was relieved she was gone, as would anyone in their right mind. She was volatile in a way that was dangerous. She was precarious, a timebomb waiting to expose the whole of the Immortals. If he and Ace had known what she would become ... well, he knew he would have rather killed her than subject the likes of the world to her and the uncanny powers she seemed to inherit from Ace. And to make matters worse, she had decidedly chosen to obsess over him.

The days went on, and Nero had hidden himself away from the coven and Six as much as he could. Normally, in Kurome, he wouldn't have had too much interaction either. Elder duties as they were tended to be focused more on tending to the histories and less so on the actual going-ons of the Vampires. It was not exactly what he had had in mind when he was ascended to the position; and it was certainly worse now that he was the Head Elder.

But here he was without his Elder tasks. He frequently checked in with the other Elders, and occasionally Ace, by email but his purpose here was to watch Six. To be certain she was using the Necare leant from other covens appropriately, and for that he would have to pull himself from his rooms and immerse himself in the strange place he found himself in.

Most recently when Six would come to him, it was less about seduction or persuasion and more attempts to get him to go hunting with her and the Necare. Thus far he had turned her down, but he was realizing that was his purpose for being there, after all. In truth, he had not gone hunting for centuries. His once Necare status had been left behind when he transitioned from Coven Judge to Elder. Not that he had forgotten how it was done. He would never be able to forget the pleasure of the hunt and the satisfaction of the kill with his own hands or fangs.

It was during this musing that Nero decided to leave his room and seek out the Necare. That was the first step, to see what Six had made of her warriors. He moved through the manor, eyes taking in the rooms he had yet to fully investigate. The manor, though a traditional plantation-style home in the South, was, like the library, decorated brightly and extravagantly. House Vampires lounged on ornate couches, dressed as scantily clad as possible while still being clothed.

Six spotted him from where she had been inspecting some new blades across the room that was once the formal dining room, but Six had turned it into her operations room. Weapons and supplies were scattered across various surfaces.

"Nero! You decided to join us, did you?" she asked, quickly meeting him halfway, her advisor, Brendin, in tow. Nero glanced at the Vampire he had known well years ago. This creature looked nothing like the one Nero had once considered a trusted friend. He had been placed with Six when they sent her to New Orleans. He was to assist, instruct, and advise, but mostly to watch. Back then he had been a strong, brave Necare, but now that Nero looked at him, he looked frail and weak, something Six, no doubt, had changed about him with her domineering and madness.

"This is Brendin," Six said, gesturing to him and making him flinch uncomfortably at the quick motion. It was then that Nero noticed him clutching his arm, dark crimson blood slowly dripping to the floor. Six had been testing the blades on him.

"Oh, I forgot. You know him, don't you?" she said, scowling at Nero, then to Brendin, himself. She loathed that she was a Coven Judge and yet was still being babysat. First by Brendin, who she immediately and effectively strove to break when she arrived there, and now Nero. Though her plans for him were not to break him mentally but break that steely façade that kept her at arm's length.

"Yes, I do. Hello Brendin, how have you been? You haven't been coming to any of the Harvest feasts for the past … has it been ten years?" Nero said, as he stepped forward and held out a welcoming hand toward him. Brendin only nodded in Nero's direction, not taking his hand but looking down at it with wide eyes. Nero let his arm drop.

He had supposed for several years now that Brendin hadn't gone to the Harvest feasts because he would be away from Six for a short period of time, which, from Nero's recent experiences, would be a blessing, but he hadn't been prepared to see this once-decorated Necare trembling and useless.

"How has Kurome been?" Brendin asked in a somewhat shaking voice, as he glanced at Six several times. Kurome had been Brendin's original coven, a coven he would have gladly gone back to now.

"It's been much the same," Nero said with a nod, now making certain he would include Brendin in his plans to return to Kurome. The Vampire before him deserved much better than this, if not the bliss of eternal sleep. Six narrowed her eyes at Brendin, silently daring him to stay any longer.

"I should go. Good evening, Nero." He paused and turned to Six. "Six," he said with a slight bow before he left the room, closing the door with more care than needed.

As soon as the door was closed, Six scowled and turned back to Nero.

"I never knew the reason he needed to be here. He does nothing at all but sit beside me and try to advise me to do things." Then she paused for a moment and snickered. "Well, he used to. Then I threatened him. I suppose that's when it stopped," she said, her face contorting to look innocent. Her attempt was unsuccessful. Nero gave her a rueful look in response but turned his attention to the activity in the room.

"I'd like to see how your Necare work," he told her as he sat down in the nearest chair and continued to glance around. There was no way to distinguish the ranks from one another, he realized. Her Vampires dressed just as casually and outlandishly as she did. While Ace had made certain her Necare wore practical clothing that would assist with blending into whatever environment they would be going into, the attire would need to be able to be fought in as well. She had seen far too many good Necare die by way of fashion rather than function. Six seemed to care less.

"Finally! We're going hunting soon. The House Vampires will be joining to get in a good meal, but we had a tip about a congregation of Werewolves. You should come and see." She was practically squealing with delight, clapping her hands with excitement at the prospect.

"Will you be changing for the hunt?" Nero asked, glancing down at her normal attire; her corset and short skirt were less than ideal for killing Werewolves. Really, he considered it more like a beacon, announcing her presence to mortals and Werewolves alike.

"Why would I do that?"

"You're looking very ... *flashy*. Is that appropriate for what you'll be doing?" Nero asked, finally meeting her eyes with a raised eyebrow.

"No one cares. Not in New Orleans, at least," Six told him with a grin, as she held out her hand for him to take.

"The Werewolves will know exactly who you are."

"And? Then I won't have to chase them down. They'll come to me." She smirked, eyes bright with anticipation as she grasped his arm, since he didn't take hers, and started pulling him along. "Let's leave now." This last bit was said as a bellow to the rest of the house, making them all go on alert.

Nero followed Six, being surrounded by quite a crowd of others as they made their way through the large property, dotted with large trees and swampy patches. The Necare that were from the other covens were noticeable against the ones from Redeamond. They dressed in darker colors and wore hoods, so as to not attract attention. He sensed that they were just as uncomfortable in these new surroundings as he was. Necare were trained to be cold-blooded killers, to remain calm and unaffected. Six's Necare seemed to have an almost opposite approach.

It was when they hit the road outside the property that they seemed to split off into smaller groups. This property was not far from the French Quarter, taking only a brief walk to get there. The streets were already packed with cars and people milling about. He was still skeptical about Six's clothing. If the Masquerade, the deception that kept the mortals from knowing of the other world hidden from them, was revealed, they would be ruined. Not just them ... but all Immortals. And he would have to kill her.

"We heard that some of the Werewolves are congregating here by this club in the Quarter. A lot more than usual," Six told him, gesturing toward the club. It was very close to the center of the French Quarter, but its entrance was on a side street rather than facing Bourbon Street itself. "The amount of Werewolves in this area is growing. In the past few months, we've seen the numbers triple. And it doesn't seem to matter how many we kill, there's always more coming. It's as if all the dens are joining together for something," Six told Nero, as she halted just at the edge of the street, waiting for Lin to move from the back of the group to her. As he came toward her, he attempted to kiss her cheek but she avoided it smoothly.

Lin scowled lightly, returning his expression to a neutral one almost instantaneously, but Nero saw it. Since they had returned to Redeamond, it seemed like Lin was lacking in the attention he was used to from Six. With Nero there, Six had no use for him. But though he was aggravated by her overt rejection, Nero wasn't staying forever. Lin felt assured she would come back to his arms ... or rather, let him return to her bed.

Their approach toward the club was halted quite a few times as various people approached them. Some just seeming to want attention from the interesting-looking people walking down the street; others more blatantly asking to be her meal for the night. Nero stood, trying to keep his composure, when internally he was horrified at the display. In the past, Vampires often acquired mortal stock, humans who would live with or adjacent to the covens to provide blood at convenience. They had since all been relegated to the facilities, living there for periods of time throughout the year to provide blood for distribution to the covens in bags, or joining them in person for special events, like they had for the Harvest.

This was done for safety. The Masquerade had to be upheld, and keeping the few families of mortals who were privy to their secrets away was deemed much more secure than the old ways had been.

"Is this something that happens normally, Six?" Nero asked in a hushed whisper, as he leaned down to her ear.

She shivered slightly at the proximity and his breath against her skin. Yes, having him come out with them was a *very* good idea.

"Most of the local people in this part of town know I'm a Vampire," she said, glancing over at Nero with her blood-red eyes and grin spread over her lips. "Those who practice voodoo fear us, though. The other humans don't seem to have much of a sense of self- preservation." She reached out and touched a girl who had approached, caressing her cheek until a deep blush flourished against her skin.

"But, Six—"

"I know, I know. The Masquerade. But it's not my fault! New Orleans is very different from London, Nero. Even different from most other cities. It's a nexus. Our world and the Mortal world collide here, and these humans see a lot of unusual things. Not just Vampires. This is a crazy town," she told him, shrugging and continuing to walk.

"You shouldn't break the Masquerade; that's important to keep the balance between our world and theirs," Nero said seriously, noticing more and more people were eyeing them as they walked closer to the club.

"You know I wouldn't break the Masquerade by choice. Don't look at them and they won't approach, unless they're especially stupid. That's what I've found," she snapped at him, quickly shooing away the few lingering humans.

They slowed as they got closer to the club, finally turning down the side street. The crowd on Bourbon Street seemed to forget they had ever walked through. Six was clearly about to start pushing her way up to the front of the line for admittance when Nero caught a scent, and once it was there, it became more and more noticeable and grotesque to his nose. It had been so long since the last time he had been hunting, but that scent he could spot anywhere. Werewolf.

His eyes rolled back as he sniffed, trying to find a location, the nearest one; that's all he wanted. He hadn't realized how much he missed the kill. How much the scent of a Werewolf set off the predator in him. Not for blood to satiate his hunger, but to satiate his killer instincts. One was close. Female, it smelled like, with a sweeter effect to the sickening stench of their kind. His eyes snapped open when he knew he'd homed in on it.

"That one," he said thickly, as his fangs grew and his eyes began to glow.

The woman he was staring down was petite, her frame slight, despite her obvious lean muscles. She had noticed them too, or at least their scent. Her eyes were already changed as she sniffed around, looking for the source. Werewolves were rather good about keeping their world separated from the mortals, but in certain scenarios, especially for a young or newly turned Werewolf, they just wouldn't be able to hold back. Sometimes when a scent hit the air, it could set them off for good or for naught. They would sniff like a dog who just found its bone, but the only smells in the air were marijuana, vomit, and Vampire.

"She's not from here. There are only male Werewolves in the New Orleans' den," Six whispered against Nero's ear, just as he had done earlier. The woman's wolfen eyes finally caught sight of Nero, and the hair on her head seemed to bristle when their eyes connected.

There was an odd sense of knowing in her eyes. She recognized him, and not simply because he was a Vampire. She knew who he was. A canine whine came from her throat, and without so much as a word to those around her, she took off in the opposite direction in terror.

As Nero began to chase after her, Six grabbed him by the hair, causing him to hiss. "Don't waste your time, Nero. I'll get her. Well ... *these* will," Six said with a wicked grin, as she lifted her hands into the air. Little pieces of metal seemed to be called by her hand from various places in her scant clothing. They were shaped like diamonds, sharply pointed and unevenly distributed so the top point was heavier and the bottom was more like the end to a throwing knife. The shape matched the red tattoos that littered Six's body.

The little diamonds went flying after the Werewolf, unnoticed by any of the passersby, sliding into their target's back quickly and without a sound, leaving, for a split second, only small slivers, like the slots that coins go into for vending machines. The Werewolf stopped, rather abruptly, and turned around with a look of utter confusion and absolute pain covering her face. Her body had tensed with the blades, but the fun part was soon to come. Nero watched in amazement as smoke started rising from her orifices before she let out a rough cough and burning blood began spewing from her mouth.

"She's…" Nero started, as he looked on her flaming body with an awed and confused expression.

"It's demon metal. Had them fashioned some years ago. Handy," Six said, wiggling her fingers as she grinned at him. "They combust anything they enter. Sometimes things it just doesn't like," she told him, her voice filled with an odd sense of pride as she watched the last few remnants of the Werewolf's form crumble away under the unrelenting flames. "Fun, ain't it?" Six asked, with her drawl coming out a little heavier. Her were eyes alight with mischievous glee as she smiled and called the metal out of the pile of dust that was still smoldering on the street, back to her.

"Quite," Nero agreed, eyeing Six for a moment as the blades hid themselves back amongst her attire. Anything made from demons was questionable at best. There were plenty of stories of Vampires in the past being seduced by the power they could wield, and then ultimately falling because of the object. But he decided not to confront her about it. Years of knowing her had taught him to choose his battles, and this was not one he would win.

He began stepping forward toward the body, but Six again grabbed his hair, a bit more gently than she had previously and reigned him back. "Ace mentioned that the Werewolf remains were strange recently. I want to inspect it myself," he said, pulling his hair from her grasp with a snarl.

He walked to the ashes and touched it; they were, in fact, sticky, like Ace had described to him. So, it wasn't just Lukis's den that had this newfound ability to choose their form at will; he had spread it to the others as well.

The dead wolf's scent was fading, but a new stench of Werewolf replaced it. He saw their shadows approach from where she had been running. Nero rid his fingers of the sticky ash and let his fangs extend in warning, as he pulled a silver dagger from his pocket. Slowly he stood and looked onto one of the Werewolves' faces. Six and the others, in their smaller group of Necare and House Vampires, were still back in the line for the club. The Nero of before would have been more than capable of taking out six or eight Werewolves on his own. But he wasn't given the opportunity to fully assess the situation. The one that caught his eye came rather abruptly to Nero, their faces but a breath apart.

"You killed Shanti," growled the Werewolf. Nero stared at him for a moment, his eyes turning a bright baby blue. Slowly, he tilted his head to the side.

"*It* had a name?" Nero asked with a hint of disgust, as he glanced down at the feet of the wolf before him, shoes now covered in his comrade. The Werewolf roared, the skin on his face distorting with rage and the hint of a change.

"I'll kill you! I'm so *sick* of your kind. Soulless monsters," he managed to get out, though his voice was growing more garbled with each passing moment.

"Are you, now? I'm quite sure we've all been sick of your kind for quite some time. Nice of you to catch up. Werewolves were always the slower of the Immortals," Nero said with a smirk, as a chuckle went through the small group of Necare behind him. "Let's get straight to business, shall we? How are you changing without the moon? You're using something unnatural," Nero said, putting the tip of sliver blade on the Werewolf's chest and pressing, not hard enough to break the skin but threatening still.

"I'd rather take off your head," he screamed, rearing his hand behind him, as if he were going to decapitate Nero in one try.

Nero smirked, amused and unperturbed by this aggressive display. Without a moment for his enemy to react, Nero dodged the attack, using the momentum to quickly slide the blade around the werewolf's torso to his back. The flesh beneath the blade parted easily as he moved around him, blood immediately pouring out and causing all the Vampires to let out satisfied hisses. Now having the werewolf in a vulnerable position, he twisted the blade into the soft meat, watching the smoke rise from the wound the silver had inflicted. "Now, tell me. How are your kind changing without the moon?" Nero asked again in a more demanding tone. The Werewolf's eyes were wide from both surprise and pain.

"I won't betray..." he began.

"We've seen it happening. There were witnesses, and we are bound to find out one way or another. The question is how many of you must die before we get that answer?" Nero asked, as he stuck another blade into the wolf's back and twisted it as well. This seemed to go mostly unnoticed by the mortals. They were either turning a blind eye to it and pretending it wasn't real, or they were oblivious to it. Both were plausible, he supposed, especially based on what Six had told him about the residents of this city earlier that evening.

The mention of others dying, as he looked out over the semicircle of his pack, made the Werewolf under Nero's blades stiffen at the thought of the rest of them falling in much the same manner that he was doing now. "Okay! It's a pill! A pill! Some Witch came up with it. It enhances our changing abilities," the Werewolf spoke out breathlessly.

"Now that wasn't so hard, was it?" Nero said, smiling sinisterly before he quickly twisted and pulled up on the silver blades, cutting off a large portion of the Werewolf's neck and shoulders in the process. The Werewolf seemed to stand shocked for a moment, his blood coating the ground around them, before he slumped, his body dropping like a ragdoll, dead.

Ace had scheduled a time to meet with Lucef in the café they had spoken in before. She sat and waited at the same brightly colored table when a different man sat down next to her.

"Well, hello, Ace. I haven't seen you in a very long time," the tall man said, his deep voice resonating as a warm smile spread over his face. This wasn't a face she knew, but the sensation she got when he was near was very familiar, and the scent he gave off, a metallic tang in the air, could mean only one person when coupled together.

"Trying to keep your profile low, Codi?" Ace asked him as she smirked. She knew exactly who he was, even behind his disguise. He grinned at her, briefly eyeing the singular mortal that sat with their back turned to them on the other side of the room.

"How do you always know it's me?" he asked, shifting seamlessly from the tall dark man to a much shorter pale man, his hair slicked back, and his features rearranged to show Japanese features.

"Codi, come now. You've known me for too long to think you can play that trick on me. I can smell you," she told him, with a smile that was rarely seen by anyone.

Codi was a Chenja. They had worked together on numerous occasions over the years, especially when she had spent time in Japan, fighting off the Werewolf den that had grown during the early part of the eighteenth century. He had effectively been her partner during that time, her being the only Vampire sent to help them and the small coven there deal with the unsavory group that had begun terrorizing the Chenjas and mortals alike. Ace liked to think of them as friends, which was ideal since following that time, Codi had been appointed the liaison between Kagami, the leader of the Chenjas, and their allies, the Vampires.

"Why are you here?" Codi asked her, noting what an odd place it was to find Ace. A café, and a very cheery one at that, was not a place he would have ever suspected to have run into her. He had been there conducting business with the owner, who happened to carry some of the specialty Japanese teas that the Chenjas exported. They exported plenty of goods to other countries around the globe, making up for their small numbers by being one of the richest Immortal species.

"I'm meeting Lucef," she told him, glancing at the door, as if to will him to appear.

"*Lucef*? As in Lukis's son Lucef?" Codi asked, his face taking on quite a surprised expression as Ace nodded.

"His father's been trying to pull him back into his grasp. He's decided he's unwilling to help Lukis in whatever his plans are, and he wants to help us instead," Ace said, shrugging a little as she told him the very short version of events. While this certainly would affect the Chenjas, Ace didn't feel it was pertinent to give him all the details yet. Chenjas reproduced sparingly, and they didn't have the numbers to match any of the other species in a fight. It was best that they were kept out of it unless it became absolutely necessary for them to be involved.

"Why would he want to help the Vampires and the Chenjas?" Codi asked, his tone full of disbelief.

"Because he hates what he comes from," Ace told him pointedly.

A moment later, as if knowing he was the topic of discussion, Lucef came through the front door with a ding of the bell. He glanced around, noticing Ace, but then immediately pausing in his approach to the table when he noticed the man sitting beside her. If his hackles could have raised, they would have.

"Who is this?" he asked cautiously, sitting slowly across from the two of them.

"This is Codi; he is a Chenja," Ace told him. Lucef eyed him warily, but eventually reached his hand across the table to shake hands. Codi took it, gripping a little tighter than was comfortable on Lucef's fingers, before pulling away.

"It's nice to make your acquaintance, Lucef," Codi said, though his gaze remained pensive as he took in everything about him.

"Will you be staying?" Ace asked. It wasn't so much that she minded Codi being there, but inevitably more would be revealed to him than she had intended at this time if he did. Not to mention his questioning of everything that was already established would eat precious time that they didn't have.

"I believe I must take my leave. I have other duties to attend to," Codi said, giving each of them a slight bow of his head before he stood from the table. "Ace, I'll check in with you soon. I expect you'll have plenty to tell me."

"Oh, I'm sure," Ace confirmed before Codi made his way lithely from the shop.

Ace and Lucef sat in an odd silence for a moment, both seeming to be sizing the other up.

"I hadn't planned for him to be here," Ace offered, having read the trepidation on Lucef's features.

"I just wasn't expecting it," he murmured, shifting his eyes away momentarily. "What was this you wanted to know?" he asked her.

"You said he thinks you're some key. A key to what?" Ace asked him, leaning forward on the table to not miss a single thing he had to say about it.

"I don't know the specifics. I had overheard him talking before I left the den. That and what his men told me when they cornered me at The Gast a month ago," Lucef said with a shrug, leaning back on his chair as if exhausted. Ace had heard that brief conversation too, or she had read some of it from their lips.

"Why are you so important? Why you?" Ace asked, furrowing her brow.

"I don't know. When I left, there was some talk of a book. Something important is laid out in it, I think. I can sneak into my father's den and steal it if you'd like," Lucef offered. Ace chewed her lip for a moment. Right now, they had very little to go on. There was no way for her to infiltrate that den the way things currently were. She looked at Lucef, his essentially mortal body, only hinting at any sort of otherness with his strange eyes. Was she really going to rely on him?

"Alright," she grumbled with a sigh. There was no other option but this for now. "But be careful. If Lukis needs you, he'll take any opportunity to get his hands on you that he can. And if this book is so important, I wouldn't be surprised if it's a bit more difficult to get to than you think," Ace said, eyes flashing in warning.

"He wouldn't expect me to come to him, and I spent so much time sneaking around there as a child, I won't get caught," he told her, an impish smile forming on his face. Ace nodded sharply, leaving the café without another word. She could not foresee this going to plan, but then again, she couldn't see another way to go about getting the information that they needed.

CHAPTER 11

L ucef made his way through the crowded street in the Shoreditch neighborhood. The nightlife was in full swing, with lines of people waiting to enter the pubs there, making the street impassable by vehicles. The misting rain didn't seem to be deterring them, their excited energy keeping the chill from the rain away. Lucef was glad for their distraction; it helped him blend in as he pushed his way through one of the unmarked side doors.

The doors opened to an unlit hallway, the loud clang of the door closing echoing down the steep stairs. There was only one way to go. Down.

Lucef hadn't used these stairs for years. He imagined no one had. It had been his secret passage to and from his father's den. A long-forgotten route. He shook off his jacket and shoes, leaving them dripping at the door. He needed to be sure there were no traces he had come or gone before he made his way down to the depths of his childhood home.

As he descended, he fought back the nauseous feeling it gave him to be back there. He had escaped this place, and yet here he was, coming back to retrieve something for his father's enemies. Quite the turn of fate. He wasn't completely sure why he was helping Ace. It may have been that though she was a Vampire, and should have been hostile to him, she had done nothing but speak to him as if he were an equal. She, at least, was not the monster that the Vampires had always been portrayed as to him.

The stairs came to an end as another set of large metal doors were there, encapsulated in the red glow of an emergency light perched above them. The signage suggested danger lay beyond that point. Lucef chuckled lightly to himself. Yes, danger, but not chemical or electrical, as the symbols suggested. This was the entrance to a long-forgotten underground hydraulic power hub. Most of the den was spread out across the city in abandoned places like this, connecting through the underground tunnels. It was for secrecy, but also protection. They could move about the city, nearly unnoticed by mortals, while at the same time having the ability to change into their wolf forms at the full moon without alerting the people above. Only the oldest and most in control of their wolf forms were allowed to run outside.

City life was hard to maintain when the beasts took over, and all they wanted to do was hunt and kill.

Lucef pulled at the chain around his neck, revealing a key. It was a narrow metal key, its bow a simple oval. It didn't look particularly interesting or special, but Lucef had stolen it years ago from his father's collection. He didn't know what it did until he had left and found himself on the streets of London, trying to hide from human authorities and Immortal alike. The key opened any door. He wasn't sure if it was some ancient magic key or simply a master key for London, but he hadn't stayed in his father's den long enough to find out. He had seen a means to escape and escape he did.

The door opened into a wide tunnel. The arched ceiling made of old stone, black and ominous with such little light to see by. Lucef crept quietly across the tunnel, the door on the other side, tucked between two curved support beams. This door was not metal; however, it was heavy wood. He tested the handle and found the door unlocked, just as it had been when he left years ago.

The guards were still careless, he supposed. He slipped in and braced his back to the door, hoping that the creak of the hinges hadn't alerted anyone to his presence. After several moments of holding his breath, he finally let it out, having not heard a sound. This wing of the den was not usually disturbed. It was the living quarters for the leader's family, and, therefore, mostly left alone.

Lucef peered down the Bath Stone hallway, eyes taking in the familiar décor. Dark green tapestries still hung around the walls to absorb sound and keep the chill away, large, wooded pillars placed strategically to give the feel that the home was not underground, but perhaps a great mansion, and of course portraits hung displaying the great Werewolves of the past. People that Lucef would never have been able to compare to.

His time there had not been completely joyless, though. He thought of his mother, who he pitied more than hated. She was simply another victim of his father, but that didn't mean she wasn't culpable to some of the wrongdoings done to Lucef.

He knew her room was close. It was in the same direction as the collections room. Lukis kept her there as if she were part of that collection. He passed the door, knowing that the study was the next door down, when he heard the weary murmur of her voice, making him freeze in his tracks.

"Disgusting..." came Deca's voice, tired and slightly pained, but also rather exasperated.

Lucef tensed, unable to help himself as he turned to peek through the cracked door of the room. There she sat, light blonde hair flowing over her pale shoulders, eyes fixed on the pewter goblet in her bony fingers. Her body was hunched with pain and weakness, scapulae protruding grotesquely, skin greyed and sagging. She looked so old, broken. Even her voice quivered as she complained to herself.

"Why must I take this?" she grumbled to herself as she shook her head. Her face was even more strange than her body, Lucef saw. Hollow cheeks and deep-set eyes looked at the contents of the cup with repulsion.

With a final sigh, she pressed her lips to the brim of the cup, quickly drinking its contents. Only a small drop escaped the corner of her mouth, leaving a dark red track down to her chin. For a moment she cringed, slamming the cup onto the table beside her to free her hand so she could grip the cushioned arms of the chair better. She began coughing hoarsely, eyes wide. Lucef had to stop himself from going to her side, but he knew her pain would be over in a moment. Seeing him might be more excruciating.

Her body shuddered, the skin rippling a little as it transformed. Once loose and thin, it was now pink and firm, stretching back over her bones. Her hair even darkened from the greying blonde it had been to the strawberry-blonde locks he had known her to when he was a child. Her cringing turned more relaxed, her back leaning into the chair, and a serene expression came over her now youthful face.

Lucef heard footsteps against the floor, pulling him from the hypnotic scene of his mother's change back to the reality of where he was and what he was doing. He ducked behind a wooden pillar, holding his breath as he heard the footsteps grow steadily closer. The door was pushed open, and he heard a small, contented sigh.

"Oh good. You've taken it," came Lukis's deep voice.

"Lukis, dear," Deca said dreamily.

"I hate that you let it get that bad again," he murmured, stepping only far enough into the room to lean over and press a kiss to her forehead.

"I hate it, Lukis," she grumbled, glaring toward the cup. Lukis took the cup from the table, moving over to the shelves that lined the wall behind where Deca sat and placing the cup into a glass enclosure. Exactly the way Lucef remembered this particular ritual happening as a child.

"But it's necessary," Lukis said with finality, returning to Deca for just a moment to brush his rough fingers over her cheek, before turning back to the hallway. "I just came to make sure you'd taken it. Rest now, dear. I have things to attend to," he said, heading back where he came down the hall with quick, deliberate strides. Deca shot up from her chair and followed him out.

"Lukis! Wait. I wanted to talk to you about..." Her voice trailed off as she moved further from the room and, subsequently, Lucef.

He breathed a sigh of relief with them both well away once again, leaving the door to the collection room at his disposal.

"Perfect," he whispered, as he crept across the hall and unlocked the heavy oak door with the same key.

Lucef glanced briefly back down the hall, making sure it was still deserted, before stepping into the dark room. The room smelled of dust, mildew, and *old*. He wasn't sure there was another way to describe it. The walls were lined with shelves, some displaying artifacts, but most were covered in books and scrolls. Mounted on the wall over a painting, with a placard that read, "The Great Battle," was the top of a Vampire skull, fangs extended. Like old Werewolves, Vampires usually turned to dust once they had died, but there, for all who entered to see, was the skeletal evidence of Vampires existing.

Lucef tore his eyes away from it, briefly glancing at the oil painting below it, before letting them settle toward the center of the room. The large glass display case stood prominently there. Within it was only the book. He approached it, looking down at it. It was clearly bound in some sort of leather, stitched together intricately. It had no title on the cover, nor did it seem overtly large, as he had expected. In fact, it was not much larger than a standard college textbook, though it certainly looked ancient to his eyes.

He carefully opened the case, pulling the gloves he had brought with him on before snagging the book from its cushioned home. He slipped it into the backpack he had slung at his back, slowly closing the case once more, before he turned back toward the hall. He had left the door slightly ajar so he could hear someone approaching, but it didn't seem to help him since not a moment after he slipped back into the hall did he heard the footfalls of his parents returning.

"I should go to the meeting, Lukis," Deca said, sounding mildly disgruntled.

"You need to rest," Lukis said, stepping back into her room.

That's when it happened. A moment that seemed to freeze before Lucef forever. The backpack, which he had only put back over one shoulder, slipped down to his elbow, hitting itself against the wooden pillar he had hidden behind again and drawing his mother's attention. Her head whipped up, eyes scouring the hallway for the noise. Her senses, at least for the hours shortly following her treatment, were increased tenfold, and she was now acutely aware that there was a scent she recognized in there.

Lucef had known his scent would potentially be a hinderance in this mission, but the moment he stepped through the familiar hallways, he felt certain that he smelled enough like his father that it would go fairly undetected. This tense moment, when his mother's nose breathed in the air of the tunnels, could be it for him. No one knew the scent of someone better than their mother.

"Lucef?" Deca asked softly, her eyes darting everywhere, trying to catch a glimpse of him. Lucef held his breath, body fully tensed as he continued to hide.

"What are you talking about, Deca?" Lukis hissed, storming back out into the hall.

"I thought I heard—"

"Lucef isn't here. You're just high from the blood."

"But I..." She couldn't complete her sentence, eyes now desperately looking around the hall, as if she could will her son to appear. Lukis, at first angry, now softened and sighed as he looked at the anguish on his wife's face.

"Alright, Deca. You can come to the meeting. Let's just be on our way," Lukis said, grasping her hand and turning her body back toward the passage they had just come from, Deca still craning her neck to look behind her until their forms disappeared behind the curve of the hall.

Lucef finally let out the breath he had been holding, taking not but a moment to secure the backpack to his shoulder properly before he quickly made his escape the way he came. He couldn't help the overwhelming pity he felt, thinking on his mother. He was but a step or two from her and it would have made her so happy to see him, but he couldn't risk it. He couldn't risk his father catching him. Then all this would have been for nothing.

He growled as he placed his shoes back on his feet, recalling the chiding way his father was toward her. He treated her like a child, manipulating her into drinking that blood. He knew she hated taking it, but it had sustained her for so long that without it, she would certainly die. It had become a vicious cycle, her beginning to fall apart, rapidly aging as the effects of the blood wore off over the course of a month; then she would take it again, being once again rejuvenated and back to this younger, ideal version of her body. But it was clear she was taking longer bouts between drinking it, since Lucef had never seen her in such a withered state before. The amount of pain she had to have been in made Lucef shivered at the thought.

He slipped back out onto the street, the lines of youth still formed at the pubs, making it easy for him to slip back in unnoticed. It was then, as he was walking and turning away from this neighborhood that he realized he'd done it.

He got the book.

A grin spread over his face as he continued walking with purpose.

He had posed taking the book as being easy to Ace, but it was clear neither of them had anticipated him having such an easy time. It had been perfectly executed.

But now, how to get it to Ace.

With his childhood memories a bit closer at hand within his mind, he pulled on his lessons about the city. Places he was welcomed and places to avoid. One such place tucked between Highgate Golf Club and Hampstead Heath was a long-forgotten mansion. It was old, even for being one of the oldest cities in the world, to have a structure not only survive here in London but be hidden away for no mortal to truly stumble upon ... well, that was quite a feat. Lucef knew exactly what that was and why he wasn't ever to go there.

Kurome Mansion.

Was it daft of him to go to the main Vampire coven alone? Probably.

But he didn't have much of a choice. That book felt like it was going to burn a hole in his backpack and signal his father as to exactly where he was, if he didn't get it to Ace soon.

It didn't take him terribly long, jogging through the streets, to make his way to Kurome, eyes taking in the high stone walls that were covered with greenery. He walked along for some time until he finally came to a gate that had been camouflaged by wild plant growth. He could tell that even in the winter months, the metal gate remained obscured from view.

The place had an eerie feeling about it, making him want to turn right around on his heel than try to enter this property, but he had come this far. Squeezing through the bars, he made his way up the long gravel pathway until he finally caught sight of the mansion itself. It was massive. Huge cuts of stone, more like monoliths than homes, had comprised its exterior structure. Its windows, though many, were darkened and covered, save for a few that had dim light spilling out onto the darkened grass below. He hesitantly approached the large woodened doors, raising his fist to knock.

Not but a moment after his knuckles hit the wood did the door swing open. Glowing eyes found his, and a hiss came forth from the House Vampire who had answered.

"What are you doing here?" Charles asked with a snarl, fangs extended threateningly as he stared unblinkingly at Lucef.

"I'm here to see Ace," Lucef said, fists clenching at his sides. The look and scent of this Vampire put Lucef in a defensive state. Everything about this interaction felt hostile, and his body was screaming at him to run. But he was supposed to be here. He had to deliver this book to Ace. His father had to be stopped. There was no other way. Charles let out a sinister chuckle, letting his eyes fall from Lucef's face to drag his gaze over the rest of his body. He was dirty from walking through old, unused tunnels and running across the city to get here.

"She doesn't see your filth, Werewolf," Charles spat.

"I'm not a Werewolf," Lucef said, getting irritated. Charles sniffed him briefly.

"You smell it."

"I—" Lucef started to try to defend himself, knowing he was just in his father's den and would have nearly coated himself in the scent, but he didn't have to explain himself. The door was nearly ripped from Charles's grasp. Ace stood there, glowering at Charles for a moment before beckoning Lucef in with her hand.

Lucef stepped between them, eyes taking in the elaborate entrance and parlor as he did so. This was very different than any Werewolf headquarters he had ever been to. He turned as Ace slammed the door, still glaring at Charles.

"Go off with William and the others," she hissed, watching as he, in the blink of an eye, disappeared from sight. Ace shook her head, approaching Lucef and gesturing for him to follow her. She led him up the stairs that curved around the right edge of the rounded parlor, down a hallway, and through a door.

Her office, he supposed, by the look of it. There was only a few chairs and a desk, the rest of the space sparsely decorated. Everything in this room was for practicality, something he was coming to see was a key part of her personality. She was focused, prudent. Even their conversations were to the point, no flowery pleasantries. He watched her as she sat behind the desk that was in the center, while he chose the chair closest to the door to sit in.

"I'm assuming, if you've decided to be so bold as to come to our coven, that you actually retrieved it?" Ace asked. Lucef grinned, pulling the backpack into his lap and unzipping it. He pulled the book from within, carefully setting it on the desk before her.

Her eyes lit up greedily, though nothing else about her facial expression changed. She carefully reached out her hand, letting her fingers lightly trail over the intricate stitching.

"This looks very much like the one we keep here," she murmured, thinking on their room of artifacts. It was difficult to cultivate things older than the Elders, but they had treasures and recordings of the Immortals that surpassed even Srinta, the oldest Vampire Ace had ever met.

"Do you think it has the same information?" Lucef asked, feeling slightly discouraged that he may have gone through all this trouble for nothing.

"Sisters, but not twins, it seems," Ace said, releasing the clasp that held the book closed and opening the cover slowly to reveal the yellowed pages within.

"What's the cover made from? I couldn't tell what type of leather it was."

Ace's eyes flashed up to meet with his, a small smirk forming at the corner of her mouth as her fingers rubbed against the cover.

"Human," she told him.

CHAPTER 12

Silence overtook Ace and Lucef as she poured over the handwritten script. Yes, this book was very similar to the one held in Kurome, but it was as if the ones who had created these had gotten the same story, just told from different perspectives. She couldn't recall who had written the book in Kurome's possession. Had it been a Vampire?

These books were not marked with their authors. They were nameless.

"Anything interesting?" Lucef asked, clearly uncomfortable with the extended silence.

"This book holds a lot. Very similar to the one we have here. A history of the world not told today. Prophecies, spells, incantations," she told him as she picked the book up, eyes scanning the edges of the pages to determine if there was a particular wear to any part of the book that would suggest a certain section had been read more often than others.

"Similar but not the same," Lucef confirmed, leaning forward a bit.

"Not the same, no."

She saw it. The darkening by finger oils, nearer to the end of the book, indicated it had been skipped to and touched many more times that the rest of it. She carefully tucked her fingernail between the pages there, opening the book to that spot and taking a deep breath as the page before her revealed quite an illustration.

It was hand-drawn and painted, but with absolute detail. The eyes of the person on the page were what stood out most to her. The inky black that seemed to melt into the light blue. Eyes that were looking at her right now. Ace looked up at him, letting her surprise show, even just momentarily.

"What—?" Lucef started, but his gaze dropped to the painting, and his mouth snapped shut. That was him; there was no mistaking it. From his eyes to the shape of his face, even the length of his hair, was the very same as the man shown there.

"I suppose we know why you're so important to your father," Ace said, turning the page. Lucef continued staring at the pages, despite his image being obscured by the pages Ace now looked at.

"What does it say?" he asked, his voice a hoarse whisper.

"It appears to be a prophecy and a ritual," Ace said, letting her hand that wasn't on the book clench. She knew what Lukis was doing now. She knew with the utmost certainty that *this* was what he was planning.

"What does he want with me?" Lucef asked, eyes seeing the less-detailed illustrations of bodies laid out on tables and bleeding cuts on the skin of each one.

"It seems you are a Chosen One, Lucef. A vessel that will take in each Immortal. Though I'm not sure how he thinks he'd control you after. You've proven that you have no loyalty to him," Ace said, still looking down at the pages, taking in all the information as quickly as she could.

Lucef shook in his seat. His stomach turned and his heart thundered in his chest, causing Ace to look up at him, wondering if he was going to be ill.

"He's going to switch our souls," Lucef said through clenched teeth.

He had seen it preformed. It had been a ritual that the Witches did with frequency, especially with their offspring that they created with mortals. Those children had power and longer lifespans, but they didn't live forever. They weren't true Immortals. They would take a new body, a mortal body, and imbue it with their blood and soul. They'd then be transferred into the new vessel, banishing the mortal's soul away to whatever afterlife they went to.

His father was going to take his body.

Banish his soul.

His father was going to kill him.

Lucef's heart and erratic breathing made the hair stand up on Ace's neck. The scent of his fear was enveloping her and, oddly, made her want to protect him rather than kill him.

"You'll need to stay with us," Ace said, having watched the haunted look grow in his eyes and the sureness of the last words he said to her.

"Excuse me?" he asked, brow furrowing with confusion, as he watched her snap the book closed with a little more casualness than he thought it could handle.

"We can't let him get his hands on you. You are the key to his whole scheme after all. Without you, he can't proceed with his plan. We'll keep you here until we know more details," she said, walking toward the door at a human's pace so he could catch up to her.

"Where will I sleep? Won't the others take issue with this?" He hastily got up from the chair and followed her.

"They will get over it. We have a room that has a bed. We have several, but the others are taken at the moment," she told him, walking down the hall. He could tell the moment he had stepped into another wing of the mansion. Its colors were slightly different, and the ornamentation on the molding had changed. This was clearly for more important individuals in the mansion. Elders or high-ranking people. Not the likes of him.

Ace stopped at Nero's door, hesitating as Lucef caught up to where she was. Her teeth knocked with frustration as she contemplated what to do. She didn't want anyone in Nero's room; that was *his*, a place only few were permitted to go, and she happened to be one of them. Her crossing this threshold and letting in another person, a person who happened to be the son of their enemy, was going against so many things that were ingrained in her that she found it difficult to move.

She had thought to put him in Six's room, but that had been taken over by Racid upon Six's departure, since he seemed to be lingering at Kurome for some reason.

"Is this it?" Lucef asked, causing Ace to close her eyes to keep from lashing out at him. She was having a bit of an internal struggle, and he was making it worse by being there for it.

"It's an Elder's room. He is off doing duties for the war," Ace said after a drawn-out pause.

"Is it ... is it okay that I stay here?" he asked, now noticing the slight strain in her expression and how her hand was frozen in mid-reach toward the door.

"There's nowhere else suitable," Ace said stiffly, finally moving her hand to turn the knob and push the door open.

They both stepped inside as she stood just in the door for a moment. Lucef smiled slightly, more in awe of the extravagance than pleased with the situation. The four-poster bed was sitting, untouched since Nero had left, its heavy velvet curtains tied open, as if waiting for his return. The room had plenty of rich velvet furniture, a desk, an easel, and shelves full of his personal book collection.

Ace let her fingers glide over the silky sheets that were spread over the bed, remembering sitting beside him while he was sick and lying there years ago. It had been the last time she had set foot in there until recently, and a large part of the reason she had chosen to stay away from this room.

Six's making, a memory Ace seldom thought of and rarely wanted to. It was the late 1800s, and Six had been a young student, sent away to a British boarding school from the Americas. When a Vampire is sick, they need to have the purest of blood. They must drink enough to wash away whatever is plaguing them. The mortals the House Vampires had been procuring were negligent, to say the least. Poor undesirables were what had gotten Nero in this mess in the first place, and yet the House Vampires continued to only provide Nero with subpar specimens. In utter despair and frustration, Ace had gone out on her own in search of someone that she could bring him that might actually rid him of his affliction. Happenstance or fate, Ace didn't know, but she found and lured this girl, who at the time went by the name Sinthia. Ace had spotted her, smelled her untainted blood, and knew she was the one. The last sacrifice to bring her sire back from the brink of certain death, as Sinthia would save him.

Nero drank her until she was nearly dry. It had been the most savage attack Ace had ever witnessed Nero wreak on a mortal. It shocked her to a point that she took pity on the girl, who lay broken and dying of blood loss on the floor beside his bed. Ace let the girl drink from her wrist and named her Six. Six, because she was the sixth made from their line of blood.

"Sinthia isn't a very vampire-like name. Your name is Six now."

Six was taught by both Ace and Nero, but always thought that Nero had made her. Ace knew Six remembered the horror of him drinking from her until she was not able to move or speak, but it had been Ace who cut her wrist, offering their sacred blood to her, and transforming her into the creature she would become.

Now it was Lucef sitting on the end of the bed, looking around at the room with a sort of amazement. No blood, sickness, or death looming in the room now.

"Is there anything we need to retrieve for you?" she asked, turning her gaze away from him so he wouldn't see the disgust that flashed across her face. Lucef was not a Werewolf, but it bothered her that he was sullying Nero's bed, nonetheless.

"I move from place to place. I try not to stay anywhere too long, so I don't have much to call my own. I should be fine," Lucef said.

"If you need anything, you know where I am," she told him dully. He nodded, and she walked out of the room, closing the door slowly behind her.

Ace paused for a moment, resting her head on the door and letting her mask drop. She hated recalling that night; it was unpleasant for Ace and probably horrifying for Six. Ace couldn't stop the images from flashing through her mind. Nero laying there, his skin gray rather than porcelain white, cheeks hollowed, and eyes dull white instead of glowing with hunger. She could have easily lost him all those years ago, and yet she had chosen to stay away from him. Chosen to be a Necare and a Coven Judge instead of stand by his side.

With a heaving breath, she moved back through the halls toward her room. Choosing, once again, to banish those thoughts from her mind. She had a job to do. New decisions to make. She couldn't go back and change what had already come to pass.

Nero had been out hunting with the Necare and Six almost every night. It had started as a distraction, something to take his mind off Ace, and of course, an obligation to his duties of assuring the additional Necare were being utilized properly. But those reasons seemed to fall away with each passing evening. He had forgotten how much he relished the hunt. How the predator within him felt so satisfied after he brought another of his enemies to their death. Each passing evening, it became harder for his thirst to be abated when they returned to the manor. With his lust for the kill also came the *need* for warm blood directly from the mortal source.

It was becoming a moral quandary for him. He knew that other Vampires still drank from humans with semi-regularity, using the donated blood only when they weren't able. He, however, had been the Elder who had gone to such lengths to make it possible and had lived purely off that blood for years. And now that he had let himself get lost in blood sport, it was getting harder and harder for him to push the aching need to lure a mortal to a darkened corner and take their essence from them.

This night, Nero had just finished beheading a Werewolf and was practically panting with thirst. He had turned away from the rest of the Necare they had come out with, eyes scanning the crowd of mortals beyond the narrow side street they were hidden on. Six wouldn't like it if he disappeared back to the manor without her. No, she would and had taken offense to that several times over the last few days. This time, he would at least warn her.

"Six," he said slowly, tearing his eyes away from the humans. She walked over to him, brushing off some of the dust that a Witch had become, her face twisted with disgust.

"Yes, Nero?" she asked, her voice sweet, though she seemed far more preoccupied in the speckles of blood across her corset that were keeping the dust clinging there.

"I need a blood bag," he said, running his hands through his hair impatiently. She looked up at him, red eyes brightening with anger. There was still fun to be had and killing to be done, and she wasn't going to cut off her time simply because he was hungry.

She stamped her foot like a child.

"But I don't want to go home!" she whined, watching him wince at her tone.

"Six—" he started, but she hissed at him.

"No. You hunt!" she ordered him as she pointed at the crowd he had just been staring hungrily at. "Go!" she ordered him again, continuing to point.

"I should just return to—" She hissed again. It wasn't like Nero to take orders from anyone. His position as Elder made it so he normally did the ordering. But the truth was, he *wanted* to hunt. He only needed the excuse, and Six gave it to him.

He watched the crowd, waiting for at least one of them to notice him. Humans were more often not likely to be aware of a Vampire in their midst. It was a feature of the Masquerade, but it was also a protection mechanism. Mortals lived their lives oblivious to the dangers that surrounded them. But sometimes one would sense the danger and either run away in fear or be drawn to it like a moth to the flame.

A fair girl with bright red hair stopped and turned her gaze down the darkened side street. She could feel the danger, but it excited her. She saw his glowing eyes, then. Not so bright that they looked alien, but as if the light had caught them just right from the streetlights. She walked away from the crowd until she found herself very close to him, close enough to smell his enticing scent. He bent down, as if to whisper in her ear, but instead enveloping her in his scent, breathing against her skin. Her head fell back in pre-ecstasy, as Nero's fingers travelled lightly up her arms.

"Will you come with me?" he whispered.

She nodded her head almost zombie-like, her eyes locking with his once he pulled his head slightly away. Leading her off to a small space between buildings, he pressed her against the wall, hands travelling from her arms to her waist. Oh, the feel of her warm body and scent of her blood through her pores was nearly more than he could bear.

"Do you want me to kiss you?" Nero asked her, his voice low and velvety. She nodded, entranced with his eyes and voice.

He bent his head back down, his nose skimming the smooth skin at her neck, taking in her rapid pulse and how much stronger her blood smelled this close. First, he kissed her neck several times, until the feeling of mortal flesh on his lips became too overwhelming to ignore. Slowly he let his fangs puncture, savoring the feeling, shivering with how much pleasure it felt to simply taste the hot blood against his tongue.

He drank from her slowly, pressing himself against her and letting himself be lost in the ecstasy of her taste. He continued drinking from her until her heartbeat began to slow, knowing if he continued, he would kill her. With much reluctance, he pulled his mouth from her neck, licking the wound that was left there, so it would close almost unnoticeably. She would think they were mosquito bites when she came out of the stupor he had caused her to be in; for now, she was asleep.

Nero slid her down the wall, positioning her such that she was sitting and leaning against it, brushing her hair over her shoulder to hide the marks before he turned back to where Six and the others were. But there were no others. Only Six remained, having watched the whole thing. She was staring at him, her gaze intense.

It took not but a moment with their eyes locked for her to be on him, pressing *him* into a wall this time, her lips against his. He remained still and shocked as she moved over him, tongue sweeping at his unmovable lips.

"Mmm ... she was rather tasty, wasn't she, Nero?" Six said, finally breaking away from him and licking her own lips to savor the taste of the young mortal's blood. Nero growled, pushing her away from him but remaining against the wall.

"You can sate one hunger, but I know you have more," Six said with a grin, unfazed by his hostility.

"I will do no such thing," he said back menacingly, pushing off the wall and walking past her toward the end of the street.

"You can't pretend you don't want it, Nero. The evidence was clear a moment ago," Six said, her voice like bells, teetering on laughter. He reeled, turning around, and immediately taking her by the neck and slamming her against the nearest brick wall. Her smirk didn't falter, though her eyes widened just the slightest bit with surprise.

"Like every Vampire, I am aroused by drinking from my prey. I am not immune to our nature, Six, but I *am* able to control myself," Nero hissed, keeping her pinned beneath his hand.

"I'm not going to stop."

"It's pointless, Six. I won't give in."

Six reached up, bringing her fingers to lightly trace the contours of Nero's Roman features.

"You can pretend I'm her," Six said quietly, feeling the grip on her neck loosen just a fraction. "Just a kiss, Nero. One kiss, and I'll never ask it again."

Nero closed his eyes. He had to choose his battles. He had to choose which ones were worth fighting with her. If she was true to her word, and one kiss was all to get her to leave him be during his time in New Orleans, it might have been worth it. He was still vibrating with the life provided from his first live meal in years while his ache for Ace was becoming visceral, because despite them having remained unattached for years, neither of them had never taken up a different partner. This felt like it would be a betrayal.

"Why?" Nero asked, keeping his eyes closed. He didn't want to look at her face. He felt her move closer, easily pushing his hand away from her neck and moving herself even closer to him. Her fingers slid up his shoulders and neck, moving into his dark hair.

"I want to know what it's like to be yours," she whispered, gripping the hair at the back of his neck as she pressed her lips to his ear. Her whole body was pressed to his, the heat of the swampy city, even at night, almost made them feel human, especially since he was warmed by the girl's blood.

"Once," he agreed, his voice a rumble.

Six pulled her mouth from his ear, running her nose along his cheek until they were nose to nose. Nero's hand moved from his side to the back of her neck, pulling her, jarringly forward and smashing their mouths together with overt force. Six greedily lapped it up, clutching harder at his hair and lifting her leg over his hip.

For a moment, Nero got lost in the kiss, his mind immediately drifting to the image of Ace's face. It was like he was kissing her, and he lost himself in the joy and lust of that until the face he saw in his mind slowly twisted to enraged. Eyes blazing with a fury he had never seen there before.

He ripped his lips from Six's, pushing her away from him and into the wall with enough force the mortar between the bricks rained dust. Six was panting unnecessarily, eyes bright and glowing as she looked him over. His hair was in disarray, eyes also glowing but not with desire, with rage. He hissed at her, balling his fists as if he'd love nothing more than to rip her to pieces before him.

"Never again," he growled, turning and moving swiftly through the streets to head back to the manor.

CHAPTER 13

Ace's nails dug deeply into the arm of her chair, extending and splitting through the upholstery and wood. It was still morning here but clearly night across the ocean. Ace saw all of it. She felt the surge of emotions from Nero, first his overwhelming thirst. She couldn't help but let the vision flood before her eyes, watching as he succumbed to his instincts and drank from the mortal. Ace's fangs had extended, her body nearly vibrating alongside his with the feel of the girl's lifeforce flowing through him.

It made her recall the countless times they had shared a meal in the past. Instincts and memories flooding her with desire so potent, she closed her eyes in the ecstasy of it.

But it was shortly after that...

"You can pretend I'm her," Six had said, and Ace stilled.

It no longer became an immediate and absolute "no"; now she felt his hesitation. She felt his longing for her and his desire surging with the mortal blood singing in his veins.

"Once."

His voice rumbled in her own chest, and the word, followed by the kiss, was like a punch to the gut.

She felt sick.

She felt angry.

A rage she had never known before boiled within her.

Then it was just the two of them facing each other for the briefest of moments in a void. She didn't even need to say a word; she simply looked upon him, her anger radiating from her. The hunger left his eyes, a pleading expression taking its place. Ace tilted her chin up, eyes narrowing, before she turned in the void, effectively cutting him off from her mind.

She stood from her chair, withdrawing her nails from the armrests before picking up the chair with one hand and throwing it against the opposite wall. The chair exploded, sending wood shards scattering across the floor, while plaster wall crumbled behind the thick wallpaper, leaving a chair-shaped indent.

She knew he didn't *want* Six; it was Ace that he truly wanted. She could feel that from the snippets of his mind, but it didn't alleviate her rage. She had intended to go to New Orleans as soon as she knew what Lukis was up to, and now that she did, she wouldn't wait any longer. It would be difficult to convince the council of her departure. Being a Coven Judge was much like a captain of a ship. You weren't to abandon your territory. But she had to go. She had to see what was happening between them for herself, and she had to be there for when Lukis's plans ultimately came to fruition.

Once night fell, she and Lucef would be on the first transport across the Atlantic. It would get Lucef away from his father, and it would eliminate the opportunity for Six to try exploiting any other weak moments in Nero.

"I thought I heard some ruckus," came Srinta's voice from the doorway, causing Ace to whip around toward her.

"I didn't think anyone would be awake," Ace said, her voice slightly unsteady with her surprise.

"My sleeping cycle has been strange for the last two hundred years, or so. I suppose it's a symptom of my age, much like Ramses was before," Srinta said, closing the door behind her and stepping further into the room. Her face was thoughtful as she approached the destruction Ace had just wrought on her wall and chair, her dark brows rising as she touched the wallpaper lightly.

Ace had no idea who she had been in her mortal life, but Srinta had always been quite an interesting beauty. Her skin, though paled by her Vampirism, was still warm, suggesting that golden and brown hue had been deeper as a human. Ace knew she had come from somewhere near the Mediterranean Sea, Ramses having been her sire and changing her during his long tenure in Egypt. Her black hair fell down her straight back in waves, and she moved with a grace that even other Vampires envied. Ace wasn't sure how humans perceived her, but she was certain that it was immediately obvious Srinta was not one of them.

"Why are you awake, Ace?" Srinta asked after several long, silent moments.

"I was comparing the books," Ace told her, gesturing to her desk where the sister books sat side by side.

"Are you finding differences?" Srinta asked, moving over to Ace's desk to look for herself.

"Many," Ace confirmed, moving to stand beside her. "Quite a few things are exactly the same, but here," Ace pointed to the mid-point in both books, "where the prophecies begin. This is all different."

Srintas eyes lit up with delight, looking at the page that had originally stopped Ace in her tracks when Lucef had brought it to her.

"It's exactly as I remember," Srinta whispered, letting her fingers run over the page that showed Lucef's likeness.

Ace's eyes snapped to the Elder's face, watching how her appearance practically glowed with recollection.

"As you remember?" Ace asked, trying to keep her voice from being accusatory. Srinta smiled lightly, turning the page over to see the ritual laid out.

"Sisters indeed. These books were written as companions. These are to be paired, not separated as they once were. When Alexandria fell, so many things were scattered. I wasn't sure this one had survived," Srinta murmured, touching the pages that didn't show a hint of damage.

"You've known about this prophecy, then?" Ace asked, her brows coming together as she tried to put together how little she seemed to have known before. There seemed to be a lot she was unaware of.

"Many prophecies have been laid out over the years, and very few have come to pass since I have been here, Ace," Srinta said, giving her a shrewd glance for a moment, before turning the pages to examine some of the others Ace hadn't yet gotten to. "Have you read every prophecy in our book?"

Ace averted her eyes, glancing at the light that peeked out from the bottom of the curtain, remaining silent. No, she couldn't feel betrayed that she wasn't informed that this book existed. She hadn't even fully read the book that had been at her disposal. Her lip curled with self-loathing. She was little better than a House Vampire.

"But this is not why I came to you this morning," Srinta said, straightening up and moving around the desk to once again look upon the broken wall. "I'm assuming you didn't check your email since last night, or I imagine you would have approached me. Nero and Six have apparently confirmed that New Orleans is not only the base of operations for the Werewolves, but they are convening there. New Werewolves and Witches seem to be arriving in droves every day."

"Just as Six claimed when she was here," Ace said, smirking a little with uncontained pride. Six may have been mad, and perhaps a touch misguided in a lot of scenarios, but she certainly wasn't stupid. She had asked for more resources with just cause.

"So it seems," Srinta murmured, her tone just slightly bitter. "We need to send more resources there. The remaining Elders and I agreed that the best course of action will be to send you."

Ace let her brows draw together once more.

"Just me?"

Srinta turned away from the damaged wall to give Ace a pointed glare.

"I've seen you take out a den practically by yourself while we were in Japan. Minimal help from the coven there or our Chenja allies. You nearly killed Lukis a few weeks ago. Several of our own Necare are already there, simply waiting for true instruction. You should be all the help they need," Srinta told her.

"And what of the coven? I'm the Judge. I can't just leave," Ace reminded, crossing her arms over her chest defiantly. She wasn't sure why she was pushing back, as this was exactly what she wanted. She wanted to go to New Orleans. She wanted to get Lucef away from Lukis, and she needed to see Nero with her own eyes.

"Us Elders can take care of the coven. Your skills and presence are needed where it's most important." Srinta moved around the desk to stand before Ace suddenly, her hands raised to touch Ace's cheeks lightly. The contact was unexpected and unusual to Ace, but she remained still, only letting her eyes widen slightly with astonishment. "You have nothing to fear with Nero, Ace," Srinta whispered.

"He was mine, my progeny, my Nero, but I never held his attention quite the way you do. Even when you were human. He would have traveled to the ends of the earth, taken countless lives, to be with you. Do not worry. Do not fear. He's not been mine or anyone else's since the moment he saw you in that window."

Ace let out a breath, her shoulders seeming to melt down, though she hadn't been aware they had been raised with tension until she did so.

"Did you see it too?" Ace asked, hesitantly meeting Srinta's eyes.

"I have not looked in for many years, but Nero is so far away and Six is ... volatile," Srinta said, tilting her head a bit and letting her face soften a bit with humor. "I was not expecting to see what I saw, but I suppose neither were you."

"Nothing to fear, then?" Ace asked doubtfully, but Srinta's face turned serious again.

"Nothing."

Srinta released Ace's face just as abruptly as she had grasped it and moved toward the door to leave.

"I have already set about transport for you and Lucef. You'll leave at first dark." Then she was gone.

Ace spent the rest of the day preparing to leave. She packed a bag with a few pieces of clothing, weapons, and her laptop, before taking pictures of the pages of the book and taking both volumes back to their antiquities room. Reluctantly, she placed the book volume that had always been in the Vampires' possession back on its pedestal, wishing she had time to look through it. Another time she would be sure to educate herself; however, that was not what her objective was now.

The mansion was still quiet, as most of the other Vampires sequestered in their various rooms, soon to rise with the setting of the sun. But other than the stray Elder or two, Ace knew there was one guest that was most likely awake who she needed to warn of their departure.

She made her way to Nero's room, finding it was much easier to knock and move into the room than it had been the evening before.

"Usually, people wait until someone answers after they knock before they come in the room," Lucef said, his head stuck in the neck of his shirt, giving her a mildly annoyed but mostly amused expression.

"Not enough time for formalities," Ace said, closing the door behind her. She tossed a duffle bag similar to the one she had packed for herself toward his feet.

"What's this?"

"Your bag. You don't have enough clothes, so I found some spares that should fit you. We're leaving as soon as the sun sets," Ace told him, though she didn't look at him. She noticed the book that was slightly out of place on one of the shelves. She assumed he had tried to amuse himself during the day by looking through the books, and she didn't fault him for that, but something about seeing that book leaning just a bit too far to the left and clearly not pushed in as much as the other books made Ace's eyes narrow.

"What's going on?" Lucef asked, squatting to look in the bag, somewhat interested in what clothes she had procured for him.

"We need to leave for America," Ace said, moving to the shelf and correcting the book, before turning back to scan the rest of the space quickly to be sure nothing else was out of place.

"How are we getting there?" Lucef asked, shoving his backpack into the duffle with ease, before sitting to put his boots back on.

"We're flying. Private plane."

"Why are we going?"

"Werewolves are converging there. I must go to help defend." Ace found another book out of place on another shelf. Had he read both of them, or simply pulled them to decide if they were worth a read?

"Why am I going?" Lucef asked, pausing in his shoe-tying to watch her move quickly through the space, following the path he had walked the night and day previous and touching everything he had.

"We might be able to throw Lukis off you. He'll think you're still in London, and it will set them back for a time. Hopefully it will be long enough for me to take out enough of their numbers; his plan will be moot before he ever makes it across the ocean."

The plan seemed solid enough to Lucef, though he had never left London before, and the idea of not only being away from his city and in a completely unfamiliar place with unfamiliar vampires sounded rather ... daunting.

"That's where this Elder is?" Lucef asked, gesturing to the bed that was made but wrinkled, as if Lucef had merely laid on top of the blankets instead of sleeping within them.

"It is."

"Are you not concerned about him?"

"I'm far more concerned about the Coven Judge there and how she'll react to you than Nero," Ace said, smirking mildly at the idea of Six having to accommodate Lucef.

"Well, that's not particularly comforting," Lucef grumbled, following Ace out the door and off on their flight across the sea.

CHAPTER 14

Nero heard the distinct sound of the creaky door to his room opening, and at least one set of footsteps moving across his room from where he sat in the bath of the attached restroom. He had immediately come back to the manor and went to wash himself. He had to clean any trace of Six from him, to rid himself of the evidence that he had lost control. The hum of the human girl's blood still sang in his veins, and he decided he would just sit there, long after the water had gone cold.

Had he stayed there through the day and long into the night? He had.

Did he have other things he needed to be doing? Absolutely.

But remaining separate from Six, especially while he waited for a response from Kurome, seemed prudent.

He had asked for Ace to come. Not only because her skills and ability were unparalleled, but because being apart from Ace when their relationship was already so fragile and broken was driving him insane. He sighed, thinking how odd it was that the years he had waited for her, at least she had been so near. Now that they were separated by an ocean, he could feel his control unravelling.

Whoever had entered his room seemed to remain, waiting for him emerge. While the idea of making them wait even longer was tempting, he had already spent far too long in this tub. He couldn't dally any longer. He pulled himself from the water, quickly drying and dressing himself, before opening the restroom door.

His eyes quickly scanned the room, surprised as they rested on the image of Ace sitting on the ornately upholstered chair near the window. Her eyes were trained on the landscape surrounding the property, head tilted back to rest against the chair.

"I wasn't expecting you to get here quite so quickly," Nero said, stepping closer to her and letting the reality of her being there envelope him. Her scent, her voice. She was truly there, and she was very clearly choosing not to look directly at him.

"I didn't have much choice in the matter. The Elders deemed I was needed here, and so here I am," she said, eyes still affixed to the window, looking out across the grounds surrounding the old house. Nero knew this coldness; she had this wall in place before, but there was an edge to it. Sharp, painful edge of anger.

His mind flashed to the image of Ace when he had been kissing Six. The rage he had seen in her eyes was greater than anything he had seen from her before. That was the sharpness, betrayal.

He moved a bit closer, making sure his figure was dominating her visual space, so she'd be forced to look at him at some point.

"Does Six know you're here?" he asked, as he tried to catch her eye. Ace shrugged.

She hadn't made any sort of official announcement when she arrived, just merely spoke to a few of the Vampires present, several of which had been her Necare. Securing a room for Lucef had seemed a bit troublesome, but one was found and that's where she had put him, then she'd made her way directly here. At first, she had assumed, as the other Vampires on the lower levels had, that Nero was out once again with Six. Her anger flared at the idea he would have gone with her again, put himself in the position again, after the scene she had witnessed, but then she heard the slight slosh of the water from the room adjacent as she took a seat.

It was very difficult for her to keep herself planted in the chair while she waited. He was just beyond that door, and she had barely held in her anger for the whole nine-hour flight there. She wanted to rant and scream. She wanted to hurt him. So, Ace stayed put, anchoring herself to the spot by not looking near the door that he hid behind.

"I'll take that as a no, then," Nero murmured, watching her face to see if there were any indications she was planning on turning those silver eyes on his.

"I haven't got the slightest idea if she knows we've come or not. Honestly, I don't care," she told him.

"We?" Nero asked, catching that slight change in her wording. He hadn't expected Ace to bring any additional Necare with her, but then again, with the number of Werewolves that seemed to be filling this city in droves, he wouldn't mind any additional help she would have thought to bring. Perhaps Makiut decided to join her in the field again after all.

"I didn't mention it ... not that you would have had time to check any messages I've sent. Clearly, you've been too busy," she started, her tone clipped. "I've brought along Lucef Lynae."

Nero's brows shot up in surprise. He knew she had been following some leads, and the emails from the other Elders he had heard she had been talking to Lucef in the past few weeks, but he certainly wasn't expecting her to have brought him.

"So, you've discovered what Lukis wants with him, then?"

"I have. He's under our protection for the time being."

"And what do you mean, I've 'been too busy'? Look at me," Nero said, his voice betraying his increasing frustration at the lack of eye contact. He reached out to turn her face, but she quickly slapped his hand away, turning her silver eyes to him and giving him a look so molten with anger, it stole any other words from his mouth.

"I saw it. Our connection ... it..." Ace let the sentence die in her throat as she took in his expression, which had deepened to a strange, strangled look. He dropped to his knees before where she sat on the chair, eyes wide with a pain that she had never seen there before and an anger in himself.

"Once, Ace. Once in over five hundred years since I first laid eyes on you," Nero whispered, raising his hand as if to touch her face again, but letting it drop.

"Once too many," Ace hissed, her eyes now glowing as she glared into his. They simply sat there for several moments. The time ticked by as Ace thought of a number of terrible things she wanted to say, but she couldn't say them. Srinta had said nothing but the truth; Ace could see it, the remorse and guilt displayed in simply the way his normally proudly held body was folded over.

She leaned forward suddenly, taking his face in her hands and relishing in the feeling of touching him once again.

"*Never* again," she whispered, letting her nails bite ever so slightly into the flesh of his cheeks. "You are for me and me alone." And without a moment's hesitation, she closed the gap between them, falling to her knees as well and pressing her lips to his. He kissed her back with vigor, arms moving around her to hold her tightly against him.

If this had been a normal sire-progeny relationship, he could have simply ordered her to do whatever he wished. Demand that she forgive him or now allow her to display her anger toward him, but something about the way they had bonded, the way he loved her even before she had been turned, made that impossible. Whether by the magic, itself, or because he couldn't bring himself to treat her in such a way, he wasn't sure.

But that didn't matter. Nero gripped her with all his strength, mouth dancing with hers as if they hadn't touched in years, not weeks. His fangs extended, eyes nearly white as Ace's silver nails dragged over his skin, leaving small razor-like cuts in their wake.

"I'm yours," Nero growled at the exquisite pleasure and pain.

The door burst open as Ace had begun ripping at Nero's shirt, and Six barged in. Her eyes glowing crimson.

"What are you doing here?" Six demanded, pointedly looking at Ace, who had stood up.

"Werewolves are pouring into your city and you're wondering why I've come?" Ace asked, crossing her arms as Nero stood as well. He looked far more disheveled than Ace, with the claw marks down his neck, but his expression remained smug. Six's grimace turned to an odd grin.

"So, you thought you'd come all alone and make the difference in our numbers? You think you, alone, can tilt things in our favor?" Six's subsequent laugh echoed the room.

"I have no idea if it will make a difference, Six. But that's what the Elders have asked of me, and as such, it's what I'll do," Ace told her.

"The Elders," Six scoffed, turning to begin pacing once she threw her hands up in the air out of frustration. When she turned back toward Ace, she got close enough to touch, reaching her finger up to touch Ace's nose. "*I'm* the Coven

Judge here, Ace. It's my house, and while you're here, you'll play by my rules," Six growled.

"I don't want your coven. I am here to help with what is about to happen," Ace snapped back, batting Six's finger from her face.

"And what is it that you think is going to happen?" Six asked, her voice practically a sneer.

"There's a prophecy that Lukis is trying to bring about. Werewolves and Witches are coming *en masse* because of what he's planning. You'd do well to *listen* to me for once, you ungrateful *child*. Stop fighting me and be *still*," Ace hissed. Ace's words held a bit more power than she was expecting. Six seemed to stiffen, her whole body growing rigid with Ace's words. Something that had never worked from Nero to Ace was apparently working on Six in real time.

"How did you...?" Six's eyes grew, bewildered at what she was feeling. Ace said that and it was as if some blanket of power fell over her, weighing her down. Ace had effectively forced her to calm. Ace turned and looked at Nero, her own eyes mirroring Six's in their shock.

"Six," Nero started, taking a deep breath. This was certainly not the way he had thought Six would come to find out the truth. Honestly, he hadn't ever been sure what a good way to have gone about it would be. Six was bound to take the news poorly, no matter how it was broken to her. "We've never corrected you and your assumptions that I was your sire, but..."

Six started trembling as she stood there. There was no way to know if it was in fear or rage. Her red eyes darted between Nero and Ace, both of whom wore scowls of reluctance and regret.

"I was the one who gave you your new life," Ace finished for Nero.

Everything about Six's life seemed to flash before her. Her pitiful human existence, a night of true horror, and waking to this new world. Was she mad? Perhaps, but she had been before she turned Vampire. How could one not, with the life she had endured and the voices that plagued her, even to this day? There had been so much about who she was that had been kept from her when she was human, and now, Ace and Nero were admitting that they too had kept this vital bit of information from her.

Everything had been a lie.

"You ... you lied to me," Six said, her voice not but a whisper.

"We just didn't correct you," Nero said.

"Why?"

"You've always been so fragile, Six. It's not an excuse, I know, but I didn't want you to feel distressed about it, especially as a new Vampire. You were very convinced that Nero was your maker. So much so that when I tried to get you to remember it, you would outright refuse," Ace told her, her tone taking on just a slight edge of pity as she watched Six's expression change from one moment to the next as she processed that information.

"Fragile. Weak. You all think I'm some stupid, insipid, worthless creature, don't you?" Six's fingers sparked as her rage quietly built within her.

"Never would I list those descriptors out regarding you, Six. You are of my blood. Our line is stronger than most," Ace told her. Six switched her gaze to Nero, with eyes burning and brows pressed together.

"You should have died. I should have killed *you* before the other Elders," Six hissed, her fingers twitching with the desire to call out the blades, but Ace stepped in front of Nero, obscuring her view.

"You'll not *touch* him again. Not to hurt him or otherwise," Ace said, again putting some power behind her words and watching as they seemed to seep within Six's small frame. Six let out a pained and utterly frustrated sound, clenching her fists.

"This isn't over," she hissed, before she turned abruptly and seemed to disappear from sight.

Her temper was flared, and the buzzing voice of Vehekan in her blades, angrily reminding her she had made a deal and now there was nothing left for her to wait on, only seemed to enrage her more. But as Six made her way through the halls, the scent of something off caught her nose. She stopped, taking it in a bit more heavily. This wasn't quite the scent a Werewolf gave off, nor was it human. She took in a breath even more deeply to be certain it wasn't Witch or Chenja, and no … no Immortal she had ever come across gave off such a scent. She let her ears prick up, listening for any strange sounds, and she did, in fact, hear the steady thrum of a heart beating. It was coming from a door not so far from her own quarters.

She went to the door, turning the knob and pressing the door open without knocking to see a man there. His shoulders were broad and muscled, hair disheveled as he pulled the shirt over his head to reveal his bare back. She watched him for a moment as he rifled through the duffle bag that was sitting on the bed, seemingly oblivious to her presence.

He seemed familiar, oddly, though she couldn't quite place from where. Or perhaps it was more of an odd feeling of *needing* to know him. Normally a person she was unfamiliar with being in her home was someone she would kill on sight, but she had heard when she returned to the manor that Ace had arrived and brought someone under her protection with her. Six had felt so blinded by Ace's presence in her home that she hadn't inquired further. Clearly this odd- smelling man was that person.

"Who are you?" Six asked, her voice like ice, seeming to make Lucef shiver at the suddenness of her questioning. He turned, shirt in hand to face her. He wasn't sure what he was expecting to see, but it certainly wasn't her. Her red hair was spiked up to impossibly long points, like a bloody crown upon her head. Pale skin was a shocking canvas for the bright diamond-shaped tattoos and clothes she wore, and her red eyes were piercing as they looked at him. It took him a moment to speak, simply from the shock of seeing her.

"Lucef," was all he managed to say, trying to suppress the smile that was threatening to break on his lips. She may have been strange-looking, but it only added to her beauty. He had never laid his eyes on someone so intriguing. As if an invisible tether had appeared between them, he felt unexplainably drawn to her.

"Lucef," she murmured, looking him over as she contemplated where she had heard that name before. "Lukis's son, yes?" she asked, stepping closer as she sniffed the air. "No wonder you smell like that."

"Like what?" he asked, mildly perturbed. He hadn't bathed since the day before they left, but he didn't think he smelled particularly abhorrent. Six didn't respond, but merely brought her face closer to him, letting her nose skim his shoulder as she took it in. Not bad ... just ... not what she expected to smell. Like musky and sweet blood.

"You're under Ace's protect, hmm?" she asked, bringing a finger to touch the tendon in his neck, letting the corner of her mouth quirk up at the way his muscles tremored with each small touch of her skin on his.

"For now," Lucef said, his voice a bit shaky. He wasn't sure what she wanted from him. It could be she decided he was her next meal, but he was peculiarly attracted to her.

Six felt a zing of pleasure touching his skin and smelling his scent. She realized, as she let her gaze meet his strange eyes, that she wanted him. How she wanted him, and how long her desire would last, only time would tell, but in that moment, with the rage that she felt for Ace and Nero, the need for the pain that she was feeling to be pushed away, she would play.

Nero's hand slipped into Ace's, drawing her attention back to him once Six was out of sight. For him, it was as if a weight had been lifted from his shoulders. It was uncanny how freeing it was now that Six knew the truth. How Ace was feeling was most likely a different matter. He turned her face to him, as her eyes were sparkling with a strange sadness.

"It's good that she knows," Nero said, brushing a lock of hair from her face.

"All these years... Things could have been different had she known," Ace said back, now wishing they had just made it clear to her from the beginning what had really happened that fateful night. Now her madness had consumed her, and there was no telling what she would do with this new information.

Nero tilted his head and went to kiss her, but she pushed him a step away.

"I should check on Lucef. I was waiting in here for far too long," Ace said, wanting nothing more than to continue what they had been doing before Six had rudely barged in, but as usual, she couldn't put off her duty.

"I'll come with you."

The two of them wandering through the halls, Ace not completely sure where Lucef had been placed as far as rooms. She had been quite firm with him that he was not to leave whatever room he was given without her. She didn't know these Vampires and didn't trust Six's coven to leave him alone. Her Necare would have never dared disobey an order from her, but she was not an authority here.

They slowed when she could hear Lucef's heartbeat. It was rapid, stressed. Not a good sound in a Vampire coven.

"I don't think I want to kill you yet," Ace heard Six say from the partially closed door. "I want a pet. Something I can play with. I can just picture you." Her voice became dreamy, and Lucef's breathing had become loud and labored. "With a little spiked collar and a leash."

"That's quite enough, Six," Ace said, pushing the door open fully. Six had Lucef on the floor and she was crouched over him, eyes sparking with delight as she looked him over.

"It's not enough. He'll be my pet."

"He is under my protection. He is no one's pet," Ace growled, stepping a bit closer. She would have to rip Six off him if she didn't move willingly. That was bound to be a problem.

"Or I could turn him. He'd be *mine* then," Six said, digging her fingers into his shoulders. Lucef laughed nervously, never taking his eyes off her pixie-like face.

"We cannot turn him," Nero said. There was no way to know what would happen if Lucef was turned. He was already a hybrid, so it was possible he could die from the change. Six's face went from delighted to enraged once again.

"Can you stop trying to ruin everything for me? I'm mad, I know it," she said, thumping her a finger against her temple. "If I'm cursed with this eternal life, I at least want to have fun doing so," Six hissed.

"We cannot turn him. It has nothing to do with how mad you may or may not be. We don't know what will happen if he's turned, Six," Ace said, looking at Lucef and having a hard time determining if he was in distress. His heart rate and breathing suggested he was, but he was staring at Six with a look of ... desire?

"No, *you* can't turn him. I can do whatever I damn well please. *She* brought him into *my* house, without my consent. You better just be damn glad I don't kill him," she said with a smug look on her face, grinning as she realized she had them in a tough spot.

"Now, Lucef," she said, turning her attention back to him. "I think I'll move you to my room."

CHAPTER 15

The screams rang through the halls, the sound changing to the chilling, mournful howl of a wolf. Lukis stood in the doorway, as four of his men struggled to restrain the woman between them. Her cries falling on deaf ears until she got hold of one of their arms, biting savagely into their skin and spurting blood over all of them when she caught an artery in her extended teeth.

"Get ahold of her!" Lukis yelled, now becoming frustrated at how difficult this was becoming.

"Troubles with the tribute?" came a deep voice from the hall behind him. Lukis turned his head slightly to acknowledge the new spectator, while keeping his eyes on the others struggling with Melissa, the Werewolf who had been selected to be the next one to give blood for the sake of his wife.

"She struggles as if she's going to die," Lukis growled.

"With this much resistance, maybe she should."

Lukis growled as she managed to kick Kyle, who was by far the strongest of the four grabbing her, square in the jaw. Originally Kyle had offered to be tribute for Deca this week, but after his capture and subsequent escape, Alexander, the man who was now watching intently beside Lukis, had suggested they give him a reprieve from that duty, at least for this month.

The audible pop of dislocation and breakage was the final straw. With a roar of fury, Lukis lunged over the table to her head, arms, and legs, pinning her down as his face, partially changing with his anger, loomed over her. She turned her head away, cowering but ceasing to fight against his hold.

"Restrain her," he ordered the four men, who immediately grabbed the manacles from the walls, cuffing them around her wrists and ankles. "You're making me regret that I don't kill my own, Melissa. Would you rather I pull every last drop from your pathetic body?" he growled deeply at her.

"No," she said, through a broken sob.

"Everyone gets a turn," Alexander said smugly, still leaning on the doorway. His silver eyes shining with mischievous glee as he watched the scene unfold.

Once she was secured, Lukis pulled himself off her, nodding at Kyle to begin. Kyle pulled a long blade from the table beside him, coming to her right arm and slicing one long straight line from her elbow to her wrist. Blood flowed quickly from the wound, pooling on the little recessed catch that boarded the whole stone slab. The blood pooled there for a moment, then quickly started flowing down toward her head where a small spout drained it into a large glass jar. It didn't take long before Kyle stopped the bleeding, putting pressure on Melissa's torn skin. Opus, on the other side of the table, watched the last remnants of the blood drip into its new container before pulling it to bring to Lukis.

"This could have been much faster and easier had you just played along, Melissa," Lukis said pointedly, glaring at the woman who was crying quietly, staring at the wall instead of at his face. Some Werewolves saw it as an honor to give their blood for Deca, Lukas's human wife, while others, like Melissa, found it disgusting. Lukis knew it caused dissension in his ranks. It even disgusted him that he pushed the issue, but he had been doing this for so long now he couldn't just stop. He couldn't let her stop taking it; she would die without the blood. He just couldn't bring himself to let Deca go.

"Still no sign of Lucef in the city. He's gone deep underground, or he's left altogether," Alexander said, following Lukis as he turned to walk back down the hall to give the blood to Deca.

"He wouldn't have left. The boy doesn't know anything but London. If he was going to leave, he would have done so a long time ago," Lukis said flippantly, glancing at Alexander's dubious face.

"Well, what then? How are we supposed to procure him if he's nowhere to be found?"

"Leave Kyle and a few others behind to track him down. No negotiations. Once Deca and I are safely on our way to New Orleans, they can capture and bring him over. I only wanted him to come willingly for Deca's sake. We can't wait any longer," Lukis grumbled, pausing far enough away from the door where he knew Deca was so her human ears wouldn't pick up on their conversation.

"Why leave this to Kyle?" Alexander asked, slightly irritated that he wasn't tasked to stay behind. He had his own motives for staying in London, but no one knew about that but him. Lukis's eyes darkened, and his fingers tightened on the glass he held.

"I need you with me. My second in command needs to be there in case things go wrong," Lukis said, his voice low with seriousness, as his gaze seemed to be looking beyond the tunnels they called home. Alexander, though he didn't like it, nodded. His other reason for staying in London would be there when he came back, and perhaps once this ritual was completed, he would finally be able approach *her* when he returned. Everything was supposed to change once the ritual was completed, after all.

"I need to attend to Deca," Lukis said sharply, after several quiet moments between the two men.

"Of course. I'll instruct the ones who will remain and meet you at the cars," Alexander said, before turning to head back toward where Kyle and Opus were most likely still cleaning up.

Lukis took in a deep breath, steeling himself for what he would see when he entered the room that held his wife. She had prolonged this treatment for far too long, and he had been too distracted to push the issue, but they would be travelling to the Americas, and she would need to be in top form to not only handle the journey and the events to come, but to survive it. As he opened the door, he held back the cringe that threatened to ripple over his body as he looked at her.

Deca was lying on their large bed. Her small frame was frail, skin translucent and blue to his eyes. Her cheeks and eyes were sunken, and her hair was far greyer than its normal strawberry blonde locks. Only a few other times in the past had he ever allowed her to go this far, and each time it tore at him to see her this way. His fragile human wife had refused to try to turn.

She was happy with her life with him as she was, even aging far beyond how he looked. But he was too selfish to let her go and had made her promise to hold on. Somehow he had kept her in this state for hundreds of years, even keeping her and Lucef alive with these treatments. Once Lucef had been born, her reluctance to keep doing the treatment dwindled. She *wanted* it. Lucef had given her more of a reason to live than Lukis had.

Lukis held back his resentment of this fact from Deca, but he was certain Lukis knew his whole life that his own father was jealous of Deca's love for her son. Now that Lucef had run away, Lukis was once again in the position of forcing Deca to drink, forcing her to stay alive.

"Deca, my love. I need you to drink this," Lukis said, approaching the bed and slowly, as not to jostle her, sitting beside her.

"No, Lukis," she said weakly, waving a languid hand in his direction as he poured some of the blood from the glass into her special goblet.

"You must. We have to go on a trip."

"I cannot keep doing this, Lukis. It hurts," she whined pitifully, her voice strange and shaky. Lukis wrapped an arm around her, propping her up with additional pillows and looking deep into her pained eyes.

"It won't hurt anymore if you drink it," he whispered, turning his eyes away to grab the goblet from the table beside the bed, bringing it close to her face.

"It *will* hurt again. Even if I take it." Lukis's jaw clenched. There were plenty of things he could say. That she should take the treatments more often and avoid most of her pain. That if she would just *stop* being so stubborn, this could be so much easier.

"We can't go until you drink this," he said.

"We can't go at all, Lukis. Lucef hasn't come home yet. If we're gone when he comes back..."

"Lucef is going to meet us where we're going, Deca. Don't you remember?" he asked, unfazed by the lies between his words that she somehow still couldn't detect.

"Lucef is..."

"Yes, he's meeting us there. Then we'll come home together as a family," Lukis said, letting his face transform into a brilliant smile. The very smile he knew could persuade her, even after all these years.

"Oh," Deca said, eyes welling with tears of joy. She reached for the goblet, though her hands shook so badly, that Lukis was the one who put it to her lips. Slowly she drank the offensive liquid down, slumping back onto the pillows, her face contorted with disgust and pain as her body slowly started to regain its youth.

Lukis stared in awe as his wife's face and body returned, the color of her hair becoming bold against the cream pillows once again. He reached out, touching her now supple cheek with his rough fingers. This was the face that he loved, and he would continue to do anything he could to keep it that way.

Ace stood at the window, looking out again. She knew she would need to close the curtains soon, as the sun was so close to rising over the horizon, but she had quite suddenly felt nervous once they had left Lucef in Six's hands. Not for what assuredly would be happening to Lucef, as there was not much she could do about that, but that she and Nero would be alone once again. She hadn't secured herself a room, having chosen to forgo that task to immediately come up to his.

Ace hadn't been sure what her plan had been when coming there initially, other than to confront him. But the words, "You are for me and me alone," had left her lips, and she realized she meant them. She meant them very deeply. She had fought these feelings for so long, shutting them down, and keeping them out of her mind as much as she could because of fear, but she couldn't deny them anymore. The moment she saw him, and he saw her, a link had been formed. Something that even the weight of time or distance could not suppress.

Nero had left very briefly to instruct some of the Necare to be on day guard, something that was not as regular at this coven, but was now very necessary. When he returned, he stood near the door, watching Ace across the room, clearly deep in thought. She wasn't radiating anger any longer, but he could feel her hesitation. Something she had not had earlier when she had tried to tear at his clothes.

It dawned on him then that perhaps he had been too soft in his approach to bring her back to him. She had been forceful, angry. And though he had not been short on anger about their predicament over the decades, he hadn't used that to his advantage either.

"Ace," he said, hoping to draw her attention, but she merely made a "mm" sound, continuing to look out the window.

His eyes roamed over her body. Her pants were tight against her legs, tucked into her standard boots, revealing her strong but rounded hips and thighs. She wore a plain black shirt tucked in and a suit jacket. Her face's silhouette was just as graceful as the rest of her look, beautifully complemented by her jet-black hair against her pale skin. The girl he had met centuries before had a dusting of freckles over her nose, but those had been shed the same night she shed her humanity.

He knew exactly what he needed to do if he was to have her fully be his again. He would always be hers, which he knew from the moment he laid eyes on her, but he had to fight to keep her, and he was certainly willing to do so every day if he had to.

He moved swiftly to stand before her, his hand reaching up to pull the curtain closed and obscure her view. Her eyes finally turned to him, but concern was still evident there.

"I'll try to find another room, though it might be too late," Ace said quietly.

"There's no other room," Nero said, not caring that his voice came out gravelly as he did so. Her eyes snapped up to his, finally seeing the primal hunger burning there. Without warning, Nero's hands found their homes, one behind her neck and the other at her waist, moving to press her body against the wall beside the window. He took her mouth with his viciously.

Ace gasped at the suddenness of it but didn't falter, meeting his kiss with a ferocity of her own. Nero's hands moved over her body, hands grasping roughly at each curve through her clothing. She moaned involuntarily as she felt the fabric of her shirt rip away from her body, letting his hands find purchase on her flesh, his mouth travelling down her neck and fangs scraping against her skin as they travelled.

"I'm yours, and you, my Ace," he bit lightly at the tender flesh over her no longer beating heart. "You are *mine*," he said, his voice not much more than a growl.

She didn't need to say anything, as her hands did their best to match his movements, tearing and pulling at the weak fabric over his body.

"Yes," she hissed, nails digging into the skin of his shoulders as he lifted her against the wall, mouth travelling across her stomach as he inched her further up.

Her eyes glowed, fangs extended, as pleasure she hadn't known in years overtook her body. Instincts that had been suppressed took over, making her practically hum. Nero looked up at her, basking in the beauty of her, loving the bite of pain she inflicted as her grip on his shoulders tightened.

He pulled her down, throwing her to the bed; the only thing left on her were her boots. He stalked over to her, hair falling into his face as he crawled over her body, his blood dripping against her torso from his shoulders.

"I love you," he whispered, reaching to spread the deep crimson droplets over her skin.

"I love you," she whispered in return, eyes glowing as her bloodied fingers ran over his cheek. It was all the excuse he needed, a growl releasing from his throat as he took her mouth with his once again.

CHAPTER 16

Six and Lucef sat on her bed across from one another, seeming unsure of what to do with themselves. Six, though happy enough to make Ace and Nero quite uncomfortable with her demands to keep Lucef as a pet, was now a bit unsure of what to do with him. He was looking around her room, taking in the strange extravagance of it. Much like the rest of Redeamond, the elaborate wallpaper adorned the walls, red-and-gold filigree busy to the eyes. Her furniture was exquisite, and she had red crystals, thousands of them, hanging from the ceiling, casting odd red reflections every which way.

Six watched him as he studied his new surroundings. She had never had anyone in her room for a purpose other than to use their body, whether that be for sex or for blood. Lucef, she wasn't exactly sure what she wanted from him. She let her eyes wander over the planes of his body: lean muscle, square jaw, eyes so strange, but beautiful. She had seen eyes like his hundreds of times as she fought Werewolves, but there was something about *his* that made her unable to look away.

"So, what do you have planned for your pet?" Lucef asked, breaking the silence that had stretched between them. She realized he was also looking into her eyes instead of taking in the room.

"You'll do as you're told and not ask any questions," she snapped, before slowly crawling across the bed to sit right in front of him. Lucef, in many other circumstances, would not have accepted this plight, but there was something about her he couldn't quite put his finger on. He was oddly attracted and couldn't force himself to leave, removing himself from her, even if he wanted to.

Six closed her eyes, leaning close and letting her nose skim across the skin of his chest as she breathed in his strange scent. She had demanded he remove his shirt before she allowed him to sit. She was hungry, but not for blood. She had satisfied that thirst when she had been out hunting. No, this hunger burned in her belly, only amplified by this musk coming from him.

"I'm going to hurt you," she said quietly, warning him of what's to come.

"I can take pain," Lucef said, his voice a bit husky.

"I hurt everyone I touch. I'm poisonous," she murmured, her hands snaking over his chest and shoulders. "But you don't have much choice in the matter. I took you."

Lucef's breath hitched as her fingers found the back of his head, yanking back so his throat was exposed. So many of his instincts told him this was dangerous, but also a growing part within him told him he liked this danger.

"I feel like I've been waiting for you," he said as she straddled his lap, letting the fingers of her other hand trail over the pulse at his carotid. Six paused at his words, letting them sink in. The electricity she felt touching him was something she had never experienced. Even the kiss between her and Nero hadn't held this powerful of a feeling.

She couldn't get enough: his scent, his touch, the way his heart beat within his chest was even soothing, instead of tempting her hunger. She didn't want to consider what any of that meant. *She* took what she wanted, and she wanted to touch him, to hurt him just a little, to mark him as hers.

"Be quiet," she hissed, pushing him back onto the bed and glaring. "Tonight, you're my pet. You'll let me hurt you. You'll let me do as I please. And come tomorrow, we'll find out if I've tired of your presence yet," she told him, internally hoping that she would. This draw to him was intense, and she hoped she would be able to stamp it out by taking what she wanted.

Lukis sat in his meeting room, surrounded by his den leaders. It had been weeks since he arrived, and in those weeks, Kyle and Opus had not found one trace of Lucef in all of London. Their conclusion was that he was either dead or had truly left the city. The idea was preposterous to him. Lucef had never left that place and had shown no indication he ever would. Lukis had assumed part of it was knowing Deca was there, waiting for him below the city. Because if there was one thing Lukis knew about his son, it was that he did love his mother.

He slammed his hand against the table. The moon phase that corresponded with the ritual was closing in on them, and the one irreplaceable piece of the puzzle, Lucef, had disappeared.

"We did get more news from London," said Joseph, the New Orleans den leader who sat at Lukis's right. "Apparently, Ace has left the city."

Lukis bristled at that. If Ace had left, she had most likely made her way to New Orleans. There was no other reason she would have abandoned Kurome, especially since an

Elder had also been spotted in the area. They knew and what was worse, they had sent some of their best.

"Ace?" came Alexander's voice from the far corner, his whole body going rigid at the mention of her name. Being Lukis's second meant he was privy to the den leader discussions.

"She hasn't been spotted anywhere, but I would argue it's very likely she'd made her way here," Joseph continued, his face turning grim at the prospect. Not only had they lost Lucef, but now Ace was probably hunting their streets, killing their men silently.

"I can scout it out," Alexander offered, trying to control the intensity in his outward appearance, his limbs vibrating with the effort.

Lukis sighed. They definitely needed to confirm if Ace was there. It would be much harder to follow through with any of their plans if she was interfering. And now that he had a taste of what she was capable of, from their fight several months prior, he had no doubt that she would be more than capable of thwarting them if given the chance.

"Yes, Alexander. You go, seek out the coven, and see if you can find any traces of her. The rest of you ... I don't know what strings you have to pull or what you have to do, but *someone* needs to track down my son," Lukis growled, his fists clenched in frustration.

Six was getting her makeup on slowly. The sun had just set, and Lucef was sleeping peacefully on her bed. He seemed to have finally gotten used to her schedule, but being that he was half-human, he needed to sleep far more than any resting she had to do. She glanced at him through the mirror, watching the steady rise and fall of his chest as he breathed.

These past weeks, she found herself soothed by the sound of his breathing, the beat of his heart, the feel of his skin on hers. It was strange how odd it felt. How right it felt.

She told herself it was simply because he was a good pet. He did as he was told, let her do what she wished, even if that meant he suffered, and that was what was satisfying her more than any other lover had before. But in these quiet moments, when she could simply listen to his sleeping sounds and watch him, she knew it wasn't simply that.

A crashing sound could be heard, wood splintering and glass breaking. She glanced again at Lucef's still sleeping form before quickly leaving the room to see what was going on. If it was a fight between Vampires, she would happily watch, but instead she realized the sound was someone raging within their quarters. She followed it, finding it curious that it was coming from Lin's room.

Lin had become increasingly irritating over the past few weeks. He hadn't seemed at all perturbed by the distraction that Nero had been when they first returned, but somehow Six's attention being on Lucef seemed to make Lin irritable. Apparently, that was coming to a head that day.

She opened the door to his room, looking around at the complete and utter destruction of his furniture. He stood in the middle of it all, body tense, eyes glowing with rage.

"Lin, you've made quite the mess," Six said, stepping inside and glancing around, her expression rather neutral if not uninterested. "I've made worse, but this is close." He turned his eyes to her, snapping his teeth.

"I heard you," Lin hissed, coming up to stand right before her and looking down at her menacingly.

"Heard me, what?"

"This morning, with that dog!" he spat, panting with anger.

"What is it that you think you heard? Me playing with my pet? I have been playing with him for weeks, Lin. What's bothered you so much about this morning?" Lin's possessiveness had become a frustration. She used Lin, just as she used many other Vampires and mortals for years. He was convenient, being that he was always there and always willing, which was why she had taken him to her bed so often. But there was nothing more to it, a convenience to sate her needs. He had apparently taken that as affection.

"You said you *loved* it," Lin hissed.

Six thought back to earlier, Lucef's eyes gazing down at her as she finally resurfaced from the blinding euphoria he had given her. Better than she had ever felt, the tingle of their skin touching only seemed to enhance how everything felt between them. She had reached up, brushing a bit of hair away from his eyes, as to not obstruct her view, before whispering to him, "I love this." She hadn't been giving any sort of grand admission. She had merely been telling Lucef she loved having sex with him.

Six tilted her head to the side, looking at Lin as if he were a disgusting insect. His jealousy had gone on enough, in her opinion. He had no reason to feel that way, since she didn't at all belong to him. Everything in this manor belonged to *her*.

"This jealousy of yours is disgusting, Lin," Six said coldly, glaring at him and crossing her arms across her chest. He seemed to explode then, a roar ripping from his throat so loud it vibrated in Six's chest. He grabbed a larger piece of debris, hurling it into the wall.

"You'd rather a weak, disgusting, half-dog than your own kind. What have I been to you all these years if not your loyal servant?"

"I never told you it was anything more than it was," Six said, glancing down at her nails as he threw yet another object.

"I have always been yours. I have been nothing but what you've wanted from me all this time." He came again to stand before her, grasping her upper arms roughly and pulling her closer to him. "You may have taken other lovers, but you've been *mine*," Lin hissed.

A laugh burst from Six's lips, starting Lin enough that he released his hold on her arms. Her laugh was eerie, almost sadistic.

"I belong to no one but myself, Lin. Everything that resides within Redeamond belongs to me. You belong to me," she said, pressing her finger in the center of his chest. "And I don't *want* you anymore." She turned abruptly, walking from the room.

Lin stood there, utterly shocked for quite a while. He didn't know exactly how he had let himself lose control so much. The slow build-up of resentment for Lucef had been manageable, but something about the word "love" coming from Six's lips as he listened outside her room that morning had sent Lin over the edge. It was disgusting; it was wrong.

Bad enough that Six had stooped to sleeping with a half-breed, and a Werewolf half-breed at that, but for her to be so thoroughly enjoying it was much worse. Their insepa-rable nature over these weeks, he had initially attributed to her wanting to establish Lucef's role as her pet. She had even fashioned him a collar and dragged him everywhere with her. All outings, that *thing* was present.

Lin needed to get them away from one another. He needed to figure out how to either draw her away from Lucef, or make sure the nearly mortal man met an untimely fate. The question was, exactly *how* would he do such a thing.

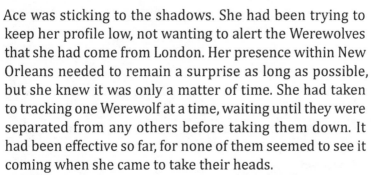

Ace was sticking to the shadows. She had been trying to keep her profile low, not wanting to alert the Werewolves that she had come from London. Her presence within New Orleans needed to remain a surprise as long as possible, but she knew it was only a matter of time. She had taken to tracking one Werewolf at a time, waiting until they were separated from any others before taking them down. It had been effective so far, for none of them seemed to see it coming when she came to take their heads.

But as the weeks grew and the time for the ritual started getting closer, she knew things would start ramping up. The Werewolves seemed to become increasingly panicked and aggressive, even to the mortals in the city. It only confirmed to her that they had no idea where Lucef was, which was rather baffling, considering Six seemed to pay no heed to Ace and Nero's warning about her taking him out with her.

It was raining rather hard, but she wasn't one to complain about clothes or hair getting wet; she came from London after all. She had caught a scent of a Werewolf not too far from the manor. The water was washing away the scent of her selected enemy for the night, but it still lingered since the track was fresh. She had picked up the scent, realizing it seemed rather familiar in comparison to many of the Werewolves she had killed recently. Perhaps a London Werewolf.

He didn't seem to notice her when she spotted him; it was probably the rain and other things blocking out her sounds as she silently moved through the streets behind. She didn't see his silhouette until they reached the open area of Jackson's Square. He passed the musicians and street artists without a glance, seeming almost oblivious to his surroundings, but it put Ace on alert. He knew he was being followed, and he was taking her exactly where he wanted her to go.

Up the stairs to Washington Artillery Park, she followed him, and down again to the Moonwalk Park, where the mortal crowd seemed to be sparse. He slowed then, moving down the edge of the Mississippi River until there was no one but the two of them there. He still had his back to her when he stopped, his shoulder-length black hair and shoulders seeming so strangely familiar that she stared at him, confused.

The waxing moon was bathing him in its light, and the way the humid breeze touched her face brought back a memory from so long ago it nearly made her gasp. It was muddied, seen through her mortal eyes, but a strong one, nonetheless. Her brother and her, watching the night sky one summer they had taken some of their father's trade to the coast. The river they sat at all those long years ago had been across the ocean of course, but the feeling was so strikingly similar, she nearly breathed to relive the feeling.

But that wasn't why she was there. She was not human, and she was not on that river with her brother. She was tracking this Werewolf and whether he knew he had been followed or not, she was going to kill him.

He slowly turned, revealing his face to her in the sparse light.

Ace froze as she looked at him. No, this couldn't be.

"Grace?" he said, his voice low, his accent like hers. The sound was so incredibly engrained in her memory, she had to resist shaking.

"Excuse me?" she asked back, brows furrowing as her old name seemed to ring in her mind. She hadn't been called that since … since she died.

She looked up at his silver eyes, glowing as they looked back at her. Those eyes she had seen recently. They were the same eyes of the Werewolf that had been watching her at the Gast. The same eyes of the Werewolf who had seemed to *see* her through the video Nyprat took.

"Grace. It's been so long," Alexander said, a crooked smile pulling at his lips.

"You've been watching me," Ace said, narrowing her eyes.

"It's my duty to protect my sister, is it not?"

She glowered at him, hands balling into fists at her side.

"My brother died," she insisted, her voice harsh as her mind tried to catch up to the fact that her brother, like the rest of her family, was supposed to have died in the attack on her home. The attack that Nero had saved her from.

"Well, I hate to disappoint you, but I'm not dead," he said, chuckling lightly and taking a step toward her.

"Nero said—"

"Nero lied," Alexander snapped. He sighed, running his hand through his hair and glancing out at the river for a moment before turning back to her. "I waited too long. I can smell it all over you."

"Smell what?"

"His scent. I should have come for you as soon as I gained control."

"Of your beast?" Ace asked, her face changing to disgust.

"I had as much choice as you about becoming what I am," he growled.

"What do you mean?"

"The attack changed me. He stole you and changed you," Alexander said, his tone matter of fact. Ace laughed bitterly, letting her eyes glow as well.

"He didn't steal me; he saved me. I *wanted* to go with him. I *wanted* him to change me," Ace said. Alexander's eyes widened a fraction, but he kept the rest of his face neutral, turning again to look out at the water.

"So, what do we do now, Grace? Are you going to kill me?" he asked, glancing at her. She forced herself to look away from his face, a face that she had mourned for so long that seeing it again made her feel both joy and a completely different sorrow.

"I'm giving you one chance. Take it or leave it. It's up to you," she said, her voice hollow.

"This won't be the last time we come across one another," he said, turning to take in her expressionless face.

"No, it won't," she said with a strange finality, as she turned and left him watching her depart.

CHAPTER 17

Ace tore through the manor upon her return, heading immediately to Nero's room where he sat, typing an email to update the Elders. Ace stood in the doorway, her body rigid as she glared across the room at him.

"Ace. What is it?" Nero asked, standing abruptly and taking in her harried appearance.

"Alexander," Ace said stiffly. Nero's fingers twitched, his eyes turning a bit darker.

"What about him?"

"All these years," Ace said, stepping over the threshold to close the door behind her. "He's alive." Nero said nothing. "You knew," she said pointedly, her eyes boring into his.

"That night, I had no way of knowing if he would live through it or not. I could have killed him, spared him the misery of dying slowly, but I left him there," Nero said, moving to the front of the desk to lean against it.

"Why?" Ace asked, her voice a mix between a gasp and a whisper.

"On the off chance … that he'd live," Nero said, his voice sincere.

"Live to be a Werewolf? Live to be the very enemy I have sworn to defeat?" she demanded, her voice breaking a bit as bloody tears flooded her eyes. Nero came to her, pulling her against him so her cheek fell against his chest.

"As a Werewolf, he would be Immortal and perhaps you'd cross paths again," Nero murmured, running his fingers through her hair.

"And if I'm the one who must kill him? I don't think..." She choked back a sob that threatened to escape.

"I would never expect you to," Nero said, his grip on her tightening. "This war is not black and white. You are not solely responsible for killing every last one of them, Ace," Nero cooed, pulling away to tilt her chin up so she would look at his face. Bloody tear tracks ran down her pale cheeks, and her silver eyes looked almost dull with the sorrow she felt. He bent his head, brushing his lips over hers and hoping that he could hold some of the burden for her, even if she was reluctant to let it go.

Lucef was perusing Six's things, taking the time to see what she considered precious. Her obsession with red was interesting, and her book collection was odd. There were plenty of books, mostly old Victorian fiction with a few more modern selections, but she had volume after volume of the same three books, all in various states of wear.

Part of his curiosity was a strange desire to know everything about her. She was strange but mostly quite mysterious. The personality she seemed to show most people was as a vengeful and demanding Coven Judge, perhaps haunted with a hint of sadistic madness. But what he saw when he touched her and looked deep into her eyes was something completely different. She could stop his heart with a look and restart it again at an unnatural stutter.

He knew he was falling in love, because what else would you call it when you'd quite literally lay your own life at someone's feet willingly?

Six had been busying herself preparing for the evening out. The thought amongst Ace, Nero, and Six had been that with Ace hunting in the shadows, and her and the Necare out more openly, they would bring the numbers of Werewolves down low enough there would be no one left to defend the den, and, therefore, they'd be able to sweep in once they located it and blot it from the map.

This plan was only amplified for her now that she knew what Lukis wanted with Lucef. Her pet was not going to be used in some sort of ritual. He now belonged to her.

"Six, why do you have so many copies of *Frankenstein*, *Treasure Island,* and *Dr. Jekyll and Mr. Hyde?*" Lucef asked, pulling one from the shelf to look it over. It was clearly one of the older copies; its cover was torn in a few places, and the binding was coming undone, he realized, when it crackled as he opened it. Six paused in her corset-tightening, eyes coming up to fall on the book in his hands. These books had been her solace, her escape from the trauma of her human life.

The memories flashed before her eyes before she could think to pull herself away.

"*John, we can't... what would happen if —*" young Sinthia whispered, her red hair tumbling from its bun as the boy before her pulled the pins.

"*Shh... Don't think about that. Just give in,*" said the boy, as his fingers tightened in her locks, his breathing ragged as his other hand slipped up her leg, pushing past her skirts to touch her silky skin past her stockings.

"Oh..." she moaned softly as she closed her eyes, relishing the feeling as his lips found hers once again. She let herself get lost in the feeling, not worrying herself with anything but how good it felt to kiss this boy and have him touch her.

But the bliss only lasted a moment. The door of the dark room they were in opened, and a large brute of a man filled the doorway.

"You little witch," he growled, the sound of his voice sending a chill of fear through Sinthia's small frame. He reached down, ripping Sinthia out of the closet by her long, red hair and against the opposite wall. She lay there, dazed for a moment, watching as her father dragged the boy from the house and slammed the door once he had tossed him aside. The man turned back to Sinthia.

"You little witch! You whore! I expected nothing less from you, you miserable spawn of the devil," he said, hatred burning in his eyes as he looked her over. Sinthia didn't have a moment to say a word in return before he took up her hair once again, the strength of his fist keeping her captive. She screamed as his other hand came down on her face.

"Put. It. Down," she hissed, moving swiftly over to him to snatch the book from his hands and replace it on the shelf. She stood with her back to him for a minute, the memories that came with that book flooding her mind. She didn't *like* to remember her life before. It was a torturous place she much preferred keeping tucked deep, where it rarely came out to bother her. But there he had gone and opened that door.

"I'm sorry," he said quietly, eyeing her tightened shoulders. "I-I didn't know," he murmured.

Six reached up, placing her hands on either side of her head as if that would block the memories from coming to the surface, but it wasn't helping.

"It's from before. I read them before I changed," Six spoke out loud. She didn't know why she had the impulse to tell him, but for some reason that was the only thing she could think of to make herself feel better.

"Was it bad? Is that why you're unhappy?" Lucef asked, placing his hand hesitantly, but gently, on her shoulder. She turned around, looking up at him, her red eyes now rimmed with crimson as they filled with tears.

"It was." She swallowed dryly, letting his touch tingle against her shoulder and cheek, soothing her. "My life before ... I was not treated well by my father. I was sent to London, to a boarding school. It was supposed to teach me manners and keep me from my less-than-proper impulses," Six said, smirking bitterly.

"You got away from him, though," Lucef said, his voice a little hopeful, but his face changed when he saw the bitter look in Six's eyes.

"I did. And then I died," Six said, pulled from him and moving to her bed. She crawled onto it, curling into a ball, and rocking slightly. "I escaped him, his horrible beatings. I didn't plan on coming back. I didn't ever want to see my family again. I was sent away, but that meant I *left* her all alone with him," Six whispered hoarsely.

Lucef followed her, sitting on the bed near her, but not near enough to touch.

"My mother," Six croaked.

"Oh, Six," Lucef said, unsure if he should pull her into his lap as he wanted to.

"I should never have been here," Six said, her voice still odd and rough from crying, reciting words her father had said to her many times during beatings. She should never have been born. Never have lived beyond her first years.

"If you weren't, then I would never have known you," Lucef told her, pulling a loose hair from her face to place behind her ear. She turned her gaze to his face. There wasn't judgement or disdain there, only concern. She had never confided in anyone about her past before, except perhaps Ace a very long time ago.

"Look at me, Lucef. I'm crazy. I've made you wear a collar, like a dog. How can you be *happy* you met me?" Six asked incredulously. He chuckled a little, pulling her easily into his lap.

"I'm not sure if this is healthy, and it's definitely not appropriate, but I think I'm in love you," Lucef said, looking down at her face that seemed to rearrange strangely from pained to surprised.

Six didn't know what to say, instead reaching up to touch his face.

Lin, from the other side of the door, clenched his fists. It was the final straw to hear Lucef say that to Six, and she didn't push him away with disgust. He moved without thinking, ripping through the manor and out the door without a second thought about the consequences of what he was about to do.

He knew exactly where to go to find who he needed to.

He knew exactly how to get Lucef out of the picture for good, even if it meant betraying his kind in the process.

Deca moved quietly through the halls of the New Orleans den. She was mostly ignored, as usual, but she couldn't simply sit still. There was nothing for her to do. Her life was pointless; only the idea that she might see her son again one day kept her going. They had been in this hot, unforgiving place for nearly a month, and Lukis's promises that she would see Lucef soon were starting to lose their meaning.

They were like so many promises he told her in the past. So many things he assured her would come to pass never did. She hated it and hated that she was strung along, her life a never-ending string of days. Dull moments between bouts of the horrific pain of aging.

She paused when she heard a commotion. Deca knew she was too far from the center of the base. Lukis always insisted she refrain from going near any of the exits, since it was easier to protect her when she was at the heart of the den, but she couldn't read the same books or watch the same television anymore. When all you had to do all day was watch the same drivel over and over, even the newness of American television faded quickly.

"How *dare* you try to tempt us, Vampire? Why would think we'd believe anything you had to say?" she heard Lukis ask. Vampire? How had a Vampire gotten into their base?

"I surrendered to your men. I'm tired of this. I'd rather give you what you want than continue as we have been," came a voice she had never heard before.

"You say he's where?" Lukis asked.

"He's at Redeamond Manor. He's fallen in love with a Vampire," the man said to her husband, his voice full of loathing and repulsion. Lukis growled, and Deca heard the telltale sound of his footfalls as he paced.

"And you'll help us take him?" Lukis asked, his voice a bit calmer than it had been a moment before. She could tell it had changed to almost being ... eager.

"I want him gone," the Vampire said, his voice inhuman in its hatred.

"Alexander!" Lukis roared, making Deca jump at the loudness of the sound. Before she had a moment to hide away, she saw Alexander step out of an adjacent room into the hall where she stood. He paused and looked at her, his eyebrows raised with surprise at her presence. She looked at him worriedly, not sure if he would reveal she was there to listen to Lukis, who would undoubtedly be furious. But he surprised her by pressing his finger to his lips, indicating that he would keep her secret, as long as she remained quiet. She nodded quickly, motioning for him to go in before Lukis took issue and came to the hall to find him, and he did, ducking into the room where Lukis was with the Vampire.

"Lin, here, has decided to help us procure Lucef from the Vampires," Lukis said.

Suddenly Deca's vision swam. They were talking about Lucef?

Lucef was with Vampires?

He was here in New Orleans?

He was in love with a Vampire?

So many questions, so many concerns, but the most pressing one was with Lukis. His fury, his demands of the Vampire named Lin had sounded less like he was *rescuing* their son, and more like they were capturing him.

The lies Lukis told her swirled in her mind as she barely paid attention to the plans the three men were making within that room. Her body shook as each memory over the years flashed before her eyes. He had been lying through it all. He didn't want to be a happy family again. He didn't want Lucef back as his son. He was getting Lucef back for some other, more sinister reason.

She moved into a closet as she realized Lukis was about to exit the room, holding her breath and hoping he didn't catch her scent in the hall as he passed. She wasn't going to allow this. If, nothing else, she would find a way to save her son.

CHAPTER 18

Six looked at the bed where she had left Lucef. She sat down on the bed beside him and just watched him, listening to him breathe deeply as he dreamed. To her, his sleeping was soothing; she loved to feel his heartbeat when they slept. She loved to listen to him breathe. He was beautiful to her, a perfect picture of something living.

He had held her for the evening and early into the morning, made love to her, and it was loving, gentle, and sweet, washing away her bad thoughts with his tender kisses. There was no pain with this pleasure, no blood spilt on her sheets. She had never had an experience like that before and she knew after that, she was just as much his as he was hers.

But her bubble of peace that watching him gave her was burst as she heard the familiar buzzing of the demon metal calling out to her. She summoned them forward, letting them meld together to show her the face of the demon within. His expression, though usually unreadable, was somehow even more angry and grotesque than usual.

<Six, pathetic, little girl. Why haven't you killed the Elder?> he asked, with a snarl coming to his horrifically scarred face. Six looked at him for a moment and tried to

ignore him by looking around the blade at Lucef until he started to talk.

"Shh! You'll wake him!" Six hissed, as her eyes darted from the demon to Lucef, making sure the sound wasn't waking him.

<That Elder has been here for months now, and you still haven't killed him!> Vehekan yelled at her, the strange, fragmented voices making her twinge.

"Because Ace is always with him!" she replied in a low voice.

<So kill her,> Vehekan hissed back at her.

"It's not that simple! She's my sire!" Six said, glaring at the blades as her hands balled into fists against the red sheets.

<You're stalling, little one. You made a deal, and you have yet to hold up your end of the bargain,> Vehekan snarled.

Lucef's eyes snapped open at Six's exclamation. He looked over at her, seeing the floating diamond before her and the way her face looked strained. He sat up slowly.

"I promised to kill them, but ... once this business is done here, I'll return to London and get the others. Why does it have to be him?" Six asked. Though Ace and Nero had deceived her for years and he was not her sire, she still felt an odd sort of affection toward him. She wasn't sure if it was Ace's influence over her, or the fact that she had thought she loved him for so many years, but the idea of killing Nero tore at her.

<If you don't, Six, we will, and your deal will be broken in the process,> Vehekan growled, before the blades split apart once more and tucked back into her clothing.

Lucef sat there for a moment, just staring at her. He was quite confused and a little worried. He had only heard Six's side of the conversation, but she had obviously been talking to *something* within those blades. She crawled across the bed to him, expecting him to flinch when she touched him or run away, but he didn't; instead, he watched her and even moved into her touch. She stroked his face and hair gently.

"Where did you get those things?" he blurted out, more loudly than was needed. She flinched a bit at the sudden noise. "Sorry," he said, waiting for her to explain.

Six opened her eyes slowly again, looking into his as she thought. It had been a while, and she hadn't thought about how or why she got them, but slowly it came back to her.

"It's alright. It was ... oh, I think 1964. I don't really know, somewhere in there. I was getting power-hungry, and I made a deal with some demons that wanted the Elders dead. I'm not sure why they want them dead, but back then I didn't care. Power was all I was after. So, they gave me these blades and told me I would be able to kill so quickly with them that no one would know it was me," she told him, looking away as if ashamed.

"Well ... as you can imagine, Ace and Nero found out about my little killing spree. They didn't know about the blades that I managed to keep a secret until recently," she said proudly. "To bribe me, they gave me a coven to keep me content and have a bit of power. And here I am," she said, as she held her arms out as if waiting for him to find her guilty and unworthy in some way. He smirked when she did so and touched her cheek.

"But you don't want to carry out the deal now?" Lucef asked.

"I don't want to kill Nero. He wasn't an Elder when I got them. He may not be my sire, but..."

"He's still important to you," Lucef finished for her. She nodded a little, taking a deep breath, but it seemed that Vehekan's patience had grown too thin, taking offense to her and Lucef's private conversation. A roar that sounded like a hundred voices rang out, making Six clutch her ears, wincing with the pain of the sudden and terrible sound.

The force of the blades pulling from her clothes forced her off the bed and onto the floor, her clothing in tatters as they hovered for a moment around her.

<If we can't rely on you to take care of him, we will,> Vehekan growled, as the blades circled her viciously, making Lucef fling himself back out of harm's way. They then slipped from the room, sliding easily between the door and its frame. Six scrambled up, dashing out the door and down the hall toward Nero and Ace's room. She made it just in time, bursting through their doors as Vehekan paused, surrounding Nero. He was alone, Ace having left with a small group of Necare to follow a suspected new arrival of Werewolves at the harbor to hopefully uncover the location of the den. Six would have been with them, if she hadn't had her unexpected breakdown.

"Vehekan! Stop!" Six yelled at the blades. They hovered, spinning in the air around Nero menacingly.

"Six... what's the meaning of—?"

"Demon metal means demon, Nero. Which you of all people should know," Six hissed, sending him a brief but smoldering glare before the blades started humming.

<Your Nero is an Elder and deserves to die!>

"When I agreed to this, Nero wasn't an Elder and therefore not part of the deal," she demanded, stomping her foot in frustration.

<Not good enough,> Vehekan growled, moving closer to Nero, close enough that the wind generated by their spinning caused his hair to flutter.

"What can I do?" Nero asked urgently, looking at Six somewhat helplessly. He knew it was no use. The demon within the metal would simply follow if he tried to outrun them.

Six reached out her hand, face contorting with concentration and anger as she tried to pull them back to her. She hadn't really breached their deal, but if Vehekan killed Nero without her approval, it would be void, and the metal, with all of its abilities, would be hers with no strings attached. The fact that Vehekan knew this and was still determined to turn Nero to ashes simply enraged her more.

She managed to get them to move a little further from Nero, enough that he could dart around his desk while avoiding them. Her eyes white with the effort, she reached out to Nero now that he was near enough to her, pulling his wrist up to her mouth.

"What are you doing?" Nero hissed, though he didn't pull away.

"If I take your blood into me, and you've already taken mine," she started, giving him a bit of a side eye, "it will confuse him." Without giving Nero a second to process what she was saying, she dug her fangs into his wrist, tearing at the flesh and feeling the tingle of his blood flowing through her. This blood was different, so different than anything she had ever tasted. It was an odd sensation, tasting him for the first time, when she had been so certain she had taken his blood before.

Fire started at her fingertips, slowly spreading over her body and then over Nero's. The blades, no longer being held back by Six's telekinesis, tried in vain to penetrate the wall of fire that enveloped them both. Nero gasped, the heat of the flames surrounding him were incredibly intense. The feeling of the blood being pulled from him so quickly and the overwhelming heat was shocking his system. His hair started showing streaks of white that hadn't been there before.

The blades seemed to stop their attempts to attack, simply spinning in place as they waited for Six to finish.

The flames died down, but her eyes were still white hot as she released Nero from her grasp. Lucef had stared in awe at the entire interaction, gripping the doorframe. There had been nothing he could have done to help either of them.

<*What did you do?*> Vehekan hissed.

"For now, you can't harm him. It will be enough time, I think, for him to move on back to London," Six said, stretching her neck and then her arms. Nero's blood gave her a surge. And strange vibration of power she hadn't ever felt before. Old blood. Ancient blood.

<*You vile creature,*> Vehekan snapped, but she twitched her finger, pulling them toward her. They followed as she headed to where Lucef stood at the door, glancing behind her at Nero's form, lying on the floor.

"Will you be alright, Nero?" Six asked, though her tone only held the smallest hint of concern.

"Ace," Nero managed to say, turning his eyes to look at her, seemingly unable to move much more than his hand.

Lucef turned, hearing the front door of the manor bang open as the hunting party returned.

"Seems she's here," Six said, shrugging and grabbing Lucef by his collar before dragging him back toward her room.

The intel they gained was valuable. Not only had Ace and the other Necare followed the shipment of new wolves to the den, but they had scouted out plenty of locations that they could lay in wait to stage an attack. Ace had instructed the few Kurome Necare to stay, watching for guard changes or any type of movement from the den that could be helpful later when they decided on their attack.

Not but a few moments away from Ace returning to Redeamond, she became overcome with emotion. Nero's strange agony had taken over her thoughts. She halted mid-step, seeing the blades, the flames, and feeling the blood draining from him. Ace didn't wait; she surged ahead of the group of Necare, bursting through the door and up the stairs with enough time to see Six and Lucef strolling away from the room that Nero and she were sharing.

She turned her eyes to the room, seeing Nero lying there, his eyes white but not glowing, white hair that hadn't been there before streaked through his hair. She rushed to him, hands hovering over his body.

"What happened to you?" she asked, struggling to keep her face neutral. Nero merely looked up at her, his gaze far away, as if unable to focus on her face. Ace's lips tightened, and her eyes glowed with rage.

Six.

With a sweep of her hand over Nero's brow, she stood and moved so quickly that she soon appeared in Six's room, where she and Lucef were settling back down.

"What did you do?" Ace hissed, standing in the doorway, hands clenched into fists at her side.

"Not me, the demon in the blades," Six said, her tone flippant as she glanced over her shoulder at Ace.

"Demon blades?" Ace asked, narrowing her eyes.

"They tried to kill him. *I* saved him. You should be thanking me."

Ace trembled, fighting the surge of fire that was threatening to spill out.

"Where is your Medicus?" Ace demanded, a growl ripping from her throat as she spoke.

"Medicus?" Six asked.

"Nero couldn't even speak when I saw him just now. Where is your Medicus?" Ace hissed. Six's face twisted somewhere between a smirk and a pitying look.

"Jag lives in the garage," Six said, but before she could add any warnings about that particular situation, Ace had already turned and gone back to Nero.

Nero had managed to sit up while Ace had been gone, leaning against the back of the desk.

"We're going to the Medicus here," Ace stated, coming up to him abruptly and crouching, as if to pick him up.

"I doubt they'll be able to help," Nero murmured, his voice not much more than a whisper.

"Tell me exactly what happened," Ace asked, sitting before him on the floor. His eyes seemed less vacant, but he was clearly still weak and in pain.

"That demon metal of Six's … seems she made a deal," Nero said with a wince.

"What was the deal?"

"She would wipe out the Elders and, in exchange, she would gain power. She drank from me to protect me," Nero said, his tone almost surprised. Though he had benefited from Six's affections for years by never being a target, once it was revealed he wasn't her true sire, he expected that would change. But given the opportunity, she protected him, risking her own safety rather than let him die.

Ace mulled that information over for a moment. She was, of course, pleased that Six had chosen to protect him, but he was clearly drained to a point that was beyond anything she had ever witnessed before. If Nero didn't see the Medicus soon … she didn't want to think about what could potentially happen.

"I'll bring the Medicus here," Ace said quietly.

It was harder than expected to find the garage. It was attached to the building but had clearly been added there years after the plantation had been built, as such that the entrance was tucked into a strange space, giving it the illusion that it was a closet with its placement rather than a door that actually led anywhere.

She entered the room, very different than the Medicus back at Kurome. It was dark and dim, the air was hazy with cigarette smoke, and the tables littered with weapons and tools, mostly for cars. A hollowed-out car on cinderblocks sat in the far corner, and that was where Ace realized the smoke was coming from, as it spiraled in the air like a snake from the frame.

"Jag?" Ace asked, as she got closer to it. From the darkness inside, a man emerged. He was not large by any means, but he gave off a foreboding air. A cigarette danged from his mouth precariously, as he pushed the long, disheveled hair from his face.

"You rang?" he asked, looking her over.

"I need you to come with me. Nero, the Elder, is in need of your services," she said, taking a step to turn and head back through the manor, when he let out a chuckle that stopped her.

"I don't leave the garage," Jag said, letting the cigarette fall to the floor so he could stamp it out.

"I don't think you understand," Ace said, letting her eyes glow slightly. "Your services are needed by the Elder sent here to help your coven. You'll come with me now."

Jag folded his arms over his chest as he leaned back against the car frame he had just emerged from.

"I don't think you understand. I don't take orders from anyone unless it's Six," he sneered.

Ace tilted her head slightly, looking over his smug demeanor. She raised her hand, looking at her nails, instead of him and watching as they started to lengthen. She then stepped forward, coming close to him.

"You'll come with me and help our Elder, or you'll do it missing a few things," she said coldly, pressing the tips of her elongated nails against his inner thigh. His smirk fled his face, eyes going wide. Six may have been a loose cannon, keeping everyone, even those in her coven, on their toes, but Ace could rival her if the mood struck her. And with

Nero in the state he was currently, one that brought out the ominous familiarity of a time gone by, she had nothing keeping her from taking out her frustrations on a sniveling creature like this.

"Okay," he whispered.

Jag trailed behind Ace through the manor, the House Vampires staring the whole way up. Nero was still on the floor, but his eyes seemed to be returning some of their spark.

"Nearly drained," Ace said, watching as Jag came up to Nero. He inspected him, opening Nero's shirt to look at his torso, which oddly looked bruised as if blood had been brought to the surface.

"He needs blood. He's lost too much of his … essence, for lack of a better term. A Vampire donor would be best, and then a live mortal," Jag murmured, now looking at Nero's eyes.

"That's it?" Ace asked, her fingers twitching with need.

"That and rest. He won't be able to do much for a few days," Jag told them, standing from his crouched position.

"The ritual is set to happen in a few days," Nero groaned.

"You don't need to be part of that," Ace murmured, glancing at Nero.

"I'll have one of the House Vampires send up a human for him," Jag said, taking his leave as quickly as possible, while Ace moved to sit beside Nero. She rolled up her sleeve, placing her wrist before his mouth.

"I'm not drinking from you," he grumbled, turning his head away.

"I'm not waiting to find another suitable Vampire donor. Take my blood," she said sternly, using her other hand to turn his head back to her wrist.

"You need all your strength. The ritual," he murmured.

"And I'll regain it much faster than you will without my blood."

He stubbornly pinned his lips closed, scowling deeply at her. She let her fingers soften at that glare, letting her hand slide around to caress his cheek. In the face of losing him, she would always go further to keep that from happening, and she knew he felt the same.

"My blood is yours. My bones, my flesh." She pressed her forehead to his. "Take it. It already belongs to you," she whispered, holding up her exposed wrist to him once more. His eyes soften at her words, letting his head rest against hers for a moment to just look into her silver eyes. Slowly, he opened his mouth, letting his fangs gentle penetrate her flesh there and feeling her blood flow into his mouth.

CHAPTER 19

L ukis was growing impatient. The moon for the ritual was quickly approaching and though they now had Lin as their ally, they had yet to get their hands on Lucef. He sat in the meeting room, which had somehow become the room where they were preparing Bridgit and Natalia. Bridgit was one of the few Werewolves who had come forward and willingly chosen to be the sacrifice for the ritual, and Natalia was the Witch sacrifice. They were being blessed by the Witches, who insisted that the days leading up to the event were very important in preparing them for their fates.

The Chenja sacrifice in the dungeons was not so willing. Strangely metallic screams would often be heard from below as they struggled to fight their confinement. Lukis smirked to himself as he recalled the horror on that Chenja's face once they realized there *was* a cage that could hold their kind. Lukis had been planning this for years, and so far, everything except for getting his hands on his son had come to fruition.

He stared beyond the women in the corner, fighting the extreme feeling of guilt that washed over him as he had regretfully reminded himself that he would also, in essence, be sacrificing his own son. A goblet of blood sat on the tabletop, its contents most likely cooled and congealed into a disgusting glop that not even a Vampire would drink. Deca was meant to meet him in that room for nearly an hour and, as of yet, still hadn't shown up.

Finally, she appeared in the doorway, her eyes looking over toward the group of women in the corner with a slightly disinterested expression before she moved around them to sit beside her husband.

"It's gone cold," he grumbled toward her, gesturing to the goblet.

"Took me a little longer to find the energy to get here than I expected," she said back apologetically. She hated that she had to lie to him, but after realizing that nearly everything about their relationship had been a lie, she was struggling to give into his demands. Her body did hurt, but that didn't mean she couldn't have gotten there sooner.

"Drink it fast," Lukis suggested, pushing it toward her while still keeping his eyes on the blessings.

"I think I'll wait," she murmured, seeing the chunks that had formed when she moved it around slightly. She would be chewing this blood at this point, and beside that, she didn't plan on ever taking another drop of it. If Lukis was planning anything that would hurt their son, she didn't want anything to do elongating what was left of her miserable life. Especially not this.

"You need to keep your strength. A lot will be happening soon," Lukis told her, glancing at her hands, which had taken on some withering over the last few days.

"The things happening don't have to do with me," she grumbled, pushing the goblet further away from her on the table. Lukis looked at her more fully. Her eyes looked sad and perhaps resigned, to what he didn't know. She had stopped asking him about Lucef over the past few days and seemed rather withdrawn.

It was against his better judgment to try to coax the warmth from her by talking about the son he would soon be forfeiting for his own ambitions, but he wanted that warmth, the love in her eyes, more than anything. There was no other reason for him to have kept her alive as long as he had if he didn't crave that light and joy she brought with her.

"Lucef should be arriving in a few days, if not sooner," Lukis said, watching as her whole body seemed to stiffen. But what he thought was in excitement was actually in fear. What would he do to Lucef once he had him?

"You don't know when?" Deca asked.

"Not exactly when, no," Lukis confirmed, though he looked at her curiously. Normally at the mention of Lucef, she became overjoyed. This was the first time where the look in her eyes seemed a bit sadder than happy.

"Deca, what's wrong?" he asked, but before she could even look his way, Alexander came through the door, walking right up to Lucef's other side and bending to whisper in his ear.

"We have a location. The plan can be set in motion," Alexander murmured quietly so only Lukis could hear. Lukis stiffened, nodding at Alexander as he waited for confirmation and turned back to his wife.

"I need you to go back to our room, my love," he said, pushing the goblet closer to her.

"I just left there," she said, furrowing her brow at him.

"If it is too much for you to walk back, I'd suggest taking your treatment," Lukis said, urging the goblet into her hands.

"I'm not drinking it, Lukis," Deca hissed, pushing it over so it spilled out over the table.

Lukis slammed his fist into the table, causing a dint to form in its surface, the impression of his knuckles clearly defined in the polished wood. He surged to his feet, coming around to pull Deca's chair away from the table before pulling her in his arms and stalking from the room. The group of women in the corner had stopped, staring as Lukis stormed from the room, Deca stick-still in his arms.

He made his way down the hall, the fury in his eyes making everyone they passed pause to watch. Once they made it the door, he opened it, closing the door forcefully with his foot before tossing her unceremoniously onto the bed.

"You'll drink the blood, and you'll stay here, woman!" he roared, moving to the small refrigerator that he had tucked inside their closet to pull the last of blood from Melissa's tribute.

"I don't want to drink it anymore! Why should I? What is even the point?" she screamed back, dissolving into tears and crumbling against the bedsheets.

Lukis set the glass of blood on the bedside table, kneeled on the floor beside the bed, and watched the wretched sobs wrack Deca's delicate and increasingly failing body.

"I love you, Deca," he whispered, reaching out to touch her face, but she swatted his arm away.

"If you loved me, you would have let me die. If you loved me, you wouldn't have driven my son away," she said bitterly, her eyes opening, full of tears to stare at him with the full force of her anger.

Lukis's eyes went cold. He turned, placing the glass back on the table, before slowly standing. There was a pause as he breathed deeply, staring at the glass full of blood. Deca stared at him, her breathing ragged from crying as she waited. She didn't see it coming when he lunged at her, grasping her roughly and pulling her up against the pillows. He pinned her to the bed and forced her mouth open. She screamed. Never before had she been scared of her husband, but right now, the combination of how aggressively he was handling her and the beast in his eyes sent a visceral terror throughout her body.

"You'll drink it, whether you want to or not. You'll live forever by my side, until *I* decide you can die," he growled, as he took up the glass of blood and poured it down her throat, stifling her screams with choking and gagging in the process. When the goblet was done, he climbed off her and moved to the door. "I'll come see you once my business is done," he said as he paused, with his hand on the doorknob. And then he was gone, leaving Deca shaking and crying against the sheets, her body renewed, but her treatment couldn't mend the broken, torment within her mind.

Six and Lucef had left the manor, for no other reason than to stroll the streets of the French Quarter at night. Oddly, she had no desire to hunt, perhaps Nero's blood had sated her better than she had been in quite some time. Regardless of the reason, they had snuck away from the Necare that had joined them. Lin had taken issue with this, of course, as his jealousy of Lucef had become even more irritating than his overt attempts at affection had been before. She simply ignored his protests, moving through the streets with Lucef hand in hand. She found she quite liked how it felt to be with him. His long fingers seemed to perfectly incapsulate her small, thin ones.

The sharp scent of Werewolf caught her nose and she paused, eyes darting around to see where it came from. Though they had left the Necare, she had expected one of them to stay near enough to take on whatever may come to bother them. The Necare knew how important it was to keep Lucef safe, and now she was feeling the tendrils of frustration at herself for deciding to take him out.

"Six," Lucef said, his voice hushed as his hand gripped hers harder. "We need to leave."

Suddenly they were surrounded. Out of the shadows Werewolves stepped, circling them.

"There's no getting away, Lucef," Alexander said, eyes glimmering as he stepped out of the shadows. The smirk that stretched over his face only proved to make Lucef growl deep in his chest. He had never changed into a wolf before, but the adrenaline pumping through him as he saw himself cornered with his Six made his skin ripple.

"You aren't ruining my fun, filthy beasts," Six hissed, trying to summon the blades. She'd make quick work of this, even if it was ruining the perfection of this evening. But the blades didn't come. Vehekan seemed to snicker in her mind, pressing the blades a little further in so the edges threatened to break her skin through the fabric of her corset.

"Don't fight it," came a voice Six wasn't expecting. Lin stepped out from behind Alexander, his hand outstretched to her. "Let them take him, and you'll be free."

Lucef let out a howl, more wolf than man. His teeth had grown, bulging fangs bursting from his mouth. He looked at Six, loosening his hold on her fingers. If he let her go, she'd be safe. The pleading look in his eyes and the feel of him pulling away enflamed Six even more. Her eyes glowed, fingers curling before her before she snapped her focus from Lucef to Lin. Nothing but hatred for him shown on her face.

"He's *mine*," Six hissed, gripping Lucef's fingers more tightly.

"You crazy bitch. You can't fight all of us," one man said while laughing in her peripheral.

"She can, and she will," came a voice from behind her. Sparks in her curled hand grew into flames, causing several of them to gasp. Alexander's face remained unchanged, smirk only deepening as he stepped forward.

It happened so quickly, Six could never have prepared for it. A minuscule change in Alexander's eyes was all the signal they needed. Six was sudden paralyzed, as her body seized up and a searing pain engulfing her. She could see Lucef pinned to the ground, his shouts and screams piercing to her ears as chains were placed around his wrists, silver she imagined, since the others were wearing gloves.

Alexander stepped closer to her, touching her chin and tilting her head up so he could look into her eyes.

"Don't you fucking touch her!" Lucef screamed, still pinned to the ground.

"You should be unconscious from that blow," Alexander murmured, inviting Lucef's outburst. His tone suggested he was impressed by Six. "Stronger than you look, indeed." He glanced over her head, quickly removing his hand as another wave of pain shot through her, and it all went black.

Alexander looked down at Six's unconscious form as Lin made it to his side.

"I'll take her back," Lin said, bending over as if he was going to pull her into his arms.

"She's coming with us," Alexander said, gesturing Opus forward from the circle.

"Lukis and I had a deal," Lin hissed, stepping in front of where Opus approached, as if his body as a shield would prevent him from taking Six.

"She's exactly what we need. She comes."

"No!" Lucef screamed, using all his strength to pull himself up to stand, rushing over and kneeling over Six's body.

"It was already decided, boy. Let Opus take her," Alexander growled down at Lucef, ignoring Lon's additional protests as Opus easily removed him from the circle.

"No! No one else will touch her," Lucef said, reaching out with his silver-chained hands to brush a lock of fiery red hair from her face.

"I told you—"

"*I* will carry her," Lucef snapped, pulling her against his chest and standing once more.

"It will not change her fate," Alexander said, placing a hard grip on Lucef's shoulder to steer him away.

"We'll see," Lucef growled.

Lin watched from the shadows as the entourage of Werewolves moved silently through the back streets to the den. There was no way for him to acquire Six. No way for him to get her back. He hadn't just betrayed his own kind, but he failed in his goal. He'd lost her.

He made his way back to Redeamond as the sky began changing, brightening from black to deep purple. The sun would rise soon. He stepped into the manor; the rest of the Necare had already returned and adjourned to their rooms. The assumed House Vampires would have followed suit, but as he looked up, he was met with silver eyes.

"Where are they?" Ace asked from where she crouched beside a sofa. A human was lying on it, her golden hair not long enough to hide the telltale bite marks that were left there. But she wasn't dead, just sleeping.

Lin cast his eyes at the ground, unable to meet her gaze. His failure would be true and complete if he had to admit it, especially if it was to *her.*

Ace checked that the human girl was secure, then approached Lin, grasping his face and forcing him to look at her.

"What has happened?"

"Taken," he gasped out. Ace's brows furrowed.

"Six and Lucef were taken?"

"They surrounded them," he started, taking in rough pants of air. "Some sort of electrical device. Like a taser, but more powerful."

"They were attacked. Captured, not killed?" Ace urged, shaking him slightly. His pants got more frantic.

"They were supposed to leave her. Just take him. She was supposed to be mine," Lin finally said, the words bursting forth. Ace let go of him as if he were on fire, her eyes wide with shock.

"You gave them up," she whispered, horrified.

"*He* is unnatural. It was wrong for them to be together," Lin hissed, his eye having grown wolf.

"You betrayed us all."

"No! They tricked me!" he screamed, reaching up to pull at his own hair. Ace surged forward, grasping him by the throat and slamming him into the wall.

"You betrayed your Judge, your lover, and all of your kind, Lin. I can't stand the *sight* of you," Ace spat, her eyes white with rage.

The screams had drawn a crowd. Ranked and House Vampires alike came pooling into the room.

"You gave them to the enemy?" came Jacob, one of Six's Necare, as he pushed forward through the crowd. He was young, but had become quite formidable under Six's leadership. And he was loyal enough for her to have him join her and Lin when they made their trip to London for the Harvest.

"I—"

"You sick bastard!" another Vampire rang out.

"Death!" they all began chanting. Even Nero came to the top of the stairs, looking down on the chaos.

Ace's fingers tightened against Lin's face, crushing his jaw beneath her fingers. He let out a strangled cry, which was met with cheers of encouragement from the coven.

"I can ... I can make this right," Lin stammered, his mouth moving strangely and his voice pained.

"There is no way to make this right. The ritual is tonight. You've just killed Six and the rest of us," Ace growled, glancing to her right to see an unused fireplace companion set beside the large hearth. She reached out her idle hand, calling the poker to her before digging her nails into the flesh of Lin's face and dragging him out the door.

The sun's rays were beginning to peek out over the horizon as Ace marched out onto the brick path before the manor. She threw him against the bricks, taking no moment of hesitation as she drove the poker roughly through his breastbone and through him, effectively pinning him to the ground. Lin screamed, his eyes wide with terror, knowing exactly what was to become of him. Ace crouched down and stared into his eyes, the prickling pain from the sun starting at the back of her neck.

"For what you've done, Lin, I put you to death," Ace hissed, standing and walking back to the safety of the manor's shadow, as the sun burst over the treeline, basking Lin's exposed body in light. It didn't take but a moment for his blood and the sun to collide, making him immediately burst into flames, his screams changing as he choked on the flames ripping through his throat.

CHAPTER 20

Ace closed the door to the manor, her eyes still burning white with rage as she looked out over the crowd of Vampires that were still taking up the room. It was silent as a tomb as she looked out at their faces.

"Back to your rooms," Nero commanded them, though he never took his eyes off Ace.

They dispersed, disappearing back into the manor, though Jag seemed to stay behind, leaning against the door-frame of the hallway that led to his garage.

"We have to go now," Ace said, her body still rigid. The ritual would be hours away, but the feeling she had, deep within herself, was that if they were going to prevent what was prophesized to happen, they couldn't wait for sundown.

"We need a plan," Nero said, descending the stairs. He looked better, though Ace could tell he still wasn't back to his full strength. The addition of the white streaks actually made him appear even more domineering and powerful than he had previously.

"We know where their den is. The Necare have been watching their movements. They decrease their guard by fifty percent during daylight hours. We can sneak in and find them," Ace said, starting to pace.

"What? With an army of Necare? You don't think they'd notice a horde of Vampires coming down on them?" Nero asked, stepping closer to her.

"Not an army, Nero. Just us," she said, stopping to face him.

"I have some things that might help," Jag said, smirking lightly as he lit the cigarette that had been dangling from his lips.

Six woke up but didn't open her eyes. She felt Lucef's arms around her, smelled his scent close. It was punctuated with fear, pain, and anger. He was holding her tightly, more tightly than he had ever before. She took a mental catalogue of what she could feel and smell. They were clearly on the ground; her feet were bare and against a concrete floor; and Lucef was clearly cross-legged as he held her. She couldn't hear any others in the room; it was just the two of them in this unfamiliar place.

She opened her eyes, looking up at him. He was glaring at the door, eyes full of rage. Slowly she reached up, touching his cheek to gain his attention, noticing how her limbs didn't quite want to cooperate with her commands.

"It hurts," Six said in a quiet moan, letting her hand drop back down when she couldn't hold it up to his face any longer.

"I know, I'm so sorry," Lucef murmured, bending his head to place a kiss softly on her cheek.

"How did they...?" she began, but taking in breaths to make words was even a difficulty.

"Lin. He gave us over," said Lucef as he sighed. Six furrowed her brow, thinking back to the moments before she went unconscious. It came back to her in odd flashes, but she saw him there. Lin slithering from behind Alexander, reaching out his hand to her as if she'd choose to come with him.

"Son of a bitch," Six whispered, trying to scowl. "Always thinking with his dick. I'm glad I let him go," Six whispered.

"I'm sure if Ace gets word of what he's done, he'll be dead," Lucef said, pulling her closer.

"He's probably already ashes at this point," Six agreed, snuggling her head into the crook of his neck. His scent and his heartbeat were so calming and comforting to her. She couldn't even be mad at Lin while Lucef was there.

The door suddenly opened with a painful screech, and Lucef looked up at the three Werewolves that entered: Alexander, Opus, and Kyle.

"No. I'm not leaving, and neither is she," Lucef said bluntly, getting their intentions by the looks on their faces.

"There are preparations that you both have to undergo for this evening," Alexander said, as the other two moved to either side of the couple on the floor.

"We aren't being separated," Lucef growled, hunching his body over her protectively. Six opened her eyes, pulling back a fraction to focused on him. She turned his face toward hers and looked deep into his black-and-blue orbs.

"They're going to, Lucef. We can't fight them this way. Just kiss me quickly," she said quietly. Lucef leaned down and kissed her, pulling her as close to him as he could. They put everything they were feeling into the kiss. Their longing, their love. Everything they wanted to say but couldn't resided there in those few moments with their lips locked together.

But they were torn apart almost as quickly as the kiss had begun. Opus ripped Six out of Lucef's arms, who began screaming like a banshee, though it hurt every fiber of her battered and sore body to do so.

Kyle then dragged Lucef to his feet, pushing him quickly out of the room. Six stared after him until the door banging closed, bringing her focus back to the Werewolf still in the room. He was large, not overly tall, but still towering over. His arms rippled as he clenched his fists, stepping toward her.

"What are you going to do? You can't kill me," Six said, smirking as she scooted herself to lean against the wall. She was regaining control of her body, but it didn't mean it didn't hurt terribly. Whatever they had used to knock her out did quite a number on her.

"No, can't kill you, not until tonight, but I can make sure you can't fight the preparations," Opus said, his voice so low it vibrated her body and put the hairs on the back of her neck on end. With no further hesitation, he drew back his fist, swinging it with full force and punching her square in the side of her head. Stars formed in her vision as she slumped to one side, but she remained conscious, if not immobilized by the excruciating pain.

The door opened again, and a group of women entered. They were clearly Witches; Six could tell not only from the scent they gave off, but the very specific ritualistic robes they wore. The women began moving her, pulling her so her body lay flat against the concrete floor. Manacles were produced and placed over her wrists and ankles, then cloths, wet with some strange-smelling oils that were wiped over her body.

"How long will this take? You have Lucef to do after this," Opus asked one of the Witches.

"Not long. We don't have much time before we have to start the ritual," she said, returning to her tasks. Six winced as they pressed on her, flinched when symbols were being drawn over her body in blood. The blood, she could tell by its scent, and then subsequently its taste when her mouth was marked, was baby blood. She scowled at them, her eyes glowing bright red with the offending taste. Even Vampires didn't kill babies.

If she could have mustered the energy to do something, *anything*, she would have fought against this, but she had been basically powerless when they came in the room, and now that the manacles were on her, she realized she wouldn't be able to move even if she tried.

Stupid magic, she thought, glaring at the women who chanted as they worked, rocking their bodies and being lost in the process.

Lucef had been taken to a room only a few doors away from where he and Six had been locked together. Kyle threw him in, pulling at the silver chains still around Lucef's wrists and hooking it to a large meat hook over his head. Lucef wasn't sure what this room had been previously, but it was tiled on all walls as well as the ceiling.

"What are they doing to her?" he hissed at Kyle, who merely chuckled as he cranked up the hook so Lucef's feet couldn't touch the floor. Kyle didn't answer, taking a knife from his pocket. He slowly opened the knife, inspecting the point and the blade for sharpness against his thick thumb. "Answer me, you fucking dog!" Lucef yelled, shaking the chains holding him.

Kyle rushed forward, pressing the knife to Lucef's throat and staring into his eyes with a menace he had never seen before.

"Do you know how much time I wasted looking for you back in London?" Kyle growled, the knife pressing a bit deeper as he spoke, breaking the skin on Lucef's neck, but only just the surface. Lucef smiled, his eyes alight with mischievous humor as he looked at the rage laced on Kyle's face. This man had been Lucef's bodyguard for most of his childhood, one of his confidants throughout his teenage years, and yet there he was, pressing a knife to Lucef's throat.

"Oh yeah? He left you behind, did he? Made you seem quite the fool when I wasn't there, eh?" Lucef asked, letting a small chuckle escape his chest.

"Boy ... there are things in this world that are bigger than you and I. You spit in the face of it all and have for ages," Kyle said, pushing away from Lucef and turning to the door.

"Who's to say we're right, Kyle? That my father is right?" Lucef demanded.

"We all have to pick a side and be willing to die for it."

"I'm not willing."

"But you will," Kyle murmured with finality, his hand gripping the doorframe roughly.

"How dare you?" came a weak voice from the shadowed hallway outside the room. Deca stepped forward, her face lined with fury as she looked past Kyle's bulky frame and saw her son hanging from the ceiling.

"Deca—"

"He's chained," she snapped, turning her furious gaze toward Kyle. He looked at her with horror, having not expected her to be there. No, this was no place for Deca and if Lukis knew...

"Lukis would rather you stay in your room," Kyle said, stepping further through the doorway to block her passage.

"Lukis would rather quite a lot, but I'm going to see my son," she said bitterly, moving past him and stepping into the tiled room.

For a moment, she simply stood there, gazing at Lucef's body, scraped, bruised, and now cut slightly at the neck by Kyle's knife.

"What have they done to you, my son?" she whispered hoarsely, moving closer to him and staring up at his face.

"They're going to kill me, Mum," Lucef said, seeing now, for the first time, that she had no illusions about what was going on. That he could finally speak to her freely. Tears welled in her eyes as she reached up to touch his face, her fingers brushing over his skin as they had hundreds of times in the past. Her baby, her son.

"There's nothing I can do to stop him, Lucef," she sobbed, the tears finally escaping and cascading down her cheeks.

"I know, Mum," Lucef murmured, wishing he could wrap her in a hug and comfort her. No, he didn't hate his mother. She was just as much a victim as he was in his father's torturous games.

"What can I do, Lucef?" He looked up at the doorway, Kyle was nowhere in sight, but he could hear movement down the hall. They were alone, if only for a moment.

"Help the girl," he whispered hastily, causing her brow to furrow.

"Girl?"

"I came in with a girl. Her name is Six. She's ... she doesn't deserve this. I can't make it out alive, but maybe she can," he said, eyes pleading with her.

"Who is she to you?" she asked, seeing that spark there as he spoke.

"She's my..." He didn't know what to call her. Soulmate? True love? What was Six to him? But he didn't have to say anything but through Deca's tears, a slight, wry smile met her lips.

"I'll try," she whispered, nodding to him as footfalls became louder, quickly approaching the door.

"Deca!" snarled Lukis as he burst into the room. "You were to stay in bed!"

"I wanted to see my son!" she snapped, turning to glare at him, though her body curled a bit into itself, as if to protect her from him.

"Back to your room, woman," Lukis growled, staring down at her, her gaze just as menacing and promising much pain later if she did not obey. With a final, fleeting glance at Lucef, she hurried from the room, leaving father and son alone.

Lukis turned after a beat of silence, closing the door soundly before returning his gaze to look upon Lucef.

"Have a nice chat with your mother?" he asked, as a smirk spread across his face. The malice behind his words was not lost on Lucef.

"Why would you care?" Lucef said, spitting at his father.

"Well, I thought it was cute that you were trying to save that little Vampire's life. What was it that you were going to say the two of you were? Were you going to tell Deca that Six is your lover?" Lukis asked, watching his son's face very closely. Lucef scowled, clenching his jaw with anger he could do nothing to dissipate.

"That's disgusting," Lukis growled, ripping his eyes from his son in revulsion as he began to pace before him. "I didn't bring you into this world to fall in love with their kind."

"You didn't *want* to bring me into this world at all!" Lucef yelled, breathing heavy. "And you married any better, father? You keep Mother alive by giving her blood of Immortals. She doesn't even want it anymore! Can't you see what you're doing to her?" Lucef challenged.

"Shut up, boy!" Lukis roared, backhanding Lucef so hard this whole body swung violently on the hook.

"What are they doing to Six?" Lucef demanded, spitting the blood from his mouth after a moment of heavy breathing.

"Preparing her for the ritual," Lukis said, pulling a handkerchief from his pocket to wipe blood from his knuckles.

"And what of me?"

Lukis stepped forward until he was nose to nose with Lucef.

"They'll be doing the same with you shortly," Lukis said quietly.

He stepped back as the door opened again. Four Witches entered, and his preparations began.

Kyle dragged Lucef from the room, his body now covered in symbols. He was taken back to the original room with the concrete floor, but initially when he was thrown in, he didn't see Six anywhere. He struggled to move his body from where it had been thrown, his body sore from being strung up for hours, but he managed to roll over, seeing Six lying on the floor, pinned down with manacles on her extremities.

"Six!" he hissed, scrambling over to her and looking down at her face. She too was covered in the odd symbols like his.

"I'm fine," she murmured, though she was far from fine. Her body still hurt, she was trapped, and she was covered in baby blood. All things on her list of "Would very much not like," seemed to be happening at once.

"I don't know if we'll be able to get out of here," he said, reaching his hands up, still bound together with chains to touch the places on her face where they had drawn.

"We won't," she said conclusively, looking into his odd eyes and letting a little smile break through. "The sun is going to set soon. I can feel it," she whispered, rubbing her nose on his lovingly. Lucef let the tears he had been holding back fall. Her words were so haunting, it made him question everything up until that moment.

Ace had given him a chance. She had tried to protect him from all this. Many of the other Vampires he had encountered, with the exception of Lin, of course, had been nothing but helpful and kind to him. He didn't know how the war had started in the first place, but he knew one thing: Vampires were trying their utmost to change, to be better, while Werewolves were still trapped in the old ways.

And Six...

He curled up beside her on the floor, letting her head nuzzle into its favorite spot at his neck. Six had become more important to him than anything that world had yet offered him, and seeing her die because of him, even if he was to follow just a few moments later, made him never want to let her go.

CHAPTER 21

Ace and Nero drove through the congested streets of New Orleans, the car Jag had leant them was equipped with sun-resistant windows to make travelling so far from the Redeamond Manor easier for them. By the time they had gotten it running and out of the garage, it had passed into the afternoon, and Ace was feeling that impending doom deep in her stomach. This wasn't just about saving the Vampires from whatever would come to pass once Lukis took over Lucef's newly empowered body; this was about her progeny, her Six, being sacrificed for the likes of a madman like Lukis.

Nero clutched the seat of the car as Ace dogged dangerously through traffic, slowing to reasonable speeds only once they were coming upon the huge, abandoned building. The ghost of a hospital was massive. Never before had Ace known Werewolves to inhabit such an overtly large space above ground, but she supposed they most likely used the lower levels exclusively to keep people from thinking it was anything other than an abandoned, post-Hurricane Katrina hospital.

Ace parked a good distance away, quieting the engine and staring out toward the emergency entrance where the

Necare had been watching their comings and goings. It was quiet. Too quiet, even for daylight hours, Ace realized as she watched the singular guard standing outside the large ambulance doors.

"There's only one," Nero murmured in confusion, having expected more.

"They could be roaming, but..." She let her eyes scan the area. There was no indication there were any others about.

"Why would they leave it so unguarded?" Nero asked.

"They don't think we'd risk it during the day," Ace said, raising her eyebrows smugly. There Lukis was, again under-estimating her by placing only one guard outside this place. He should have learned his lesson when he tried to attack Kurome, but apparently, he liked to continue to make mis-guided assumptions. Just because Vampires didn't like going out in the day, didn't mean they were trapped within the confines of their houses and coffins. For as old as he was, Lukis should have known better.

"Should we take him out?"

Ace considered it, looking at the man who was now starting to doze off against the wall in the evening sun. It would be easy enough to do so. They could come upon him when he's about to fall asleep and slit his throat with her silver blades, but his dead body would be an indication to whoever came to take over his post that they had Vampires in their midst. And the shift change was due to happen in about an hour, with a doubled guard.

"We can sneak by him," Ace said conclusively, pulling the hooded jacket as far forward over her face as she could before stepping from the car. Nero followed suit, the two of them slipping into the shadows of the trees surrounding the hospital. They edged around cars, moving as quickly and silently as possible. There was a wide gap between where the final car was and the singular door entry beside the ambulance bay. A gap that if the guard happened to rouse from his light slumber, it would make them plain targets.

Ace watched him as he scratched his nose lazily, eyes still closed, but breathing shallow and uneven. It took ten minutes, but still she watched, feeling the heat of the sun, now much more brutal against her slightly covered form than it was through the shade of the trees. Finally, his breathing became deeper and even, with a small, wheezing precursor to a snore beginning against his lips. She waved for Nero to follow her, taking quick but silent steps along the gravel toward that door. They both slipped inside, careful to avoid any squeal of the hinge as they did so.

For a moment they just stood there, taking in a breath in the dimly lit ambulance bay. It was both out of relief and also to take in the scents of the building.

"I wasn't sure it would work for a moment," Nero whispered, pulling the hooded jacket from his head.

"Me either," Ace said, shedding hers altogether.

The room smelled like a hundred Werewolves and a dozen Witches had been through there, though Ace knew that more had in all likelihood. She glanced around at the various doors that lead out of the bay. Which one would lead them where they needed to go?

Nero stepped up to one, pressing his ear to the door to *see and hear* what was beyond it, shaking his head when it was fruitless. Ace began doing the same, the two of them systematically narrowing the chances down until there was only one door left.

She placed her hand on the cold knob and turned it, finding it was locked. "They're smarter than I thought ... locking their doors," she whispered with a smirk, glancing at Nero.

"How very grown-up of them," Nero murmured, returning her smirk with one of his own. If it hadn't been for their duty, the combination of his smirk and the new streaks in his hair would have been enough for her to want to take him in the darkness of that room. But this was neither the time nor place for such a thing. If they made it out of this alive, Ace felt certain she would be the one pinning Nero to the wall.

She used her nails to quietly pry the door open, pausing for a moment to make sure no one was suddenly rushing to their location, but it remained mostly quiet. The only sounds were distant. Their eyes glowed as they walked down the darkened stairwell. At the bottom there was yet another door, but this one had a window. They flanked the window, which was cascading light into the small space.

"How many?" Nero asked, glancing out just as Ace was from her side.

"Five, maybe?" she speculated, trying to gain a sense of the layout.

"I don't see any on my side," Nero murmured.

Ace glanced again. The group of Werewolves were travelling the opposite way down the hall, carrying a large stone slab.

"It's clear, we can try to dart into one of those empty rooms," Ace said, seeing one in particular that was darkened, the door slightly ajar.

Nero nodded and Ace opened the door, moving silently into the hallway. The group of Werewolves were turning a corner as they slipped into the darkened room. Another set of five Werewolves started down the hall on the same path as the first. This time they were holding what looked to be a cage. Ace's eyes burned with rage as soon as she realized who was inside the cage.

"Let me go!" Codi shouted, though his voice was weaker, and he was visibly recoiling from touching any of the sides of the cage.

"Shut up, Chenja," growled the Werewolf at the back. "You haven't escaped in weeks. What makes you think we'll suddenly let you go now?" Alexander said with a sinister chuckle.

"You'll bring down the wrath of my mistress! She will not accept this as anything but dishonor on Lukis's part," Codi said bitterly. As they passed by, Ace stuck her head from the room, hoping Codi would look past Alexander's shoulder at her. Just as they were about to round the corner like the other group did, Codi's eyes caught hers.

She pressed her finger to her lips quickly, indicating that he needed to stay silent about her being there. She now had so much more at stake than simply the fate of the Vampires. Six, Lucef, and now Codi were all lined up for their horrible fates. Codi nodded back at her, clamping his mouth closed, and looking at where they were headed.

Ace glanced in the direction where they came from and didn't see or hear any indication others were close behind. She gestured to Nero to follow her, as she walked down the hall and glanced around the corner where they had gone.

The sun would be setting soon, and with that, a throng of Necare would descend on the den, ready to help Ace and Nero with whatever remained of their enemies, but for now, the two of them were on their own and the ritual would soon begin.

They approached a set of double doors, and Ace's hair rose when she felt the magic in the air. She glanced at Nero, her eyes glowing of their own accord. They looked through the small windows at the top of the doors. The room, which must have been a cafeteria previously, was filled with Werewolves and Witches. At the center of the crowd was five stone slabs. Ace watched in horror as Alexander ripped Codi from the cage he had been trapped in, getting assistance of three additional Werewolves to subdue him while he was forced upon one of the slabs, cuffs being places over his hands and ankles, and a collar at his throat.

The central slab, Ace saw Lucef fighting against his confinement, his entire body covered in strange symbols. He screamed and roared, his eyes bulging with effort as he tried in vain to rip himself from his enclosures. Six lay on the slab to his right. Her body languid, head turned to watch Lucef.

"How? How do we get in there?" Nero hissed, staring out the window just as Ace was in abject horror.

"We slip in. They're too focused on the center to notice who comes from behind right now," Ace murmured. They slipped in, unnoticed as Ace had assumed. There were hums and growls resonating around the room; chanting from the Witches was a low murmur.

This was an Immortal slaughter. It was the only way Ace could think of it. It was disgusting to see them all lined up like this, bodies marked and bound.

Was this Lukis's plan? To rid the world of Immortals completely?

He was going to murder each of these beings one by one, imbue his son with god-like powers, and then rip his son's soul from his body so *he* could inhabit it.

What on earth could he plan to do once that was done?

The Witch sacrifice entered from a door at the back, the crowd parting to let her pass. She was shaking, her eyes darting around with nervousness as she carefully climbed onto the slab beside Six's still form. Kyle approached her, taking her hands and placing them in the cuffs like all the others. A moment later came Bridget, her eyes sullen as she moved from her position in the crowd forward. Alexander reached out his hand for her, grasping hers firmly and pulling her a bit toward the slab next to Codi. The effect of the two women willingly placing themselves there was chilling.

Alexander and Kyle both stepped aside, slipping into the front of the crowd to wait, like everyone else. But the room grew tense, and the minutes ticked on. Lukis did not appear. Ace looked around and noticed frowns and concern flooding the faces of the onlookers. One girl behind her whispered to another, "Lukis is never late ... I wonder what's going on."

Then suddenly the door behind the stone slabs slammed opened, and Deca stalked into the room. She completely ignored the Werewolves that watched her, with a few belatedly trying to catch her arm, and went straight to Lucef's in the center.

"Mum?" Lucef asked, as his eyes widened. He had stopped trying to get to Six when the final sacrifice had been placed on the slab, feeling it was inevitable now. They were all going to die there, and there was nothing he could do. Blood ran down his arms from where he had cut his wrists on the cuffs, and his breath was ragged with effort. "What are you doing? Do you know what Father will do to you?" Lucef hissed, as Deca started to try to remove his cuffs from his bloodied wrists.

"I don't care what he'll do," Deca said, her voice holding a fury that Lucef had never heard from her before today, the same fury she had unleashed in that room on Lukis earlier. Just as soon as she started to loosen the cuff on his right arm, Lukis walked in with a furious glare.

He stood in the doorway, ignoring the crowd who was incredibly intense, and looked at Deca with a sour face.

"Deca, step out here into the hall with me. I need to speak with you," he said to her in a cold voice. Deca straightened up and shook her head, continuing to work at the chains.

"No. I'm busy," Deca said stiffly.

"I *said* that I need to speak with you! Come here now!" Lukis growled. She didn't move, continuing to work the cuff off her son's wrist. He stormed over to her, grabbing her wrist and ripping her away from Lucef.

"Mum! NO!" Lucef screamed, watching in horror as Lukis dragged her through the crowd and back out the doors he came in. Alexander stepped forward, landing a forceful slap on Lucef's face just as the door slammed closed once more.

Lukis grabbed Deca by the shoulders, slamming her against the wall and shaking her slightly.

"What the hell do you think you're doing?" Lukis snarled.

"I'm doing what I believe is right. What *you* should see is the right thing. We can't kill our son," she said back, her voice stronger with each passing word. She looked into his furious eyes, the emotion not changing even the slightest amount with her words. "You don't even think lying to your wife of eight hundred years, killing your son, forcing four others to die ... you don't think any of it is wrong," she said with disgust. She shook her head, and tears streamed down her face. "So, I'm doing the right thing for you."

"I kept you safe, my love! I've kept you ALIVE!" he yelled.

"Alive, but in pain!" Deca screamed back at him. "Don't you see this isn't how things should have been? You are planning to *kill* our *only son*, Lukis! For what?" she sobbed, clutching at her chest as if her heart would burst forth from it.

"It's the only way," he growled, reaching up to caress her cheek, but she flinched from his hand.

"Don't touch me," Deca demanded, jerking out of his grasp.

"You will stay and obey. I already told you, you have no say. You will live and die at my pleasure, Deca. You are mine!" Lukis roared.

"I am not your dog! If you want a dog, take up with one of the wolves out there who so desperately want your attention," she said bitterly, turning on her heel and marching down the hall.

Lukis stood there, his fists clenched and eyes burning. He couldn't afford to chase after her; there wasn't time if the ritual was to be completed. But he would make time to force her to see reason. Once he had his abilities, he would be able to force her to do whatever he wanted.

He turned, stalking back into the ritual space to be met with awkward stares of the crowded room. He approached the center, eyes glancing over the sacrifices, making certain they were all appropriately chained, before he nodded his head toward Alexander, signaling for the ritual to begin.

CHAPTER 22

A ce's mind was racing. The sun had to have set by then, but she wasn't sure how long it would take for them to get there, and the dread she felt when she realized it might take them some time to find this room, since the hallways were like mazes in this abandoned building made her body tense. Their back up could be too late. Her eyes turned to Six, who up until this point had appeared to be basically catatonic. Ace could not lose Six. They may have had their differences. There may have been many regrets about how things were done in the past, but Six was her blood. Her progeny.

But as Ace's eyes looked over the still form of Six, she realized she wasn't completely still. Six's hand was slowly, ever so slowly, slipping through the cuffs at her wrist, with tiny, barely comprehensible sparks shooting from her fingertips and swirling to the hinges, heating and loosening them. She was going to make an escape, Ace just hoped there would be back up, because timing would be everything.

Ace's focus was taken from Six's small movements when Alexander and a woman that clearly was a Witch stepped toward Lukis. Alexander held a black box in his arms, covered in similar symbols as the sacrifices. The Witch opened the box, her words, the language of the ancients, rang out louder and different than the other words that were being chanted in the background. The magic became thick in the air with her words, heavy with the burden of power. Witches may have been weak physically, but their powers were unquestionable when they were in control.

Within the box, there seemed to be five vials of liquid. Potions Ace suspected to facilitate in the ritual. The book had listed out several things that would need to be done in the previous months' moons to fully prepare for this. This ritual was not something that could be done on a whim. Lukis had been planning and preparing for this for years.

The Witch approached Lucef first, gesturing to Lukis to come toward his son. With a grin of sadistic pleasure, Lukis came behind Lucef's head, grasping his head and forcing his mouth open. The Witch poured the liquid down his throat, leaving him gasping and sputtering once his father released him.

"What was that?" Lucef hissed, eyes glaring up at his father. Lukis said nothing, staring down at his son and waiting. It only took a moment, but Lucef felt a ripple through his body. It was as if every cell came alive, vibrating and screaming. He shut his eyes as a scream ripping from his mouth. He seemed to be glowing, and Ace had the impression his body was ... open. As if the potion he had ingested and the words that were said had unsealed him, making him ready to receive the others into him.

The Witch waited, watching until Lucef's eyes went white, his body's glow pulsing, before she stepped to the first sacrifice, the Witch. No one had to hold her mouth open; she willingly opened it, letting the liquid flow down her throat. Her body seized after a moment, her eyes wide and staring blankly above her. They systematically moved through each of the others, going to the Werewolf, Bridget next, then Codi, who also had to be forced to drink much like Lucef had, and then they approached Six.

Ace turned to Nero, her eyes pleading silently with him to go check, to go see where the Necare were. He squeezed her hand lightly, nodding before he disappeared silently through the doors from where they came. It was now Ace, alone in this room, unable to make a move until Nero was back with their small group of Necare to help battle this massive group of Werewolves.

"Don't ... don't touch ... her..." Lucef said, his voice faint as he struggled to maintain himself in the here and now.

"It must be done, Lucef," Lukis said, pulling Six's lips open. Her eyes glowed for the first time since she had been in that room, finally focusing on Lukis's face as she glared up at him. Her hand wasn't quite free yet, so there was no way for her to fight back against what was going to happen.

Ace clenched her fists so hard, blood started pooling in her hands as she watched Lukis pour the final vial of liquid down Six's throat. Six, however, resisted the feeling as the others had been unable to do, not shivering or shaking as it took hold in her body. She already had things try to take hold of her all the time as a Vampire and she managed to resist them, so it was no far feat for her to do the same here.

The Witch then took up a dagger, clearly blessing it with whatever words she was speaking, before handing it over to Lukis. He went to each slab, touching the blade to his lips before he began cutting at each sacrifice's arteries. Blood began flowing quickly, flowing into recesses Ace hadn't noticed were in them. The chanting grew louder, and now the Werewolves were also taking part in it.

Six, ignoring the way the cuts in her wrists and ankles made moving and control difficult, continued her struggle with the cuffs, managing to get one hand free, though her fingers didn't want to cooperate with her. She knew it was too late for her now that she had ingested that poison, and her blood was spilt. She was part of this ritual and there was no going back, but what she could do was take as many of these monsters as she could with her.

The blood, once it began dripping off a divot in the slabs, seemed to snake through the air instead of following the force of gravity. All four of the sacrifices began to shake as the blood got closer to Lucef's form. Lucef seemed to be unable to move or do anything but scream as the blood started flowing into him. The force was clearly painful as it did so.

Ace's eyes pooled with bloody tears as she watched Six and Codi clearly withering where they lay. Six's free hand raised, her eyes closing with the effort she had to put forth to summon a demon blade from within her corset. One came to call, but wobbly. It was as if Vehekan had vacated his position within them, making their powers less stable than they had been. She wondered if it was because he was certain she would die, or if he had considered her saving Nero just cause to depart.

But just as Six began sending the blade spinning toward Lukis's head, Ace saw Six burst into flames, her final focus not on if the blade hit its target but on turning to Lucef to blow him a farewell kiss. Then she was gone. And quite suddenly, the room elapsed into silence.

The blade dropped just before it was about to hit Lukis, falling to the floor with a clang. Everyone watched with bated breath for Lucef to move. If this part of the ritual wasn't successful, then the spell and ritual to place Lukis's soul there would be moot. But Lucef opened his eyes slowly. As rapidly as his thoughts were swirling in his mind, his eyes were changing. From normal, to red, to all black, and to a regular blue, his eyes changed almost unconsciously, as if just his thoughts made them do so.

Ace heard the sound of Nero returning, the Necare behind him, slinking into the room and behind their enemies. She didn't have to wait any longer, but in her mind, it was far too late. Bloody tear tracks down her cheeks. She pushed through the crowd forcefully, making all eyes turn toward her. Lukis's satisfied expression quickly twisted into a shocked grimace.

"How did you get in here?" he demanded.

"You should very well know we can move during the day. It's just very dangerous for us," Ace said, coming even closer to Lukis to pick up the demon metal blade that had just barely missed its target.

"Well, you're too late anyway. I've already killed your Vampire. Leave us or I'll rip you apart where you stand," Lukis growled. Alexander stiffened from where he stood beside Lucef's slab, glaring at Lukis.

"I'm not completely too late. I can stop you before you take your next step," Ace said, eyes burning into his.

"You waited until she was dead before you tried to stop me?" Lukis asked, smirking lightly as he gestured to the empty slab where Six once was.

"Why should I have? I'm far outnumbered," she said, gesturing to the Werewolves around her. Her eyes rested on Alexander for a moment, whose expression was pained, then turned back to Lukis. She could not let her mind wander to what Alexander may or may not feel about her at the moment. He was the enemy. He assisted in killing Six. If he died that night, she would be able to wash her hands of whatever feelings it brought up in her when she realized he lived.

"And why step forward now?"

"If *she* would die, I'll finish what she started and take you with her," Ace hissed.

"You'll die before you escape this building if you try it," he growled.

"A challenge," Ace said suddenly, bringing everyone to attention. Immortals were many things, but one thing they didn't budge on normally was rules. If a challenge in one-on-one combat was requested of a Werewolf, even if it was by a different type of Immortal, the request could not be denied. Lukis snarled.

"You dare challenge me?"

"You and me, Lukis. We fight. If I die, you proceed with your ritual. If you die…" She paused, her stare turning quite sinister. "I take Lucef with me or I slaughter every last Werewolf and Witch in this building."

Lukis laughed, the sound offensive against the stone and marble in the room. The Werewolves behind her shifted nervously, growls and murmurs rumbling through the crowd.

"I don't think it's much of a fair fight, Ace. I can't change in a challenge, and you already have weapons at your disposal," he said, recalling her nails from their previous fight.

"I think it's plenty fair, since I can clearly see the two guns you have under those robes. You scared to face me with only my strength and my nails, while you have guns at your disposal?" she taunted.

"It doesn't matter, Lukis. She's challenged you. You either take the challenge, or you forfeit and give in to what she wants," Alexander rumbled, his hands having tightened holding the box that the sides were crushed under his fingers. Lukis's head snapped over to where Alexander stood, a growl in his chest.

Lukis whipped the edge of his cloak away from his side, his hand immediately reaching for one of his guns, but Ace was ready. She easily dodged the first shot, listening as it struck a Witch that was behind her squarely in the forehead. She used the momentum of her dodge to place one foot on the slab that once held Codi, nothing but a pool of mercurial-looking liquid remained, vaulting off and landing before Lukis, too close for him to shoot her. Her nails already extended, she plunged them deep into his chest, the thin silver easily finding their way between ribs.

"Do I feel your heart fluttering, Lukis?" Ace asked, slowly inching her nails deeper. "I do. It's vibrating my hand."

He realized that he was trapped. One scrape of her silver nails against his heart, and he was dead. If he moved, it could also pierce his heart.

"This was too fast; we barely had any fun," he whispered to her, their faces close. She smirked, fully intending on finishing this here and now, but she was surprised when she was hit forcefully from behind. Lukis took the opportunity, grabbing her fingers and pulling them out of his chest, before kneeing her in the stomach, sending her flying into a slab, shattering it with the blow.

"I hope you enjoy dying," he snarled, pulling his other gun from its holster and aiming them at her.

"I already did," she said coldly, as she regained her footing. Alexander, who had evidently thrown the box at her, moved away from Lukis's line of sight, though his eyes never left Ace, just as Lukis began firing.

Ace continued to dodge them, the green hue of the metal telling her exactly what kind of bullets these were. The same ones he had used at Kurome. Bullets flew, Lukis clearly not caring who died in the aftermath of this fight. The crowd began trying to disperse to get away from the fight. Witches near the front lines of the battle screamed as they were shoved aside by the stronger Werewolves.

Lucef's eyes opened, causing a glaring light to pour into the room. Lukis shielded his eyes for a moment, blinded by it momentarily, giving Ace the opportunity she needed. She ran and stood between his outstretched arms, moving one of his hands so the barrel of his own gun was touching his temple. And then everything seemed to stop. She heard a hundred guns cock, the barrels faced toward her and subsequently at their leader, who she now had in a headlock, his gun at his temple and her silver nails trapping him at his neck.

"Shoot at me, and you shoot him," Ace hissed at the crowd, but they were soon distracted as the Necare that had been hiding amongst them began taking them out. Screams and roars filled the room as Ace kept her hold on Lukis. "I'll not kill you just yet," Ace whispered in his ear. "I think there is someone else who wants to do that honor."

And she used the gun to hit him in the head so hard, there was an audible crack heard, and he fell to the floor unconscious.

She glanced around the room, watching the Necare do their worst.

"Any that we don't kill can be captured," Ace yelled over the sounds of battle.

"Did you kill him?" came Nero's voice from beside her suddenly. He was splattered with blood, his fists looked like they had been having a great time playing in someone's torso.

"Just unconscious. He'll heal soon enough. We need to get him secured."

"I can do that," he offered, reaching out to take her hand.

"I'll tend to Lucef," she whispered, turning her attention to his still-imprisoned form.

The fighting seemed to cease quickly enough, many of the remaining Werewolves and Witches having fled, but there were plenty dead on the floor of this horrid place.

"Lucef," she said, seeing now that his eyes were back to their normal blue and black. "Lucef, you know what

happened couldn't have been done any other way. I couldn't
have stopped Six's death," Ace said to him, staring at his face.

He, out of nothing more than emotion and instinct,
broke the chains and grabbed Ace's throat, trying to crush it.

"You could have stopped him!" Lucef sobbed, tearing
rolling down his cheeks.

"No. No, I couldn't have. You were already linked in
the ritual. I would have killed you," she told him, her face
showing her own sorrow.

"You'd rather have me live than your own progeny?" he
nearly screamed with anger, his fingers tightening on her
throat. Ace took his hands from her throat forcefully and
glared at him, though more bloody tears ran down her
own cheeks.

"All of you were linked. All of you would have died,"
Ace said quietly, keeping his hand in hers. Lucef breathed
heavily for a moment, looking in her eyes and knowing it
was true. His whole body shook, wracked with sobs that
simply could not be quelled as he held onto Ace.

CHAPTER 23

Deca stood in the door of her bedroom. She had heard the gunshots, the horrible sound of fighting, and then ... it was quiet. She was scared to go further. If Lukis had succeeded in his plans, he would be furious with her if she left their room, but if he didn't...

She then saw a man carrying Lukis down the hall. It was rather an odd sight, given that Lukis was a significant amount wider than him, though he was clearly well-built as well. He looked over at her, his blue eyes softening behind his curtain of long black-and-white hair as he passed. She wasn't sure what his expression was for, only that Lukis was clearly unconscious. She knew if he were dead, there would be no body for that man to lug around.

She stepped from the room, hurriedly making her way back to the ritual space. When she entered, the scene was much different than she had left it only an hour before. Instead of a room filled to the brim with growing Werewolves and heavy with magic even she could feel in the air, it was covered in a dozen or so Vampires, all of whom were busily moving about, cleaning what she suspected was the ashes of quite a few dead Werewolves, as well as the bodies of several dead Witches.

Her eyes turned to the only two who were still. Lucef and Ace still sat, hand in hand on the slab where he had been shackled to previously. She didn't know who that woman was, but she wasn't the Vampire that had been chained beside him earlier.

"Lucef," Deca said quietly, causing his eyes to turn to her.

Ace stood, touching his shoulder lightly and nodding toward Deca, before moving far enough away from them to provide at least an illusion of privacy. Slowly, Deca walked toward her son. Her eyes filling with tears as she saw his expression. Pain, excruciating pain was screaming out from his features. But this wasn't physical.

"Lucef, my son ... I'm so sorry," she whispered, pressing her delicate hand to his cheek.

"I don't wish to speak of it," he said quietly, his voice shaking. Deca nodded in silence and kissed his cheek softly. She had no intentions of remaining as she was. She had one final thing to do, and then she would happily leave this plain of existence, letting her body fade and die as it kept trying to do.

"I love you, Lucef. I hope you know I never wanted any of this. I..." she trailed off, her voice breaking as her eyes welled with tears.

"I know, Mum," he said, as he let out a breath.

"Do you forgive me?" Lucef looked up at his mother's face, the same youthful face he had grown up looking at was staring back at him, but instead of the complete and utter joy he used to see there, all he saw was sorrow.

"There's nothing to forgive. You did *nothing* wrong other than love the wrong person for too long," he said, pressing his hand over hers at his cheek. She gave him a teary smile.

"You, despite all the odds, have grown into quite a good man."

"Mum, why are you saying this?" he asked, his brow furrowing as he looked into her face.

"I'm saying goodbye. I need to leave this world. It has been too long," she told him, looking down at her other hand that he had clasped in his.

"You aren't going to kill yourself!" he said, not able to even consider the idea.

"I'm going to let death happen as it should with me. I'm not going to drink any more of that foul blood. I'll just drift slowly to death as I should have long ago," she whispered to him.

"And what will you do until then?" he asked, wanting to focus on anything other than what had just come to pass.

"I have to be the one to take care of your father," she said, glancing behind her at a discarded gun she had spotted when she first walked in. Lucef had wanted to do it himself, but as he looked at his mother, her frame slight, her body weak, but her face set with determination, he knew it was her task to complete. He brought his mother's face to his, giving her a kiss and nodding, before she turned and left the room again, heading to where she saw the man carrying Lukis.

Nero was chaining the now unconscious Lukis to the wall of, coincidently, the same room Lukis had been prepared in for the ritual. Once he had him securely restrained, Nero stood back to look at him, mild pity meeting his eyes.

"Why don't I just kill you now?" Nero asked aloud, even though he knew there was no one to hear him. But suddenly there came a voice.

"Because someone else is coming to do so," Lukis said, as he opened his eyes slowly. The dent in his head had already begun to heal, but his eyes were still not focusing on anything. "I'd rather be killed by her than a Vampire like you,"

Lukis said, his voice clearly trying to be forceful or insulting but coming out more as a whine.

"I don't care what you prefer," Nero said with a smirk, crossing his arms over his chest. He knew exactly who was being given his life, and clearly, she deserved to be the one to do it. "But I am a man that understands dignity and honor. I'll wait for her outside," he said, as he turned and exited the room, leaving Lukis with his head rested against the wall, waiting.

Nero walked out to the ritual space and saw Deca beside her son. She was still looking down at her shaking hands as Lucef watched her cautiously.

It was only a few moments later when Nero saw her. Deca walked slowly down the hall, a gun clutched in her small hands. Her face was bold, determined, a far cry from the fearful woman he had seen just a few minutes earlier when he was bringing Lukis past her room. She looked up at Nero, eyes glistening with unshed tears.

"Just in here," Nero said softly, opening the door for her. She stepped inside, pausing for a moment until she heard the door click close before she let her eyes rest on Lukis. Her eyes roamed over him. This was a man she had loved for over eight hundred years. She had loved him enough to suffer in horrible pain. She loved him enough to believe the lies he told her. She loved him enough to follow him away from her home and across an ocean, only for him to try to murder their son.

She realized as she looked at his face, still full of hatred and deep ugliness she had never fully witnessed before the other day, that this was not the man she married. He had changed. He had become twisted and cruel from the power bestowed on him. He had become the monster that he had feared she thought him to be all those long years ago.

"Lukis," Deca said, watching as his eyes struggled to focus on her.

"Yes, Deca. I know why you've come," Lukis said quietly in response, looking away from her.

"You'll look at me," she snapped, causing his eyes to return to her face. "You don't get to be a coward in this. I deserved better. For years, I endured your lies. I endured all that suffering! And for what?" she asked through clenched teeth as she walked toward him.

"I—" he started, but she started to speak again.

"But I've loved you," she said in a much softer voice, as she got very close to him. "I've always loved you, Lukis," she whispered, as she brough her face as close to his as she could, touching it softly with her free hand.

"And I, you," he whispered back to her, staring into her eyes, which were so tainted with grief and sorrow it pained him to look within them.

"You haven't loved me for a very long time," she whispered bitterly, knowing it was true. She parted their gaze and looked at her other hand that held the gun.

"Just one last thing before you..." he said trailing off, his throat suddenly having gone dry as he glanced at the gun, and tears threatened to pour from his crisp blue eyes.

"Yes, Lukis?" she whispered, looking back at him.

"A kiss?" he asked her. His eyes seemed to be pleading more than his words as tears flowed down his cheeks softly, like little falls of water down a smooth stone. "My last request of you," he whispered to her. She smiled at him and nodded as tears of her own fell down her cheeks.

"Of course, my love," she said, as she leaned forward and kissed him softly. She held the gun with her free hand and just as their lips touched for the last time, she put the barrel to his temple and pulled the trigger.

Slowly she parted from him and looked at his face. His lids were closed softly over his cruel, cold eyes, and his lips curved up just enough to show a hint of a truly happy smile on his face. Deca's face wrinkled into her sorrow, as she watched his body slowly start to crumble into dust.

Ace seemed to snap herself back to reality as Nero re-entered the ritual room. She had done all the leadership she could for the day, deciding that she would instead let herself be vulnerable, at least to him. He approached her, tilting her face up to his by her chin and looking over her blood-stained face.

"You've lost too much blood recently. Between me and these tears," he whispered, brushing one tear track and smearing it over her pale skin.

"I'll feed when we get back," Ace murmured, glancing over at Lucef, who still sat slumped on the slab. "He needs to get out of this place."

Nero nodded his agreement, reaching to take her hand and pulling her over to Lucef.

"Lucef, we're leaving," Nero said, his voice authoritative in a way that only an Elder could. Lucef glanced up, his tears had stopped, but his face was trapped in a sort of painful shock.

"You're leaving me?" he asked, his voice breaking. Ace reached out, taking his hand in her free one.

"You're leaving with us," Ace said definitively, tugging lightly, indicating he should follow. The three of them walked from the room, Nero stopping them briefly to give orders to Jacob, telling them to wrap everything up and head back to the manor. The Werewolves had dispersed, but they would be back. There was too much left there for them to completely abandon it, and the wolves from other dens would be heading back to their home cities.

They made it back to where they parked Jag's car, slowly driving back through New Orleans to the manor. Lucef didn't say a word on the ride back. He simply stared out the window of the back seat, eyes unseeing as they passed the sights. Nero held tightly to Ace's hand as he drove them back. He could feel her mounting tension the closer they got to the old house.

Once they parked, Ace took in a breath, turning around in her seat to look at Lucef.

"There was nothing we could do," Ace said to him.

"I could have figured out a way for her to escape before they had captured us, but she wanted to fight them. She didn't want to leave *me*. And now she's left me here alone," Lucef said bitterly.

"I never got an opportunity to tell her how I felt. Not really. I should have professed it to her. I should have—" He choked as a sob wracked his body. Ace glanced at Nero, her own eyes welling once again.

"She knew," Nero said, just before he opened his door and climbed out. Ace and Lucef made no moves to get out, so Nero came around, opening each of their doors and reaching his hand out to Ace to assist her.

Jag came out to put the car away, reading the solemn faces and deciding against making any comments. They made their way through the garage and into the main house, all three of them silently walking up the stairs. Lucef stopped, strangely abruptly once he got to their room, because though it had been Six's room for many years, she had clearly relinquished some of the ownership to him when she made him hers. He held his hand on the knob, knowing that when he entered, she would not be there. His knuckles turned white, teeth clenched, as he forced himself to turn it and walk inside.

Everything about the room reminded him of her.

The bed was still unmade from the night before, the clothing she had tried on but decided not to wear draped over a red velvet chair. Even her silky night dress she had planned on wearing after their night stroll was waiting for her. Waiting, but she would never again come to see these things. Lucef slumped on the floor at the foot of the bed, eyes reviewing all the memories they had compiled together in that room.

It was hard to think that just over a month ago they had met for the first time; now Six was an essential part of his life, and he felt hollow without her. His sorrow turned to rage as he thought about it. Thought about everything he had been through over the past several years. So many times he had evaded his father's men; so many times he had moved about the city, avoiding the Immortals that ran through the city, at least as much as a half-Immortal could.

Ace appeared in the doorway just as Lucef's anger became visceral and overwhelming.

"*You*," he growled, coming up to her so fast she didn't have time to react. He grabbed her throat, slamming her into the nearest wall. Not knowing his new strength, he crushed her throat with the force, causing a quiet, choking sound to come from her mouth. "You got me into all of this. *You* are the reason she's dead!" he screamed. Ace's eyes welled with fresh tears.

What could she have done differently that wouldn't have made for a worse outcome? Left him to be taken by the Werewolves in London? Killed herself and Nero, and potentially Six and Lucef as well as all the Necare that were on their way by trying to get them out before the ritual began? Should she have killed them all by intervening while the ritual was happening?

What could she have done?

But she couldn't say any of those things out loud, her windpipe was still crushed under his hands.

"I'm sorry," she mouthed to him instead, her eyes pleading.

He let her go abruptly, and she slid down the wall from where he had been holding her up.

"How could you just do *nothing*?" he asked quietly as he looked away. Ace, still in surprise, waited for her throat to heal for a few moments, then she spoke.

"I weighed it all. I tried to find the best time with the least amount of deaths," she whispered hoarsely. "But don't think, not for one moment, Lucef, that it didn't feel like my heart was being torn out watching her die."

He turned back to her, surprise evident on his face as she left the room so quickly, he barely saw her move. Ace made it back to her and Nero's room, immediately finding a wall to lean against. She gasped in air she didn't need, but somehow the pain and guilt were so crushing it was causing her diaphragm to spasm. Nero came behind her, lacing his fingers through hers against her stomach, taking in long, deep breaths that pressed his chest against her back.

Slowly, his efforts worked, and Ace's breathing slowed to match his.

She let her head lean back against his shoulder, realizing now where she had rushed to as she looked up. It was the portrait of her, the deadly fiery look in her eyes that he showed in that painting, were nowhere to be found on her own face now.

"Look what's become of me," Ace murmured quietly.

"Nothing has become of you. You are simply you," Nero whispered into her ear.

"This sniveling creature. I'm not worthy to remain here while she's dead and he's..." she trailed off, thinking of what a mess Lucef was. Ace turned in Nero's arms, looking up into his blue eyes.

"I don't know what I'd do if I lost you, Ace. I think I'd become much madder than Lucef seems to be. I'd have to be put down like a dog," Nero confessed, brushing the hair from her face.

"We spent years—" she began, but he cut her off with a rough kiss on her lips.

"Apart, yes, but I knew you were there. You knew I was there. If the near month I spent apart from you in this city were not enough of an indication ... I would never make it a day if you were truly and finally dead," he said, his eyes fierce.

He lifted her, and she naturally wrapped her legs around his waist, happily letting him take her to bed. This was less about taking one another but rather about comfort. Slowly, carefully taking their time to remove their clothing as they caressed and kissed each other's skin with reverence. It was about devotion without words. Soothing pains, even if only for a few minutes. Vowing to never lose one another.

CHAPTER 24

A few days following the ritual, Deca was found by Alexander and Kyle weeping over the ashes that were once Lukis Lynae. Alexander had instructed Kyle and the remaining living London Werewolves to return home with her so she would be comfortable as she aged and eventually passed away. It had been weeks now, and she had become a frail, quickly withering woman. Her eyes had begun to set deep, and wrinkles were forming all over her rapidly graying skin. She sat in her room, at a loss for energy, slowly touching the soft curtains that hung around her bed that she used to share with Lukis.

At first, she had holed herself away, not wanting to see anyone, but as she became more and more feeble, they insisted on at least coming in to help her bathe, use the restroom, and eat. She was nearing the end and though she was pleased that it would soon be over, she was sad for the life that was stolen from her. She knew Lucef was not going to come and see her. They had said everything they needed to say to one another that day, but the ache she had deep within her, the desire to see him, to know him still tingled in the back of her mind.

A knock sounded at her door briefly before Kyle stepped inside. The past several days, when the Werewolves could smell the death quickly approaching her body, he had been stopping in, inquiring to her about who would be the new leader. The worries had come when Alexander remained in New Orleans. The former New Orleans Alpha had been killed by the Necare at the ritual, and as such, Alexander felt he needed to remain there to pick up the pieces of the now very broken den.

However, that den was dissolving. They had lost too many to fully protect themselves, while the fighting with the Redeamond Necare was fierce and bloody, almost too open for the Masquerade in some cases that many Werewolves had chosen to move to other cities with smaller dens across the United States. Alexander had still not returned to London, though.

"Are you feeling well this evening, Miss Deca?" Kyle asked, looking over her gaunt face, trying to train his expression to not show how horrified he was by her appearance. She smiled a little at his attempt, still seeing the disgust there.

"I'm feeling like death, Kyle. What is it I can do for you?" she asked. He squirmed a little at her abruptness, casting his eyes at his shoes instead of her face.

"I know that Alexander was deemed Lukis's second, but he has not returned to London, and New Orleans has been disbanded. Once you've passed—?"

"He will return," she said, interrupting and finishing his sentence for him.

"There is no guarantee that he will return, madam."

"Get me the phone," she demanded, holding out her hand. Kyle stared at her, confused for a moment.

"Why do you need the phone?" he asked, furrowing his brow as he unconsciously reached for his back pocket.

"I'm going to call him."

The phone rang for several long moments, Deca staring straight into Kyle's eyes. She may have been a dying human, but she was still in charge until she passed. That was how it worked.

"Evening, Deca," Alexander said when he finally answered.

"Hello, Alexander. I'll make this brief, since neither of us has time to waste. I will die soon. Give or take a day. If you plan on taking Lukis's place, you better get yourself back to London as quickly as possible, or Kyle here thinks he's to be the new leader," Deca said, eyeing Kyle with suspicion.

"Does he now?"

"Yes. How long will it take you to return home?" she asked, smiling cheekily over at Kyle, who merely blushed and looked away again.

"I'm in the city now. I'll make my way there shortly," he said, hanging up the phone abruptly.

Alexander gave one last look of longing toward the window on the second floor of Kurome Mansion from his place on their wall, watching the dark-haired woman in the window. It was only a matter of time, now that he was to be Leader of the Werewolves, that his true plan would be able to come to fruition.

Ace was sitting in her room at her desk back in London. They had been back for a few weeks and she, like she did every night since her return, was reading the update that was sent from Redeamond. The Necare had systematically began wiping out the remaining Werewolves in the area, enough so that the den had finally disbanded. It gave her a mild feeling of relief, knowing that the den was gone for good; however, it also meant that Redeamond was no longer a necessary coven. Those Vampires would have to be relocated, and Brendin would no longer have any authority.

"What's new? Anything?" Nero asked from the doorway. He had two glasses and a bag of blood in his hands.

"Redeamond reports the den is gone. Werewolves have dispersed to other cities," she parroted the report.

"Mmm ... we'll have to have a council meeting to decide on the best course of action for placement of those Vampires," Nero said, moving further into the room and setting the glasses and bag on her desk.

"I thought as much. I forwarded this to all of you," Ace said, now moving on to scour other websites for possible sightings of Immortals. So much had happened in New Orleans that it had become obvious to the mortals. One fight had even been caught on video and posted on the internet for all the humans to see, though there were plenty of people who thought it had been a hoax; it was enough that others had jumped at the chance to say it wasn't true that it had caused some concern for them. Now she kept a vigilant eye on message boards to see if anything came up.

"Ace, you should get back out. Your Necare are missing you," he murmured, pouring her a glass and holding it out for her to take. She pulled her eyes from the screen, looking at him with mild confusion.

"What do you mean? I've been right here," she said, taking the glass and putting it to her lips.

"You've stayed in you room or mine since we returned to Kurome. Mostly yours. Not once have you gone out to hunt or investigate," he said, crossing his arms over his chest.

"These are important," Ace said, gesturing to the computer.

"You are a *Necare*, not just a computer worm. There was a time not long ago that you absolutely hated me for not letting you leave the mansion to hunt, and now you barely do anything at all," Nero said, reaching forward to grasp her face. "Do you know how many times I've woken in the day to find you've been gone? So many times, I've been close to coming up here then to bring you back to bed with me, but didn't, thinking you wanted to be alone?" he asked, moving his face closer to hers.

"Why haven't you?" she whispered to him, closing her eyes and leaning into his touch.

"I ... haven't been sure. You've been distant," he whispered to her, standing up straight. Ace didn't know what to say. She hadn't meant to become so terribly distant from everyone, especially not him, but she felt like she had to remove herself. She had to keep herself busy and not by killing or plotting or planning. No, those things got her into trouble. Her plans went horribly wrong. Her plans had killed Six. No, she would simply research and let others *do*.

Nero watched her expressionless face for a moment as she stared off, picking up the glass, and turning away from her. He didn't know what was going on in her mind, and she certainly wasn't letting him in on the secret at the moment. After what they had shared following the ritual. After the silent vows they had made to one another, he thought she would ... well, he thought she would go back to normal, and he wasn't sure how to cope with the fact that she wasn't.

"I'll be in my room if you need me, Ace," Nero said as he walked out of the room, closing the door behind him, once she was back to the blue light of her screen.

She had watched him leave and stared at the door for a moment before she took a paperweight from nearby and threw it at the door. She screamed in anger and started to throw things around the room before she dissolved into tears once again on the floor. She balled her hands into fists and pounded them on the hard wood.

Did she want to be this shell of the person she used to be? No. She hated what she had become over these past few weeks. She hated that the idea of going out with her Necare made her fear their deaths. In the past, she would have thought herself weak. She would have pitied the sad creature she had become. She leaned against the wall, staring at the ceiling as she calmed herself.

This was not who she was.

"Dammit..." she whispered in a growl, as she stood up and walked through the darkness of her room, opening the door. The light poured through the darkened space, and she walked out into the hall.

She descended the stairs, her presence turning the heads of the House Vampires convened there.

The whispers began almost immediately, but she ignored them, pushing through the room to the main hall, where she slammed into Lotte, sending them both reeling back.

"Ace," Lotte gasped, regaining her footing. "I'm so sorry—"

"My fault," Ace said, cutting her off.

"Are you headed to the training rooms?"

"Nero," Ace said flatly. Lotte nodded, and Ace began to turn.

"We really need you back in the field with us. Makiut is good but..."

"Not as good as me?" Ace offered, letting a small smirk grace her lips for the first time in quite a while. Lotte grinned in return.

"Exactly."

"Soon," Ace said, realizing it was true before she quickly moved away from Lotte, returning to her original plan.

Ace wanted to be herself again, but she needed a reminder of who that was. The only person who could do that for her had been ever so patiently waiting for her to realize that, and she was going to him now.

She stopped at his door, taking in his scent. She had thought it had only been one day since she shared his room, but she could tell by how faint her scent was there that it had been at least a week. She cringed internally, hating what she was doing to herself and to him. With a deep intake of breath, she opened the door and stepped inside. Nero was at the windowsill, the glass of blood he had poured for himself in her room still in his hand, but untouched.

He said nothing, though she knew he sensed her. The rain was pouring outside, the grounds still as a tomb.

"Nero, I—"

"Decided to talk to me? To come out of your hole?" he asked her, slowly turning. She understood his bitterness. She felt it toward herself too.

"I'm sorry," Ace muttered to him, fighting back more tears. She had been lost, adrift after what had happened. Changed, not by magic but by the decisions she had to make. Nero noticed her face, stained from the tears of anger just a few minutes before, and now fresh ones with guilt, sadness, and yet even more self-loathing. He walked over to her and put a hand on her chin, tilting it up to him. Immediately, he regretted his tone. This is what he wanted, after all. For her to come to him finally.

"It's alright," he whispered to her, kissing her cheek and pulling her against his chest.

Ace looked up, gently pressing her lips to his before pulling away, her eyes bright and burning.

"Nero, I need you to remind me," she said quietly, her voice shaking slightly as she said the words.

"Remind you?" Her eyes became a little more determined, clutching at him a bit harder.

"Remind me of who I am, Nero." Her voice was a bit bolder, matching her expression.

Nero's face brightened with realization, his eyes lightening to glowing blue. He didn't need to say more, pressing his lips to hers fiercely. The kiss went to desperation and primal instinct in minutes. Ace was tearing at his clothes and clawing at his skin. Everything about it was fast, hard, and painful. The pleasure was insurmountable.

They lay against the floor afterward, not having made it to Nero's bed, basking in it for a moment. Nero held Ace close, realizing that the centuries before he found her, he had been everything a Vampire was meant to be: cruel, cold, heartless, brutal. He had been something to fear, something to hate. He had never known joy until he saw her in that window. He had only found peace when he had her like this, in his arms. And he had never been impressed with any other, until Ace showed him how incredibly powerful she truly was.

She was his everything, and there was never going to be a day or night that passed that he wouldn't want to show her exactly that.

She turned her eyes up to look at him; they were glowing, alive, like they had been before. She would be wounded. There would be times she would falter, but he now knew he was the one who could bring her back from that, just as she brought him back from the brink of becoming a complete and utter monster all those years ago.

CHAPTER 25

Deca lay there, pale and sweating. Alexander had arrived shortly after their phone call ended, and they began the preparations for him to take over as leader. But days had passed, and her body had deteriorated even more. Her skin was translucent and thin, sagging over her bones. He sat beside her bed, holding her boney fingers as lightly as he could manage, not wanting to cause her any more pain. He had spent a great deal of time with her, having been so close to Lukis, and he hated to see her this way, but he understood her choice.

"Alexander," she whispered in a hoarse voice. "I'm going to die today. I know I am." Her eyes were hazed over, ghostly orbs still somehow staring into his soul. "Please, Alexander. Do well for me?" she asked, her hand shaking with the effort to squeeze his. He looked down at the small, withered fingers and tried to smile.

"I promise to do my best, Mistress Deca," he said quietly.

"I want you to promise me two things," she started, stooping to take in a harsh, wheezing breath. "Lucef … you leave him alone." Alexander nodded, having already promised this countless times over the last few days. "And don't forget that *nothing* is worth losing the one you love," she whispered fiercely, tears falling down her wrinkled cheeks. She took in a short, final, ragged breath before her body tensed one final time, and the small, remaining bit of life left her body.

Ace sat gingerly on the roof edge looking down at the city street. She took in a deep breath of the night air, catching a scent she hadn't smelled since they had gotten back from New Orleans over six months previously. She hopped off the roof, quickly following the scent through the streets, down alleys, and small gaps between buildings until she came upon him, standing in a long-forgotten graveyard hidden behind buildings.

Lucef stood at the center of it, staring down at a small, dilapidated headstone. Ace approached him, being sure to make plenty of noise so he'd be forewarned of her presence. She cast her gaze down to where his was looking, reading the dates and name listed. It was a Sinthia Corbet from 1887. Six had gone missing in 1886, but they didn't determine her officially dead until the following year. Somehow Lucef had found her grave, the only one Six had ever been given.

"I wanted a place to go," he whispered, still not looking up.

"I did too, but you seem to be much smarter than me," Ace said, smirking lightly as she glanced up at him. A small chuckle seemed to come from within him, and he finally glanced at her. He didn't look much different, though his eyes were now human blue instead of the changed Werewolf blue and black that they had been before.

"I'm sorry I disappeared," Lucef said quietly.

"I sort of disappeared too," Ace admitted, folding her arms around her torso, even though she was impervious to the cold night air. Her fingers hit the hard metal of the demon metal she had been carrying around ever since Six's death, and it finally dawned on her what she needed to do with it. "I have something for you," she murmured, pulling it from her pocket and placing it in his outstretched hand. His eyes sparkled as he looked at it, hands moving over the blade as if it were precious.

"How did you get this?" he asked, his voice awed.

"I picked it up right after. Everything has been a bit of a muddle until recently," she said, though she was pleased at the expression on his face. It was much better than the swift changes between all-consuming sadness and absolute berserker rage that he had been shifting between the last time she had seen him. They had been concerned about letting him go without supervision, if only because they feared he'd break the Masquerade, but he somehow managed to completely keep himself off the map, that is until that evening.

"Thank you," he whispered after a very long moment.

"Where have you been?" she asked, now taking in his appearance. He was dressed worse, somehow, than he had been when they first met. His clothes tatters over his muscular form. He laughed at the way her face changed as she looked him over, brushing his shoulders.

"The streets, Ace. I went where no one would think to look for me, and it worked rather well. Anytime I'd ramble on, mortals would just think I was a crazy, homeless man."

Ace was impressed, if not disgusted. The idea of living in the streets of London was rather sickening.

"You could always come home with me," Ace offered, reaching out her hand to him once more. She took care of her own; she would always take care of her own. And somehow in the short course of them knowing one another, Lucef had become one of hers. He took her hand, squeezing it gently.

"Not now. I may pop in from time to time, but I'm still working through it," he told her gently, hating to see the disappointment on her face but also knowing it would be worse if he simply disappeared again on her.

Ace nodded in understanding, stepping away with a smile.

"You know where to find us, Lucef," she said, before turning and heading back through the crevices and alleys to where her Necare were.

Nero kissed Ace's head as they lay together and tried to slip out without disturbing her, thinking her asleep.

"Where are you going?" Ace asked him, her eyes still closed as he walked to the door.

"Council meeting," he said, pulling his clothes on from earlier. Ace groan, rolling over so she could watch him. The council still being down a member had made things increasingly difficult on the remaining Elders. And Nero's absence for several months, though he had been working as much as he could while he had been in New Orleans, had also caused its own set of problems.

"I suppose you must go," she said, smiling as he smirked in her direction.

"It is important," he said, finishing the last of the buttons on his shirt, before leaning over the bed to kiss her gently. Though the way she smelled and seeing her lying there, combined with the taste of her lips, made him hate to leave, he had to tear himself away.

"I'll be back as soon as I can," he said, before closing the door quickly behind him.

Ace sat up, running her fingers through her hair to fix the muss before deciding she might as well get her own clothes on. The hunt that evening had been short. Not much to do since the London den had been laying low.

Ace heard a new leader had been appointed, but there was no information on who it could possibly be, and until they had that information, it was just tracking small groups of Werewolves to see what they were up to. Turned out, they were not up to much.

Ace thought about heading down to the antiquities room. She had promised herself she would read through both books, assuring herself she would never be caught off guard by some strange prophecy, but as she exited Nero's room, she found herself face to face with Dava.

"Ace!" Dava said excitedly, her eyes sparkling with that strange look of pleasure that Ace had known too well. Ace stopped in the middle of opening her door and looked at Dava, rolling her eyes. Dava was the last person she wanted to speak with presently.

"What, Dava?" Ace said in an irritated voice.

"I've just been sent here. The council wants to speak with you. Go! Hurry and get ready!" Dava said, pushing Ace back into the room. Dava turned the light on and went to Ace's wardrobe, which had been moved from her room there. Her desk had also been placed in the room, but hers sat against a wall in the corner instead of facing the bed like Nero's. Quickly Dava threw Ace her boots, which she hadn't bothered putting on again. "Put them on and go down there." Ace took her boots from Dava with a raised eyebrow.

"Alright. Calm down, would you?" Ace asked, slipping them on and walking to the door. This seemed like an oddly out of character amount of excitement for Dava, especially since she wasn't demanding to have Ace change her clothes or put on makeup.

Thankfully, Dava didn't follow as Ace moved down the stairs to the lower level. She approached the large wooden doors, raising her hand to knock, but the door swung open for her. She stepped into the large, cavernous room, eyes glancing at the remaining Elders with a questioning stare.

"You called on me?" she asked.

"Ace, we have called you here to ask you a very important question," Srinta started, her face as stoic as usual, but Ace saw an odd glint in her eyes.

"I am here. Ask whatever you wish," Ace said, growing slightly impatient.

"We offer you a position on this council. How do you respond?" Srinta asked.

Ace froze. The sound of Srinta's request echoing within the space. She didn't know what to say. Had she thought this was a possibility? Of course, she had. But she expected centuries of being a Judge before it was even an option. And beyond that, she had just barely over the last few months gotten back to herself enough to go hunting with regularity. She wasn't willing to give up the fight.

She glanced at Nero, whose eyes were bright, eager, and excited. He wanted this for her, with her, she realized.

"I will accept, but only under one condition," Ace said, pausing to look at each member of the council pointedly, lingering especially on Nero, before she continued. "I can continue to hunt werewolves," she finished.

Fredric and Georgith both smirked and leaned back in their seats, shaking their heads slightly as if she was mad to even think of such a thing.

"Accepted," Srinta said, causing the two male Elders to startle.

"That's unheard of!" Fredric said.

"Unheard of for you, Fredic. Elders only stopped fighting when our numbers grew to a point where we had soldiers to protect us. If Ace wishes to continue, there is no rule saying she cannot." She paused, waiting for further argument, but both Elders chose to remain silent. "Now, you'll need to read the—" Srinta began but Nero held up his hand. "What, Nero?" she snapped, annoyed at further interruption. Nero smirked.

"She's already read all of the Elder Scrolls. She knows how to do everything. We worked on it together when I started to study it," Nero said, looking at Ace with pride. Ace smirked back, and Srinta sighed. Srinta had always been one for tradition and the fact that Ace had already done everything, save for officially becoming a member of the council, was not tradition in any sense of the word.

"Alright then. We'll give you a week. Use your time well to review," Srinta said, as she stood up and left the room through the side door, the other two following suit right after her. Nero stepped down from his throne and closed the distance between them, grasping Ace by her shoulders. He was beaming with pride, eyes glowing as he looked down at her for a moment, before bending to press a kiss to her lips.

Ace woke with a start. It was still daylight outside, but a storm had rolled through, casting the day in an eerie twilight. Nero had left the curtain open on the window beside their bed, letting Ace sleep, while enjoying the pattering on the window unfettered. She wasn't sure what had startled her. She hadn't been dreaming about anything, nor had she heard a sound that would have caused her to bolt up in bed, but there she was.

Nero was across from her, his desk facing the bed. She looked up at him, expecting to see a surprised expression on his face with her sudden outburst, but instead there was a look of shock.

"What is it?" she hissed, frantically glancing around to see if there was something worthy of that look on the bed near her, but it was only the sheets.

"Your stomach," Nero murmured. Ace looked down at her bare stomach. It looked absolutely normal to her. Nothing remarkable about it. It hadn't changed since the day she died. But then she saw it. She felt it. A small movement in her lower abdomen, small on the outside, but she felt a rather large flutter on the inside. Her mouth flew open in shock.

"What is that?" Ace hissed, scrambling from where she sat to stand before him.

"I..." He was at a loss for words. This was not unheard of, but it was incredibly rare. So rare, in fact, it was considered a myth.

"Nero," she hissed, grabbing his face, since his eyes were squarely on her stomach. "What is that?"

"You're with child," he finally managed to say, finally meeting her eyes.

EPILOGUE

First there had been pain. Pain and fire. Her body and soul were being torn apart over and over again. Then it was darkness. Never-ending darkness, silent and cold. She tried to scream, but she couldn't even hear her own voice, let alone feel air in her lungs. She couldn't feel her body anymore.

Did she have a body anymore?

Then her eyes opened, and she did have eyes and saw stone walls. No ... not stone. These walls were the ground, a cave, something. There was nothing man-made about the walls that surrounded her, but there was a red light coming from somewhere that was illuminating it. She tried to move her head to get a better look, but she found she couldn't, though she was aware she had a head to move.

Her eyes darted to and fro, trying to take in what little she could see of this unfamiliar place, but all she could see was the ceiling ... and perhaps a chain?

She heard a door open, creaking heavily before it closed abruptly. Heavy footfalls shook whatever she was lying on, and she tried to move her eyes to the furthest edges of her periphery to see what had entered the room, but it was still just out of her view.

"Awake, finally, I see," came a gruff, inhuman voice. It sounded more like a growl than a voice, but she managed to understand it either way.

"How long have I been asleep?" she asked, trying to think back, but the time in the places before were unmeasurable.

"A few years, at least the way you think of it," said the voice.

"Where am I? Hell?" she asked, her red eyes darting, fingers clenching into fists. The voice laughed, and suddenly there was a charred, mangled face before hers. His eyes were black voids, mouth more like a tear in his flesh, revealing row upon row of ragged, sharp teeth.

"There is no heaven or hell, Six. Only the afterlife. But you must pay penance before you can leave this place," the demon said.

"Leave this place?"

"Move on to other parts of the afterlife."

"What penance am I paying?" Six hissed, narrowing her eyes as she fearlessly glared into his. He laughed, the sound ringing against the curved walls and ceiling of the cave-like space, chilling her to her bones.

"You were a Vampire, weren't you?"

"Any evils you may attribute to my Vampirism are necessary in our survival," she countered.

"How about the deal you broke with Vehekan?" he offered. That sent a chill running down her spin. Vehekan was still punishing her? "As I thought," he said, turning away from her, and once again he was out of her view.

"What penance are you planning on inflicting on me?"

He let out a frustrated sigh, grumbling and slamming something metallic down.

"Torture, Six. You're to be tortured. One long day of torture to last for years. It is only my job. I do not have all the answers, Vampire-girl. So please stop asking them."

Six smirked, pleased that she had gotten a demon to essentially beg for her to shut up. This may be a very long day, but at least she would have fun tormenting him right along with her.

Book Club Questions

1. Ace and Nero evolve their relationship over the course of the book. What would you most like to see for them in the future?

2. Now that Ace knows Alexander is alive, and her enemy no less, do you think there's any chance for them to reconcile?

3. Lucef is now the most powerful Immortal being on earth, yet he's decided to remain in hiding. What are the chances that he'll rejoin the millennium-long war once again?

4. Why do you think Ace chooses not to use her additional powers often, relying primarily on her silver nails?

5. Explain Six's madness and where you think it stems from.

6. Now that Ace is an Elder, what other fundamental restructuring of the Vampires do you think will take place?

7. The war is now at a standstill; what do you think will be the catalyst that will bring it to violence once again?

8. What characters would you most like to see return or be expanded upon in the next book?

9. Srinta mentions that there are more prophecies that have yet to be fulfilled in the books. What do you think Ace will find there when she delves into them? Who do you think made them?

AUTHOR BIO

Chelsea Burton Dunn is a Kansas City native—the Missouri side, not the Kansas side. That matters to locals. Where is that you might ask? Right, smack-dab in the middle of the country. She has two beautiful children and is married to a superb partner, but let's not forget their two snuggly cats and eager-eater of a dog.

Having always been a little strange herself, she instantly fell in love with paranormal, supernatural, and fantasy books, movies and TV shows as a child. Did everyone think it was a phase? Absolutely. Was it? Absolutely not. Being weird is a blessing, not a curse. She's always embraced that part of herself and those around her.

She started writing from a very early age, initially starting and completing one of the *Deadman's Handbooks* in high school. She is a lover of music, having her other love and talent be for singing. She performed on main stage operas in the children's chorus from grade school to high school.

Chelsea loves to delve into the difficulties of life, love, and loss, while spicing it up with a little magic and monsters. As she liked to say when she was younger, "The monsters in my head need to come out to play every once in a while," so giving them life on the page seemed appropriate.

You can see more about Chelsea, her projects, and find her social media platforms by going to:

www.chelseaburtondunn.com.

HORROR, THRILLER, & SUSPENSE

Paranormal & Urban Fantasy

Amanda Fasciano
Waking Up Dead
Dead Vessel

Beau Lake
The Beast Beside Me
The Beast Within Me
Taming the Beast: Novella
The Beast After Me
Charming the Beast
The Beast Like Me
An Eye for Emeralds
Swimming in Sapphires
Pining for Pearls

Chelsea Burton Dunn
By Moonlight
Moon Bound

J.M. Paquette
Call Me Forth
Invite Me In
Keep Me Close

Kait Disney-Leugers
Antique Magic
Blood Magic

Lyra R. Saenz
Prelude
Falsetto in the Woods: Novella
Ragtime Swing
Sonata
Song of the Sea
The Devil's Trill
Bercuese
To Heal a Songbird
Ghost March
Nocturne

Megan Mackie
The Saint of Liars
The Devil's Day
The Finder of the Lucky Devil

Paige Lavoie
I'm in Love with Mothman

Robert J. Lewis
Shadow Guardian and the
Three Bears

Valerie Willis
Cedric: The Demonic Knight
Romasanta: Father of Werewolves
The Oracle: Keeper of the
Gaea's Gate
Artemis: Eye of Gaea
King Incubus: A New Reign

Discover more at
4HorsemenPublications.com

9 781644 509869